DELIVERY TO THE LOST CITY

A TRAIN TO IMPOSSIBLE PLACES NOVEL

P. G. BELL

illustrations by Matt Sharack

FEIWEL AND FRIENDS
NEW YORK

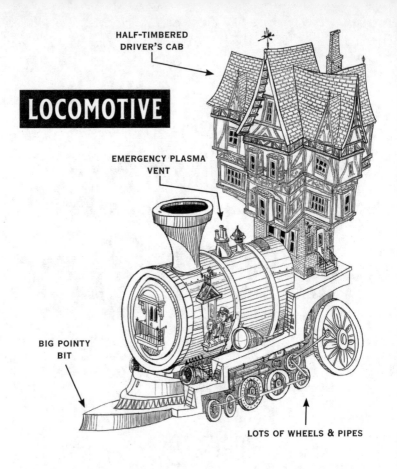

LOCOMOTIVE

HALF-TIMBERED DRIVER'S CAB

EMERGENCY PLASMA VENT

BIG POINTY BIT

LOTS OF WHEELS & PIPES

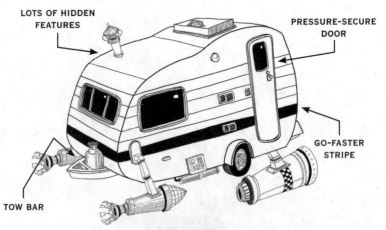

LOTS OF HIDDEN FEATURES

PRESSURE-SECURE DOOR

GO-FASTER STRIPE

TOW BAR

H. E. C.

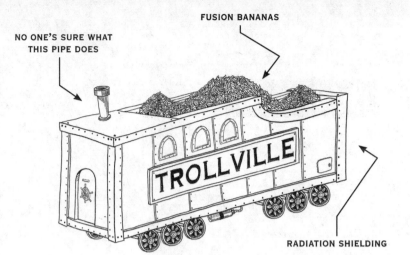

NO ONE'S SURE WHAT THIS PIPE DOES

FUSION BANANAS

TROLLVILLE

RADIATION SHIELDING

TENDER

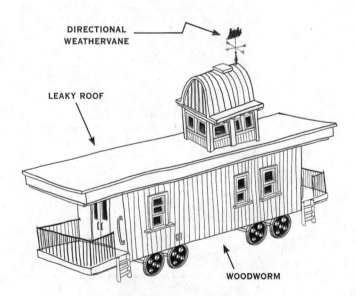

DIRECTIONAL WEATHERVANE

LEAKY ROOF

WOODWORM

SORTING CAR

For Anna, for everything

A Feiwel and Friends Book

An imprint of Macmillan Publishing Group, LLC
120 Broadway, New York, NY 10271
mackids.com

Our books may be purchased in bulk for promotional, educational, or business use.
Please contact your local bookseller or the Macmillan Corporate and
Premium Sales Department at (800) 221-7945 ext. 5442 or by email at
MacmillanSpecialMarkets@macmillan.com.

Library of Congress Cataloging-in-Publication Data is available.
ISBN 978-1-250-19007-9 (hardcover)
First edition, 2021

BOOK DESIGN BY TRISHA PREVITE

Printed in the United States of America by
LSC Communications, Ltd., Harrisonburg, Virginia.

Feiwel and Friends logo designed by Filomena Tuosto

1 3 5 7 9 10 8 6 4 2

1
THAT FRIDAY FEELING

It was Friday afternoon and school had just finished, but Suzy couldn't muster any excitement for the weekend that lay ahead. Instead, she was sandwiched between a dozen other pupils in the dilapidated bus shelter outside the school gates, watching the rain hammer down, and worrying.

The bus was late.

This wouldn't usually bother her, but today was different. Today was *important*, and she had to make sure she got home on time. So it should have been a relief to see her parents' car race into view around the corner, but Suzy just let out a groan.

"Oh no," she muttered. "Not this again."

The car accelerated toward the shelter, then screeched to a stop at the last second, ejecting a wave of dirty water from the gutter. Suzy just had time to shield her face with her backpack before the wave broke, drenching everyone in the shelter. There was a collective cry of shock and dismay from her schoolmates.

The passenger-side window wound down, and Suzy peered through her dripping hair to see her mother at the wheel. She was a small, dark-skinned woman with a round face and red-tinted braids. She must have just finished her shift at the hospital, because she was still wearing her scrubs.

"Sorry I'm late," she said. "Hurry up and get in."

Suzy's soaking clothes did nothing to dampen the hot prickle of embarrassment she felt as the other pupils turned, as one, to glare at her.

"Mom!" she hissed. "Look what you've done!"

Her mother looked confused. "I told you I was going to pick you up."

"And I told you not to," Suzy said a moment before someone shoved her hard in the back, and she went reeling out into the rain. She turned to see who might have done it, but the group had already closed ranks and she was faced with a wall of carefully neutral expressions. She sighed, and turned back to her mom. "Fine," she said shortly. "Let's go."

She climbed into the passenger seat, wound the window back up, and tried not to feel the sting of all those eyes on her as they pulled away.

"I told you to take an umbrella this morning," said her mother as the school faded from view behind them. "Now look at you. You're soaked."

Suzy briefly considered responding to this, but settled for trying to make herself comfortable, despite her clinging cold uniform. "You and Dad can't keep doing this," she said. "You never used to drive me everywhere. I can take the bus like everyone else."

She watched doubt and worry chase each other across her mother's face for a moment, before she finally got them under control.

"I know," her mother said. "But we're your parents. We enjoy doing these little things to take care of you."

"Is that why you've started phoning the school every day to check up on me?" she asked.

Her mother's expression slipped a little, confirming Suzy's suspicion that she hadn't been meant to know about the phone calls.

"I think *every* day is a bit of an exaggeration."

"Every day for the past three weeks, and twice this morning," said Suzy. "The school secretary called me into his office to complain about it. He says he's going to block your number if it carries on."

3

Her mother drummed her fingers on the steering wheel in annoyance as she negotiated the traffic. "I knew I should have gone straight to the headmistress."

"You just need to stop worrying about me," said Suzy. "I'm fine!"

"But we *can't* stop worrying about you, darling," her mother said. "You gave your father and me such a shock."

Suzy rolled her eyes. "I know, and I'm sorry. But that was three weeks ago. I thought you'd be over it by now."

"Over it?" Her mother gave a strange, humorless laugh. "We discover that you've been sneaking out of the house in the middle of the night with a bunch of ogres—"

"Trolls," Suzy corrected her.

"—to deliver mail to other planets—"

"Other *worlds*, Mom. They're called the Impossible Places."

"—filled with witches and dragons and heaven knows what else."

"A lot of them are friendly."

"And that your *life* has been in danger!" her mother continued. "You were in a train crash! And an earthquake! That's not the sort of thing your father and I are going to just 'get over.'"

Suzy folded her arms and sank down in the seat. "I'm starting to wish I'd never told you about it."

4

"Thank goodness you did," said her mother. "Otherwise we wouldn't be able to protect you at all."

"You weren't supposed to protect me," Suzy muttered. "You were supposed to understand." But buried deep within her resentment was a sickly twist of guilt. Her first adventure to the Impossible Places might have been largely accidental, but her second had been deliberate. She had chosen to leave her parents behind, under the influence of a sleeping spell, while she faced danger and excitement in some of the stranger corners of reality. It hadn't been fair on them. But that was exactly why she had decided to tell them the truth. She had expected a little shock and disbelief at first, but she hadn't expected them to panic. And then to keep panicking for three weeks solid.

They had confiscated her postal uniform, her delivery satchel, and her copy of *The Knowledge*—the encyclopedic handbook for all Impossible postal operatives. And when an invitation to rejoin the crew on their delivery rounds had appeared last week via remote spell, her parents had refused to let Suzy reply. They hardly let her out of their sight anymore, except to go to school. For the first time in her life, Suzy was grounded. She hated it.

Why couldn't she make them understand? Yes, the Impossible Places were bizarre and sometimes dangerous, but they were also wonderful. She had experienced things there that she wouldn't have been able to imagine just a few months ago. She had befriended ghosts, met a king, battled a giant robot, and saved an entire city from destruction. And she hadn't done any of it alone, because she was part of a crew now—the crew of the Impossible Postal Express, the fastest troll train in existence. She had saved their lives and they had saved hers, several times over. They were her friends, and she missed them. The possibility that she might never be allowed to rejoin them filled her with dread.

Which was why, the day before yesterday, she had proposed a plan she hoped would fix everything. With her parents' permission, she had returned the crew's invitation with one of her own: an invitation to dinner.

She still didn't think her parents were entirely persuaded by the idea, but she had successfully argued that they couldn't reasonably ban her from seeing friends they had never met. This was the perfect opportunity for them to get to know the crew and learn more about being a postie. She was sure that, once they really understood what she had been trying to tell them, they would drop their objections. At the very least, they might finally learn the difference between trolls and ogres.

But that meant that tonight had to go perfectly. It was her best, and possibly last, chance to change their minds.

If she failed, she might never see the Impossible Places again.

⤖

Her father was waiting for them in the front doorway when they finally pulled up outside the house. He was tall and pale, with a long face and a mop of ginger curls. He was drying his hands on a dishcloth and had already changed into his best shirt.

"What took you so long?" he said as Suzy and her mother hurried out of the car. "They'll be here soon!"

"I know," said Suzy's mother, planting a distracted little kiss on his cheek as she brushed past him. "I just need a shower and to get changed." She dropped her bag in the hall and pounded upstairs.

"Hello, sweetheart," said Suzy's father as she hopped in through the door. "How was school?"

"Fine, thanks," said Suzy, dumping her bag next to her mother's. "Is everything ready?" She didn't wait for an answer but raced down the hallway and into the kitchen.

The whole room sparkled—she had never seen it so clean, and all the usual detritus that cluttered up the counters was absent, replaced with a few small vases of flowers and a scattering of tea lights in jars. The kitchen table was covered with a white cloth that Suzy hadn't realized they even owned, and that in turn was almost lost beneath a small mountain of food. There was a bowl of baked potatoes, three types of cheese, sliced ham, roast beef, chicken wings, steamed peas, carrot sticks, bread rolls, vegetarian pizza, pasta salad, Caesar salad, burgers, sausage rolls, and a large pot of her mom's octopus curry.

"Wow. Dad. This looks incredible."

"I should hope so," said her father. "I took the afternoon off work to get it all ready."

"Really?"

He smiled. "I'm treating it as a diplomatic summit," he said. "A first contact between two peoples."

"And a bear," said Suzy.

Her father nodded. "Hence the salmon, as per your instructions." He pointed to the huge baking tray in the center of the table, from which the somewhat surprised-looking head of a whole roast salmon stared out at them from its nest of tinfoil.

"Brilliant," said Suzy. Bears liked salmon. She had looked it up online.

Her father tousled her hair. "You're not the only one taking this dinner seriously," he said. "In fact, I think it might be one of your better ideas."

"Thank you." Suzy leaned into him. "I'm sure they're going to love it. And you and Mom are going to love *them*, too. I promise." She pulled him into a soggy hug.

"Hey, mind the shirt," he said. "You'd better get dried and dressed. Your friends will be here soon."

"Right," she said. She let him go, but had only taken one step toward the door when the whole house began to shake.

"What's happening?" said her father, lunging to steady a pile of buttered bread rolls before they tipped onto the floor.

Suzy heard her mother shriek, and a moment later, she reeled into the kitchen, still soaking wet from the shower and fastening the cord of her fluffy pink bathrobe. "Is it an earthquake?"

Suzy grabbed the counter for balance. "No," she said, a smile spreading across her face. "It's a train!"

There was a tortured screech of brakes, and then the fridge door was blasted wide-open, hurling a carton of milk and half a dozen eggs across the room to decorate the opposite wall. A cloud of yellow steam billowed out from inside, filling the room and making the three of them choke.

"What was that?" Suzy's father's voice came from some-where in the middle of the fog. "And why can I smell bananas?"

"It's the Express!" said Suzy, trying to dispel the steam with a wave of her hand. "They're here!"

2

GUESS WHO'S COMING TO DINNER

The clouds of yellow steam filling the kitchen began to dissipate, and Suzy was finally able to fight her way through them to the fridge. She steadied herself in the puddle of orange juice that was pooling in front of it, and looked inside.

She was only a little surprised to discover that the shelves and most of their contents had vanished, and the interior of the fridge had expanded to form a shining white space the size of an aircraft hangar. A set of train tracks ran from a dark tunnel mouth in the rear wall, almost up to the fridge door. And standing on the tracks was a huge old steam train. Not a normal steam train, though—its locomotive, the *Belle de Loin*, was oversized and misshapen, as though it had been put together out of spare parts by someone who had a pretty good idea of what a train should look like, but had never actually seen one before. Its wheels were a confusing mix of different sizes, its boiler sprouted pipes and valves in strange places, and its driver's cab was a lopsided Tudor mansion, complete with mullioned windows and warped wooden beams. Behind it was a tender, piled high with the fusion bananas that were the *Belle*'s fuel.

A simple red wooden carriage was coupled behind this. This was the sorting carriage—the traveling post office in which the mail of a hundred different magical worlds was carried and sorted. And behind that, at the very end of the train, was a small and slightly shabby-looking caravan with the letters *H.E.C.* stenciled on its door: the Hazardous Environment Carriage. It didn't look like much, but Suzy knew that it was capable of withstanding the most extreme conditions a postie could face, from the freezing depths of outer space to the blazing hearts of active volcanoes.

The sight of the train took her back to the first night she had seen it, almost three months earlier, and she felt her heartbeat quicken. She would never get entirely used to seeing it—it always carried the promise of adventure.

"What on earth?"

Suzy turned at the sound of her father's voice and

realized that her parents had joined her. They stared into the fridge with a mixture of terror and disbelief.

"Mom? Dad?" said Suzy, swelling with pride. "This is the Impossible Postal Express. Isn't it fantastic?"

Her father looked around the suddenly cavernous fridge. "I put some yogurts in here this morning," he said. "Where have they gone?"

Suzy gave him a look. "Dad, the yogurts aren't important."

"But they were probiotic," he lamented.

Suzy was spared having to reply when one of the windows of the locomotive's cab swung open and J. F. Stonker, driver of the Express, poked his head out.

Suzy's parents gasped in astonishment. Stonker was a troll. Small and round and wrinkled, he looked a bit like a gray potato, except for his absolutely gigantic nose—at least a foot long—and the enormous handlebar mustache that hung beneath it. A pair of sharp blue eyes blinked down at them from beneath the peak of his railwayman's cap.

"Good evening!" he said. "Are we all right to park here?"

Suzy's parents just stared at him with their mouths open, so Suzy answered for them. "Yes, that's fine, Stonker. But what's happened to the Express? The carriages are in the wrong order. Isn't the sorting carriage supposed to be at the back?"

Stonker turned and looked back along the train as though he had never seen it before. "Ah, you spotted our little mistake," he said. "Well done. We got a bit mixed up at our servicing check last week and put them back together wrong. I was rather hoping no one would notice."

Suzy laughed. "It's good to see you."

"You too!" he called back. "Stay there, we'll be right out." He disappeared back inside and shut the window.

Suzy let out a little giggle of excitement. "This is going to be brilliant!" she exclaimed. "I can't wait for you to meet everyone."

Her parents nodded, a little vacantly.

"Please try not to stare at them," said Suzy. "I know they seem a bit unusual, but you'll soon get used to it and...oh no!" She looked down at her soaking-wet school uniform. "I can't meet them like this! I need to get changed. And so do you, Mom." She made a run for the hallway, skidded to a stop, and hurried back. "There's no time right now. I'll introduce you to everyone first."

Her parents didn't reply. They were still gawking, dumbfounded, into the fridge, although they shuffled aside as Stonker stepped out of it and into the kitchen.

"Suzy Smith!" he said, hopping neatly over the puddle

of orange juice and opening his arms wide. "How the devil have you been?"

"I've been okay, thanks," she said, hugging him. "Thank you for coming!" She gestured toward her parents. "This is my mom and dad."

Stonker pivoted on the balls of his feet and swept his cap off his head. "Mr. and Mrs. Smith," he said. "J. F. Stonker, at your service. Absolutely delighted to make your acquaintance." He offered them his hand, and after a moment's hesitation, Suzy's father stepped forward and took it.

"Um, yes," he said. "Sorry. Hello."

"Splendid, splendid!" said Stonker, pumping first Suzy's dad's and then Suzy's mom's hand so vigorously that they became a blur. "You must be so very proud of your daughter."

"Er, well, yes," said Suzy's mom reflexively.

"And I believe you already know Fletch?" He nodded to the fridge, where another troll had emerged. Fletch was older than Stonker, with skin as brown and creased as old tree bark. Tufts of wiry hair escaped from his ears and nostrils, and he wore his usual ensemble of dirty overalls and scuffed work boots. He directed a brief nod of recognition at Suzy's parents, tramped straight through the puddle of juice to the table, and helped himself to a seat.

"How's it goin'?" he said, picking a chicken wing off a

nearby plate. He cast a critical eye over the mess of eggs and milk on the wall. "You've redecorated."

"Yes, we remember Fletch," said Suzy's mom curtly.

Suzy grimaced. Fletch was lovely once you go to know him well enough, but he didn't exactly make a good first impression. And three weeks ago, at this very table, she had revealed the truth about the Impossible Places to her parents by waking them from the depths of a sleeping spell and introducing them to him. Perhaps that hadn't been such a great idea.

Then her mom gave a strangled little squeak and retreated behind her dad.

"What's wrong?" Suzy asked.

Her mom peered out from behind her dad and pointed with a quaking hand to the large yellow bear that was squeezing its bulk out of the fridge. It reared up onto its hind legs, and the pink ribbon tied in a bow around its head scraped the ceiling. Its fur was brushed and gleaming, and even its blue denim overalls were clean and neatly pressed.

"Ursel!" said Suzy, running over and throwing her arms around the animal's waist. "You look great!"

"Rrrrorlf," Ursel replied, baring her huge fangs in a smile.

"Mom, Dad, this is Ursel. She's the Express's fire-woman."

Ursel stuck out a paw, making Suzy's parents flinch. Suzy laughed. She had forgotten just how scared she herself had been upon first meeting Ursel.

"It's very nice to meet you," her dad said, hesitantly taking the paw in both his hands and shaking it. He gave a nervous little laugh. "You're much bigger than I imagined!"

"Grrronf," said Ursel. "Hhhhrk rowlf."

"Pardon?" said Suzy's dad.

"Ursel says she'll take that as a compliment," said Stonker, with a slight smile. "But please think very carefully before you give her any more."

Suzy's dad nodded hard enough to make his teeth rattle.

"She also wants to know if this is a traditional form of human dress, Mrs. Smith," said Stonker, indicating her bathrobe. "Suzy was wearing one the first time we met her."

Suzy's mom blushed. "I was just going to get dressed," she said. "In fact, if you'll excuse me..."

"Wait, Mom," said Suzy. "This isn't everyone. Where's...?"

"Hello!" came a voice from the fridge. "Did I miss anything?"

Suzy broke into a huge grin as a young troll stepped into the kitchen. He had pale green skin and large eyes,

18

and wore a red-and-gold postie's uniform that was several sizes too big for him. He clutched a small gift-wrapped parcel and looked around the kitchen with undisguised interest.

"Hello, Suzy!" he said. "So this is where you live! Wow!" He bustled over and gave Suzy a quick hug, then headed straight for her parents. "Hello there," he said. "I've really been looking forward to meeting you both. I'm Wilmot Grunt, Postmaster of the Express, but please just call me Wilmot." He laughed. "Suzy is the very best postal operative I've ever worked with."

"She's the only postal operative you've ever worked with," said Fletch.

Wilmot pressed his lips together in annoyance. "True," he said. "But she still does an exceptional job, and I count myself very lucky to have her on my staff."

Suzy glowed with pride. This was the sort of thing she had been hoping for. It seemed to be having the desired effect on her parents as well, as they visibly relaxed.

"That's very nice to hear," said her dad, managing a smile. "Thank you."

Suzy's mom stepped out from behind him and nodded at the parcel Wilmot was holding. "Is that a delivery?" she asked.

"Oh, this!" Wilmot looked at the parcel as if he'd

forgotten he was carrying it. "No, this is for you." He stepped forward and presented it with a flourish.

"It's not often the whole crew gets invited to dinner, you see," said Stonker. "So by way of thanks, we all clubbed together and got you a little something."

"Oh." Suzy's mom accepted the box and turned it over in her hands. "That's very kind of you."

"It's nothing, really," said Stonker with a dismissive wave. "Just something to help out around the house, that's all."

"You can open it now, if you like," added Wilmot eagerly.

Suzy's mom only hesitated for a moment before her curiosity won out and she tore open the paper to reveal a plain wooden box with a hinged lid. Suzy and her dad both huddled round her as she opened the lid and looked inside.

A puff of air escaped, brushing past Suzy with a faint smell of woodsmoke. They looked into the box.

"It's empty," said Suzy's mom.

"Well, it is now," said Fletch, as though this were the most obvious thing in the world. "You just let it out."

Suzy felt a nervous twinge. "Let what out?" she said.

"The boggart," said Stonker.

"The what?" asked Suzy's dad.

"Boggart," said Fletch, helping himself to a hot dog. "It's your basic household spirit. Roams around the place keepin' things neat and dusted. Turns up little odds and ends you might have lost—keys, loose change, that sort of thing. Pretty handy, really."

Suzy's mom gasped. "You mean we've got a *ghost* in the house?"

Stonker chuckled. "Dear me, no. We wouldn't lumber you with a *ghost*. This is a spirit, and quite an unobtrusive one at that. Keep it fed and warm, and you'll hardly even know it's here."

Suzy's dad looked around the kitchen in alarm. "But where is it? I can't see it."

"'Course not," said Fletch. "Invisible, innit?"

Suzy was scanning the room as well. She didn't see anything, of course, but she caught a vague sense of movement from the corner of her eye, as though something small and very fast had just darted under the table, too quick for her to identify. When she turned to focus on it, there was nothing there.

"What does it eat?" she asked.

"Just leave a saucer of milk out at night, and it should be quite happy," said Stonker.

"I thought that was hedgehogs," said Fletch.

"Is it?" Stonker twirled the end of his mustache as he

considered this. "I'm pretty sure it's boggarts. Anyway, just let it make a home for itself in the fireplace and I expect it'll take care of itself."

"But we don't have a fireplace," said Suzy's mom.

"Really?" Stonker looked surprised. "How on earth do you keep the place warm?"

"With central heating," said Suzy. She got down on her knees and scanned the floor, looking for movement rather than detail. She let her eyes unfocus, and a few seconds later, she detected another little flurry on the far side of the room, zipping along the skirting board and hopping into a cabinet that stood ajar beneath the sink. "What happens if we can't feed and house it?"

Stonker's silence made her look up.

"Well," he said, shifting awkwardly, "I believe they *can* get a little obstreperous if neglected."

"A little what?" said Suzy's mom.

There was a crash from inside the cabinet. Suzy leaped to her feet as the door swung open and the contents were ejected one by one. Tins of shoe polish, a roll of trash bags, a sink plunger, and a dustpan and brush all sailed through the air, forcing Suzy, her parents, and the crew to take cover behind the table.

"A little rowdy," said Stonker as a bottle of fabric softener whistled past his head. "Oh dear."

"What does it think it's doing?" said Suzy's mom.

"It can't be getting rowdy already," Suzy's dad replied. "It's only just arrived!"

"Hhhrunk," said Ursel, who was too big to hide behind anything, and simply swatted aside any projectiles that came too close.

"Me?" said Stonker. "No, of course I didn't feed it while it was in the box. I thought you had."

"Unf," said Ursel, shaking her head.

"Me neither," called Fletch.

"Nor me," said Wilmot, who was crouched beside Suzy. "Sorry. Was I supposed to?"

"For goodness' sake, make it stop!" cried Suzy's mom as another cabinet door sprung open, and the boggart disgorged an avalanche of pots and pans across the floor.

"We need milk," said Suzy. "Cover me!" She dashed across the room in a crouch while Ursel kept pace with her, shielding her with her body. Suzy found the carton of milk that had been hurled from the fridge—it was leaking badly, but there was just enough left inside to fill the small measuring cup that she retrieved from the floor. Then, being careful not to spill a drop, she approached the open cabinet. Ursel plucked a saucepan lid out of the air a second before it would have struck Suzy in the forehead, and raised it as a shield, her great forearms surrounding Suzy in a protective circle.

Suzy placed the cup on the floor in front of the open cabinet, and the barrage of kitchenware stopped abruptly. Then she and Ursel beat a hasty retreat to the far side of the room, and watched.

There was still nothing to see, but Suzy thought she could hear a faint snuffling sound. Something dipped into the milk, causing ripples across its surface. The snuffling sound grew louder.

"See, Mom?" Suzy whispered. "There's nothing to worry about. Everything's under control."

The cup arced through the air and upended its contents all over her. The boggart gave a piggish snort, and blinking the milk from her eyes, Suzy thought she saw something leap off the floor into the sink. There was a splash, a gurgle, and then a groan of pipes that quickly spread out through the walls and the ceiling, until it sounded as if the whole house were coming apart.

No, no, no, no nooooo! thought Suzy as she saw her parents clutch each other in fear. *This isn't how it's supposed to go!*

As quickly as it had started, the noise died away, leaving just a comfortable ticking in the radiators.

"You know," said Stonker, "I'm beginning to think maybe it *was* hedgehogs."

"Not much we can do about it now," said Fletch. "It's got into the plumbin'."

"What on earth is it doing in there?" said Suzy's dad, looking fearfully around the room.

Suzy wiped the last of the milk from her face and stood up. "Perhaps it's trying to keep warm," she said. "We don't have a fireplace, but we do have a hot water boiler."

"You mean our central heating is haunted now?" he said.

"Sir," said Stonker. "You fail to understand. *Ghosts* haunt. House spirits *inhabit*. Your boggart is simply making a new home for itself, that's all. You'll probably find it calms down now."

Suzy didn't think he looked quite as confident as he sounded, but she also realized that her parents needed some reassurances, and quickly—her mother's lips were pressed into a thin line of disapproval, and her father still looked as though he expected monsters to emerge from the walls at a moment's notice. So far, this dinner hadn't quite been the success Suzy had hoped for.

"We'll get this mess cleaned up in no time," she said breezily. "And then we can eat. I'm sure Mom and Dad have got lots of questions for everyone."

"Oh yes," confirmed Suzy's mother darkly. "Lots and lots of questions."

3
WHO YA GONNA CALL?

It took less than ten minutes for everyone to mop up the worst of the mess and take their seats at the kitchen table. Suzy sat down next to Wilmot and directly across the table from her father, who had apparently already begun asking questions.

"...so yes," said Wilmot, "while it's true that trolls prefer to live under bridges, we don't really hold strong opinions on billy goats."

"I see," said Suzy's dad, propping his elbows on the table and steepling his hands in what Suzy jokingly thought of as his "I'm listening" pose. "But Suzy tells me that you don't have anywhere to live at the moment. Is that right?"

"Sort of," said Wilmot. "Trollville, our hometown,

suffered a lot of damage in the recent earthquakes, so we're technically homeless until they finish rebuilding it."

"I'm so sorry," Suzy's dad replied. "That must be dreadful for you."

"Oh, we're luckier than some," said Stonker, slathering butter on a slice of bread. "Most of the city's population has dispersed all over the Impossible Places. But the Express is as much a home to us as Trollville, so we've taken up a life on the rails full-time. And I must say, I think it rather suits us."

"Grolk." Ursel nodded before reaching over to spear the baked salmon through the gills with one claw. She tipped her head back and flipped the whole fish straight into her open maw. For a few seconds, the only sound in the room was the crunching of fish bones and a deep, satisfied growl from Ursel. Suzy's parents sank back in their chairs slightly.

"Is, er... is the fish... all right?" asked Suzy's mom. Ursel raised one claw in the closest equivalent a bear can manage to a thumbs-up.

"And you're making deliveries again?" Suzy asked Wilmot. Just asking the question opened an uncomfortably empty feeling deep in her chest, as though part of her was suddenly missing, but she knew she needed to steer the conversation toward the Express.

"Almost nonstop!" said Wilmot. "In fact, this is our

first evening off in weeks. But we've finally cleared the backlog of undelivered mail and we should be back to something like our normal schedule soon. Speaking of which, it would be great to have your help again. When are you going to join us?"

Suzy gave her parents a meaningful look. "I'm not sure."

"Well," said her dad slowly, "that's a conversation that your mother and I still need to have."

"How about having it right now?" said Suzy.

"No, thank you," said her mom. "We'll have it when we're ready."

"We don't want to rush into any big decisions," said her dad.

The exchange was interrupted by a shrill ringing noise, loud enough to make Suzy wince.

"What's that?" shouted Suzy's mom, covering her ears. She glared around the table, hunting for suspects, and her eyes finally came to rest on Wilmot, who was suddenly squirming in his seat.

"Sorry!" he called as he hurriedly patted himself down. "It's in one of these pockets…" Suzy watched, bemused, as he threw his greatcoat over his head until he was just a pile of twitching red fabric. She turned a questioning look on the rest of the crew, who all shrugged.

The ringing grew louder as Wilmot finally reemerged from inside his coat, holding something aloft. It was an antique telephone receiver, with a rotary dial and a pair of small brass bells that looked as though they'd been salvaged from an old alarm clock bolted onto it. "Do you like it?" he shouted to Suzy. "It's my new mobile phone! Mom gave it to me for emergencies."

"Then you'd better answer it!" Suzy shouted, sticking her fingers in her ears. She could see all the glasses on the table starting to vibrate.

Wilmot extended a long telescopic antenna from the top of the phone, and the ringing stopped abruptly. Everyone at the table let out a sigh of relief.

"Hello?" said Wilmot, sticking the receiver deep into one ear. "Mom?"

"Newfangled contraption," muttered Fletch. "What's wrong with a good old-fashioned courier fairy, that's what I'd like to know."

Suzy's mom had uncovered her ears, but didn't look any happier. "We don't normally allow phones at the dinner table," she said to no one in particular.

"Mom, please." Suzy put a calming hand on her arm as Wilmot hopped out of his seat.

"Hello?" he said into the phone. "Mom, is that you? I can't hear you." He began to jog on the spot.

"Now what on earth is he doing?" said Suzy's mom, staring at Wilmot in bewilderment. But Suzy had no answer.

"Rrrolf, hrunf grruk," said Ursel, picking a fish bone out of her fangs with a claw.

"What did she say?" asked Suzy's dad.

"She wondered how else you expected him to use a mobile phone," Stonker said. "You have to keep moving or it stops working."

"But...but why?" asked Suzy's dad. "That doesn't make sense."

"I suppose it wouldn't be mobile otherwise," said Stonker.

"Runf," said Ursel, with an emphatic nod.

Suzy barely heard any of this. She was too focused on Wilmot, and the worried frown that was gathering on his brow. Two of his words had lodged in her mind and she couldn't shake them loose: "For emergencies."

"I still can't hear you, Mom," he shouted into the mouthpiece. "Hang on a second." He set off around the table at a brisk jog. "Is this better? Can you hear me now?"

Suzy shuffled her chair in to give him more space as he jogged past. She saw her mom watching him as though he had gone mad. Then, suddenly, he stopped.

"Oh!" he exclaimed. "It's you! How did you get this

30

number?" A few seconds passed and his frown deepened. "I see. Tell me everything!"

Everyone else had gone quiet now, and even Suzy's parents were watching Wilmot expectantly.

"Really?" Wilmot said, narrowly avoiding knocking a vase off the sideboard with the tip of one ear as he jogged past it. "Wow! That sounds serious."

The others twisted in their seats, watching him as he completed another lap of the table.

"You can always count on us," he said, starting to sound short of breath. "Come rain, shine, or meteor shower, the Impossible Postal Express will . . . Yes. Yes, of course I'll shut up and get a move on. Sorry." He came to a halt, retracted the phone's antenna, and stashed it away inside his coat. "Well!" he said, drawing his sleeve across his brow. "That was unexpected." He looked around the circle of concerned faces. "We've got a delivery to make."

"But we're off duty," said Stonker. "Can't it wait until tomorrow?"

"I'm afraid not," said Wilmot. "It's extremely urgent. Top priority!"

"Why?" said Suzy. "Who was that? It didn't sound like your mom."

"Oh, it wasn't," said Wilmot. "It was Captain Neoma at the Ivory Tower. Or Lady Meridian, to use her proper title."

31

Suzy sat bolt upright. "What?"

"Now wait just a minute!" Suzy's mom stood up and raised her hands for quiet. "Lady Meridian. Suzy's told me about her. She's that terrible old woman with the army of statues, yes?"

"No," said Suzy. "You're thinking of Lady *Crepuscula*. She lives in the Obsidian Tower."

"Then who's this Lady Meridian?" her dad asked.

"She lives in the *Ivory* Tower," said Suzy. "The one inside the moon. With the library in it. Remember?" She could see her mom gathering herself for an argument, and braced herself, only to be interrupted by her dad.

"So there are two towers?" he said.

"Yes," Suzy replied.

"And two Ladies?"

Suzy looked between him and her mom, and felt some of the fight go out of her. She sighed. "Look, Dad, it's really simple. Lady Crepuscula is in charge of the Obsidian Tower. It's big, it's black, and it's a prison for the most dangerous criminals in the Impossible Places. The living statues are sort of like prison guards."

"I'm with you so far," he replied. "Carry on."

"Lady Meridian is in charge of the *Ivory* Tower," said Suzy. "It's big, it's white, it's inside the moon, and it's the largest library anywhere in existence. It contains all the knowledge of the Impossible Places, and my friend Frederick works there. He's the Chief Librarian."

"But didn't you say something about an old man running the place?" said her dad. "Or did I imagine that?"

Suzy screwed her eyes shut. Had either of her parents really listened to a single thing she'd told them?

"That was *Lord* Meridian," she said. "He used to be in charge of the Ivory Tower, but he was evil and we helped overthrow him. The new Lady Meridian used to be his head of security. Her real name's Neoma."

"And she wants us there on the double," said Wilmot, edging toward the fridge. "I don't know exactly what's happened, but she says the future of the Ivory Tower is in jeopardy. Apparently we're the only people who can help."

Stonker jumped to his feet. "Well, why the blazes didn't you say so?" He turned to Suzy's parents and bowed so low that the tips of his mustache brushed the floor. "Mr. and Mrs. Smith, it's been a pleasure."

Ursel pushed away from the table, although the movement did more to push the table away from her. It shuddered across the kitchen, its legs squealing against the floor, forcing Suzy's parents to scramble clear.

"Hhhrownf," Ursel growled.

"Ursel thanks you for your hospitality," said Stonker. "And says you have a lovely home."

"Um . . . she's welcome," said Suzy's mom, with a faltering smile.

"I'll just take a few of these to be gettin' on with," said Fletch, stuffing sausage rolls and a slice of pizza into his pockets. "Lovely spread, by the way. Really good grub, that."

Suzy jumped up. "Wait for me," she said.

"Oh, no you don't, young lady," said her mother. "You're not going anywhere."

Suzy skidded to a halt in the doorway. "But you heard Wilmot," she said. "The Ivory Tower needs us!"

Her mom folded her arms and drew herself up to her full height, which was only an inch or so taller than Suzy. She had a knack of making it feel ten times as much, though. "You're grounded, remember?"

Suzy's face fell. "But, Moooooom!"

"Your mother's right, Suzy," said her dad. "She and I still need to reach a final decision about all this magic business. Until then, we don't want you running off anywhere without us."

"But, Dad!" Suzy was aghast.

"No more *buts*, said her mom. "Your parents' decision is final."

Stonker cleared his throat. "Perhaps we should just see ourselves out," he said, shuffling discreetly toward the fridge.

"Wait," said Suzy as a new idea broke across her mind. "Take us all with you."

"I beg your pardon?" said Stonker.

Suzy turned back to her parents. "How about it?" she said. "Come on a delivery with me."

Her parents looked at one another in bemusement. "We can't do that," said her mom.

"Why not?" asked Suzy. "The whole point of this dinner was to help you get to know the crew and find out what life on the Express is like. But this is even better! Come with me to the Ivory Tower and you can find out for yourselves."

Her father was wavering already. "Go to the moon...," he said, with a faraway look in his eyes. "Just like Neil Armstrong."

"Better than Neil Armstrong," said Suzy. "Because he didn't get to look around inside it." She waggled her eyebrows in what she hoped was an encouraging fashion.

"Oh, no you don't," said her mom, stepping between them and breaking the spell. "I can see what you're doing, Suzanne Smith. Don't think you can get around me by using your father, just because he's a bit lax."

"Hey!" said Suzy's dad. "I am *not* lax. I'm just giving Suzy's proposal the consideration it deserves, rather than dismissing it out of hand."

"Is that what you think I'm doing?" said Suzy's mom, rounding on him.

"Well, aren't you?"

"I'm trying to keep our daughter safe."

The others were shuffling discreetly toward the fridge now, and Suzy was beginning to wish the floor would open up and swallow her. Or maybe swallow her parents. "Mom," she said. "The Ivory Tower isn't dangerous. It's just a library, and anyway, you'd both be there to supervise me." She gave her mother a hopeful smile. "You're always telling me that experience is the best teacher. Remember?"

Suzy's mom looked around the group of expectant faces. She pursed her lips. "I can't go dressed like this," she said.

"I don't see why not," said Stonker. "Suzy did." He met Suzy's frown with a mischievous smile. "But I can give you a few minutes to get changed, if you'd prefer."

Suzy's mom fixed him with a hard look. "I will be two minutes," she said. "And don't leave without me."

"Upon my honor," said Stonker.

"And you," she said, turning to Fletch. "You're not going anywhere until you get that boggart creature out of our plumbing."

"Why?" he said. "It's not doin' any harm. You just need to remember to give the toilet bowl a kick before you sit down on it, that's all."

"Out. Of. Our. Plumbing," said Suzy's mom. "I'll be right back."

Suzy gave a silent sigh of relief as her mother hurried out of the kitchen. For a moment, she had felt close to losing everything. "Sorry, Fletch," she said. "Do you think you'll be able to get the boggart out without hurting it?"

"Yeah, should be fine," said Fletch. "I know a bloke who can come and snake the drains."

Suzy nodded, then frowned. "Please tell me that doesn't involve actual snakes."

"Nah, 'course not," said Fletch. "Technically, they're a species of multi-headed worm."

"No," said Suzy, firmly. "No more creatures in the plumbing. Isn't there some other way to get it out?"

Fletch puffed out his cheeks. "I could probably whip up an ectoplasmic plunger," he said. "Might take me a while, mind."

"That's fine," said Suzy. "Take all the time you need."

They all turned as her mom reentered the kitchen, dressed in a tracksuit and sneakers. She was carrying a coat hanger, from which hung a long red coat with elaborate gold brocade, a matching waistcoat, and black trousers.

"My postie's uniform!" said Suzy.

"I still don't think this is a good idea," said her mom.

"But if we're going on a delivery, I suppose you'd better have it." She handed the uniform to Suzy. "Are we ready?"

"We are now," said Suzy. She hugged the uniform, savoring the feel of the heavy fabric against her face. "Let's go."

"High time," said Stonker. "To the Ivory Tower!"

4
GOLD STAMP SPECIAL

Suzy always felt a few inches taller in her postal uniform, and she stepped out of the sorting carriage's storage cupboard with a flourish.

"Deputy Postal Operative Smith, reporting for duty," she said, bracing herself against the rocking motion of the train as it sped across reality toward the Ivory Tower. The sorting carriage was a warm, homely place, lined with shelves and pigeonholes, all of which were filled with neatly ordered stacks of mail. Wilmot looked up from his desk in the center of it all, his eyes shining with excitement. He was holding a delivery form printed on shimmering gold paper. "Splendid!" he said. "This could be a very big day for us, Suzy. Neoma says her delivery is the most urgent thing we've ever had to handle. Absolute highest priority!"

"You mean we're going to do an express delivery?" said Suzy. She had committed the various classes of delivery to memory before her parents had confiscated her copy of *The Knowledge*. "Door to door in five hours?"

"We could," he replied. "But there's one category even higher than that. A Gold Stamp Special! The rarest, most exclusive form of delivery a postie can make!" He waved the form at her.

"How come I've never heard of it?" asked Suzy. "It's not mentioned in *The Knowledge*."

"Because there have only been a handful in the entire history of the Impossible Postal Service," said Wilmot. "My dad never had one. Not even my grandpa Honks." His eyes went wide. "I'd be the first postie in my family ever to deliver one," he said in an awed voice. "Mom will be so proud."

"Wow," said Suzy. "But what does Neoma need delivering that's so important?"

Wilmot's eyes snapped back into focus. "Oh. She didn't actually tell me," he said a little sheepishly. "But whatever it is, it's eating the books at the Ivory Tower and they need to get rid of it immediately."

"Eating them?" said Suzy, alarmed. "Is it some sort of creature?"

"I really don't know," said Wilmot. "But Neoma insisted that only the Express could help, and that if we didn't stop whatever we were doing and get there immediately, she'd hunt us all down and grind us into goblin fodder."

Suzy pulled a face. "It doesn't sound like she's changed much."

"Oh, I don't know," said Wilmot. "There's a chance she's joking about the goblin fodder bit." He pulled his satchel over his shoulder and slipped the form into it. "If we can deliver a Gold Stamp Special, we'll each get a medal from the Postmaster General, and our names engraved on the Central Post Office wall of fame for future generations to admire!"

Suzy's thoughts turned immediately to her parents. Surely a medal would be enough to convince them to let her continue as a postie? She'd had it all planned out in her head for days now—she could carry on at school, but join the crew at weekends and for a few weeks in the summer holidays, on the understanding that it wouldn't affect her grades. This delivery could be just what she needed. "Have you seen my parents?" she asked.

"I think they're in the cab with the others," said Wilmot. "Let's go and see."

Thanks to a clever bit of dimensional engineering, the door in the wall behind Wilmot's desk led directly into the locomotive's cab, which was hot, humid, and full of noise. Part kitchen, part machine room, a twisted mass of pipes and valves covered the front wall, curving like tree roots around an ancient-looking hearth, in which a blue fire roared. As Suzy and Wilmot entered, Ursel was tossing a few bunches of bananas into the flames. They crackled and flared, and the whole train strained forward with a renewed burst of energy.

"Be ready to hit the ground running, ladies and gentlemen," said Stonker. "We're almost there." He was darting feverishly around the various dials and levers protruding from the pipework, managing the boiler's temperature, its pressure, and the locomotive's speed.

Suzy looked around the cab. "I thought my parents were in here," she said. Stonker pointed to the front door, which stood ajar.

"Try out there," he said.

Suzy stuck her head out and was surprised to see her parents on the gangway that ran along the side of the *Belle*'s boiler, just above the wheels.

"Hello, sweetheart!" shouted Suzy's dad above the howl of the tunnel. "You look very smart!"

"Dad!" Suzy shouted back. "Mom! What are you both doing out here?"

"Your father was worried we were missing something

exciting," said her mom, who was gripping the gangway's handrail with both hands. Her eyes were screwed shut.

"I thought a tunnel between worlds would look a bit swirlier," said Suzy's dad. "Or maybe *whooshier*, somehow."

"Sorry, Dad," said Suzy. "But it turns out that wormholes aren't really that interesting. It's all about the destinations."

As if on cue, the Express raced out of the tunnel into the dazzling white heart of the moon. It was an immense, spherical space, crisscrossed with a web of railway lines that hung suspended in mid-air. Trains shuttled back and forth along them, hurrying in and out of the hundreds of tunnel mouths that lined the curving walls. And right at the center of it all, running from the top of the sphere to the bottom, was a gigantic pillar of shining white stone, set with a rainbow of stained glass windows: the Ivory Tower.

"See what I mean?" said Suzy.

She hadn't seen the tower since her first adventure to the Impossible Places. Back then, the Express had been out of control and she had been too preoccupied with the thought of impending death to truly appreciate the view. Now she found herself preoccupied with her parents' reactions.

"Amandine! Look at this!" said her dad. He gave his wife a nudge, and she opened first one eye, then both eyes wide.

"Oh my goodness!" she cried. Her fear seemed to evaporate immediately, and she leaned forward over the rail. "There's so much of it!"

Suzy joined them at the railing. "Do you like it?" she asked hopefully.

"It's remarkable!" said her dad, a huge smile on his face.

"It's beautiful," said her mom. "And this has been in the moon all this time?"

Suzy nodded, relief and excitement washing through her. "And look, that's Center Point Station," she said, pointing to a sleek, curving building of white stone and glass that floated in mid-air in front of the tower. A dozen of the railway lines flowed into it. "That's our stop."

The Express began to slow as it swooped toward Center Point, and less than a minute later, it eased in beneath the station's arched glass roof and came to a halt at one of the platforms.

"You're all here," said Wilmot, hopping out of the cab's front door. "Excellent. Let's go and see what all the fuss is about, shall we?"

The concourse of Center Point Station was busy with creatures from all over the Union of Impossible Places. Suzy spotted a few trolls, some clockwork people, something that looked like a walking rosebush, and a gaggle of giant hermit crabs with neon pink shells as she and her parents followed Wilmot through the crowd. Even she found the throng of strange life-forms a little bewildering, so she wasn't surprised to see that her parents' sense of wonder was now tempered by trepidation, especially when they had to dodge out of the path of a large ogre-like creature with a glowing horn sprouting from its forehead.

"Are you both okay?" she asked. They nodded nervously in return.

She was so preoccupied with them that she almost walked straight into one of the pillars holding up the roof. She turned around just in time to avoid a collision, and found herself staring into a face that made her recoil in shock—it was owl-like, complete with feathers, a hooked beak, and large, lamp-like yellow eyes that stared angrily into hers. Instinctively, she threw up her hands to protect herself.

"What's wrong, sweetheart?" asked her dad.

It took Suzy a breathless second to realize what had happened. The face was just a picture on a poster, mounted on the pillar, and it was surrounded by angry red text.

WANTED

REWARD FOR INFORMATION
LEADING TO CAPTURE

"Is that the one you told us about?" asked her mom, putting a protective arm around Suzy and leveling her most disapproving look at the poster.

"Yes," said Suzy, who still felt a little shaken. She had known that Tenebrae was still at large, of course, but hadn't expected to be confronted with him quite so suddenly, even if he was just a poster. She looked around and realized that there were Wanted posters on every pillar in the station, and at every ticket office. Some of them bore Tenebrae's face, while others had a picture of Aybek, the former Lord Meridian, who had controlled the Impossible Places from the Ivory Tower until Suzy and the crew had exposed his plans and overthrown him. She shrugged off her mother's arm and approached one of them.

WANTED

FOR CONSPIRACY, ESPIONAGE, HIGH TREASON,

AND SUNDRY OTHER OFFENSES:

AYBEK ARANRHOD

(FORMERLY LORD MERIDIAN)

Her parents drifted after her. They were looking increasingly worried, and Suzy knew she needed to get them away from the posters and focus their minds on something other than dangerous criminals. She forced a smile.

"There's nothing to worry about," she said. "Wherever Aybek and Tenebrae are, they're worlds away from here. Let's catch up with Wilmot." She linked arms with them both and steered them away through the crowd.

They found Wilmot at the rear of the concourse, where a noisy mob of creatures clustered around the entrance to the drawbridge that extended across the gap between the railway station and the tower. Most of them looked angry.

"There you are!" said Wilmot, hopping from foot to foot with impatience. "Something's definitely wrong. Look."

He pointed to four women with bobs of brightly colored hair—one green, one orange, one red, and one blue—who blocked the row of turnstiles that marked the entrance to the drawbridge. They wore body armor over silver jumpsuits, and each sported a heavy-looking plasma rifle. A large neon sign above the turnstiles read WELCOME TO THE IVORY TOWER. NOW FREE AND OPEN TO THE PUBLIC. Someone had spoiled the effect somewhat by hanging a hand-painted cardboard sign beneath it that read CLOSED.

"Suzy!" hissed her father. "Those women have guns!"

"Don't worry, Dad," said Suzy, trying to keep her own anxiety in check. "They're the Lunar Guard. It's their job to protect the tower."

"We have a right to use the library!" shouted a gelatinous orange slug-thing at the front of the crowd. "I thought you were supposed to be open to everyone now!" There was a low chorus of jeers and mutterings.

"And I'm telling you again," said the guard with the green hair, "the management reserves the right to close the library without notice, which is exactly what's happened."

"When are they going to open it again?" shouted a minotaur in a ball gown. "I've got important medical research to do!"

"They'll open it as soon as they're ready," the guard replied.

A jagged figure made of glowing blue crystal cupped its hands around its mouth and yelled, "You're hiding something!" This prompted a fresh chorus of jeering and booing from the crowd. For the first time, the guards started to look uncomfortable.

"No one's hiding anything," said the guard with the orange hair. "But we're dealing with a security situation and no one gets in until it's resolved."

The crowd descended into animated chatter.

"I bet it's the old Lord Meridian," Suzy heard someone say. "He's taken over again."

"That's why no one's been able to find him anywhere," said a sparkling cloud of red gas. "He's been hiding here all along."

"They probably welcomed him back with open arms," muttered a nearby gnome.

Wilmot, who had been watching the crowd with mounting concern, put his hand up. "Excuse me!" he called. "We're from the Impossible Postal Express. Lady Meridian sent for us."

The crowd turned to stare as the green-haired guard pushed her way through to him. "You're the posties?" she asked.

"Postmaster Grunt and Deputy Postal Operative Smith, at your service," said Wilmot, clutching his lapel to show off his badge. Suzy did likewise.

The guard scrutinized them both through narrowed eyes, then looked Suzy's parents over. "What about these two?" she said.

"They're observing our delivery," said Suzy. "For, er…"

"For health and safety purposes," said her mother, narrowing her eyes right back at the guard. "And this tower of yours had better be safe, or I'm going to complain to your supervisor."

The guard stared at her. Suzy's mother stared right back.

Suzy cringed, but didn't dare intervene.

"Just get in there as quick as you can," said the guard. "Her Ladyship needs you." She led the way back through the crowd to the turnstiles, and for the second time that day, Suzy was uncomfortably aware of hostile eyes boring into the back of her head as she passed.

"How come they're allowed in?" said the gelatinous blob. "That's not fair!"

"It's a conspiracy!" someone shouted as the rest of the crowd muttered and fussed.

The guards unlocked the turnstiles and waved Wilmot, Suzy, and her parents through onto the drawbridge.

"Sorry to ask," said Wilmot as they passed through, "but what exactly *is* going on?"

"Trouble," said the red-haired guard. "Her Ladyship will tell you all about it."

The four of them hurried along the drawbridge toward the tower. "Well, this is all very exciting, isn't it?" said Suzy's father. Suzy was used to him highlighting the positive in any situation, but even she thought he sounded a little uncertain. It was a feeling she was beginning to share.

A pair of large glass doors marked the entrance to the tower. They swung open in welcome, and the four of them stepped into a tall, circular atrium, pierced from top to bottom by shafts of colored light from the tower's stained glass windows. The walls between the windows were lined with bookshelves, but to Suzy's surprise, they were almost entirely bare, and a small army of white-robed library assistants were scrambling up and down ladders, stripping the remaining shelves of their contents. More library assistants and even members of the Lunar Guard hurried back and forth, through doorways and down staircases, carrying armfuls of books away. Every one of them looked tense and nervous.

Even more surprising were the piles of abandoned books littering the floor. There were thousands of volumes of every shape and size, lying in disorderly heaps that reached almost as high as Suzy's waist. Their spines were cracked and their pages creased. Their *blank* pages.

Suzy picked a volume up at random and leafed through it as she and her parents followed Wilmot through the mess. Every page was completely empty. Even the cover was featureless. She put it down carefully on the nearest pile and selected another, but it was blank, too. She looked again at the mounds of discarded books surrounding them and realized they were all the same—there was not a single word in any of them. Something about the sight sent a little chill through her.

"Is this normal?" whispered her mother, looking around in confusion.

"No," said Suzy. "Definitely not."

"Quickly now!" a voice she recognized rang out across the atrium. "Those volumes of Vogon poetry should have been in the archive ten minutes ago. And you there! Where are you going with those four-dimensional pop-up books? They're supposed to go to the lower stacks, not the upper reading room. Come along—we've lost too many books already. We need to get whatever's left to safety."

Wilmot wove through the chaos to a circular reception desk in the center of the atrium, where a tall female troll with honey-colored skin was directing everyone through a megaphone. An ancient-looking troll sat behind the desk with his fingers in his ears.

"Hello, Mom," said Wilmot, waving his arms at the troll with the megaphone. "Is everything all right?"

"Oh, hello, Wilmot dear," said his mother, lowering the megaphone. "Thank goodness you've come."

"Yes," muttered the elderly troll behind the desk.

"Thank goodness!" He pulled his fingers from his ears with a loud double pop. "And young Suzy as well. You're both a sight for sore eyes." He reached up and used his sleeve to absentmindedly polish the steel plate that covered half his scalp.

"Mr. Trellis!" said Suzy. "And Mrs. Grunt! I didn't realize you'd both be here."

"I've found my second calling in life," said Mr. Trellis. "Library Assistant Bertram Trellis, at your service."

"The Old Guard has joined the staff at the Ivory Tower until Trollville is rebuilt," said Mrs. Grunt. "And right now they need every able pair of hands they can manage." She gave Suzy's parents a quizzical glance. "Are you here to volunteer?"

Suzy's dad looked a little lost. "Um, no. Sorry. We're with Suzy."

"They're my parents," said Suzy. "Mom and Dad, this is Gertrude Grunt. She's Wilmot's mom, and she ran the nursing home for retired posties in Trollville."

Gertrude reassessed Suzy's parents with a quick look, and smiled. "Delighted to meet you both," she said hurriedly. "But I'm afraid the pleasantries will have to wait. I need to make sure we get as many of our surviving books to safety as possible before Her Ladyship arrives with the package for you to deliver. Mr. Trellis, could you call her and let her know the crew of the Express is here?"

"Righto," said Mr. Trellis, and reached for the phone.

While he placed the call, Wilmot looked around the atrium in surprise. "Did the package do all this?"

"This is just a fraction of what it's done," said Gertrude. "It's drained almost every word in the tower. Hundreds of millions of books, wiped clean. We're doing everything we can to save what's left, but . . ." She shook her head sadly. "I fear it's too little, too late."

Suzy tried to imagine the whole library bled dry. All the knowledge, history, and culture of the Impossible Places, erased. It was catastrophic.

"Don't forget the souvenirs!" a new voice echoed around the atrium. Suzy turned and saw a small, round female troll, with the same eyes and honey-colored skin as Gertrude, hurrying toward them. She wore a baggy white T-shirt covered with black writing, and was pushing a clothing rack on wheels. The rack was filled with identical white T-shirts on hangers.

"Hello, Aunty Dorothy," said Wilmot. "What are you doing?"

"They put me in charge of the new gift shop," said Dorothy, proudly. "They might not be works of great literature, but someone needs to help me move these T-shirts out of harm's way."

Gertrude tutted. "Dorothy, this really isn't the time."

"Well, I'm not going to be the one to explain to Her

Ladyship why all her souvenirs are suddenly blank," said Dorothy.

Suzy squinted at the text on Dorothy's T-shirt. "What does it say?"

Dorothy straightened the front of the T-shirt so Suzy could read it. In jaunty black text it said:

MY FRIENDS WENT TO THE IVORY TOWER AND ALL THEY GOT ME WAS THIS LOUSY REASSURANCE THAT IT'S NO LONGER AN INSTRUMENT OF CLANDESTINE AUTOCRACY.

"Would you like one?" said Dorothy. "They're on sale."

Suzy gave her an apologetic smile. "Thanks, but I don't really get it."

"No one gets it," said Mr. Trellis. "These T-shirts are terrible. But until someone can persuade Her Ladyship to give up control of merchandising, we're stuck with them."

"What's wrong with my merchandising?" said a voice. Mr. Trellis jumped. A woman with a flowing mane of neon pink hair was approaching the desk, carrying a glass cylinder the size of a hatbox, fixed to a squat metallic base.

"I'm sure it's not my place to say, Your Ladyship," said Mr. Trellis. "Please don't fire me."

"I'll fire you out of a cannon if you keep calling me 'Your Ladyship,'" the woman said, setting the cylinder down on the desk. "My name's Neoma. Please use it."

Neoma was solid and square-shouldered. She wore a gleaming white version of the Lunar Guard jumpsuit beneath a floor-length white cape, fastened around her shoulders with a gold chain. Suzy couldn't help noticing that she still had her old plasma pistol strapped to her thigh.

Before Suzy could say hello, her dad stepped forward with his hand out. "Lady Neoma," he said. "I'm Suzy's father, this is her mom, and we'd just like to say what an honor it is to be here inside the moon."

Suzy cringed, while Neoma looked at his hand as though he had smeared it in something.

"You're welcome," she said, and stepped around him. "And you," she said when she caught sight of Suzy. "I hear you're the one who stopped that giant robot from obliterating Trollville last month. Ripped it in two down the middle, in fact."

Suzy felt her parents tense. "Maybe," she replied.

Neoma's features softened into the barest suggestion of a smile. "Well done. And take it from me, you never forget your first killer robot."

At last she turned to Wilmot. "Hello, Postmaster," she said. "Are you ready for this delivery? It's got to go out immediately, and I mean right this instant. Top priority. All other duties superseded."

"We came prepared," said Wilmot. "What will we be delivering?"

"We're a library," said Neoma. "Take a guess."

Wilmot blushed a little. "A book, then," he said. "All right. But where's it going?"

"That bit's complicated," said Neoma. "I don't know."

"Then how are we supposed to deliver it?" asked Suzy.

Neoma raised a finger for silence and looked around the atrium. The last of the guards and library assistants were just staggering out of sight down a winding flight of stairs leading to the archives. "Mrs. Grunt," said Neoma. "Give me the megaphone."

Gertrude handed it over, and Neoma raised it to her lips.

"You can bring it down now," she shouted. "We're ready for you."

A few seconds later, three figures appeared on one of the winding staircases leading to the upper reading rooms. Two of them were Lunar Guards, their plasma rifles primed and glowing, and between them was a small, skinny boy with pale, pinched features and a mop of ash-blond hair. He wore an off-white tunic and carried a large leather-bound book at arm's length. He looked as though he expected it to explode at any moment.

"Frederick!" said Suzy as he and his escort arrived.

"Mom, Dad, this is my friend I was telling you about. He's the Chief Librarian."

Frederick flashed them something that was halfway between a smile and a grimace, but didn't take his eyes off the book. It was thick, and its cover was pitted and black with age, like a medieval Bible that Suzy had seen in a museum once. Its title, picked out in curling silver script, was *The Book of Power*, and it was sealed shut with a tarnished metal clasp.

"What should I do with it?" said Frederick. A few beads of sweat stood out on his forehead.

"Just put it down gently," said Neoma. She slid off the desk as Frederick, holding his breath, laid the book down where she had been sitting and took a big step back.

"How's it looking up there?" said Neoma, resting a hand on the butt of her pistol.

"Bad," said Frederick, wiping his forehead with his sleeve. "We were too late to save the whole Gothic romance section. A squad of library assistants got some of the funnier Zardonian joke books to safety, but every collection from Advanced Magical Practice all the way down to Unnatural History has been wiped. There's nothing left."

"This all sounds very serious," said Suzy's mom. "Suzy, I thought you said this library wasn't dangerous."

"Mom, please!" Suzy scowled, but saw that the guards

had their plasma rifles trained on the book. It was enough to make her pause. "Actually, what *is* going on?" she asked.

Now that he was no longer holding the book, Frederick seemed a little calmer. "Right," he said. "Yes. Hello, Suzy. Good to see you again." He gave a shaky smile, and for the first time, she saw the bags under his eyes. He looked exhausted. "This is the oldest book in the Ivory Tower's collection. In fact, it's been here for as long as the tower has existed, even though it doesn't actually belong to us."

"What do you mean?" asked Wilmot.

"According to the records, it was loaned to us just after the founding of the Union."

"But that was thousands of years ago!" said Wilmot.

"Hundreds of thousands," said Gertrude. Dorothy nodded vigorously in agreement. "It was a very long-term loan," said Frederick. "But it finally expired this morning, so now the book's overdue."

"So you need the Express to take it back where it came from?" said Suzy.

"That's right," said Frederick. "Except that we don't know where that is."

Suzy shrugged. "Don't your records tell you?"

"You don't understand," said Frederick. "*Nobody* knows where it is. It's from an Impossible Place that's been missing for almost as long as the book's been with us."

59

Suzy looked at him in confusion. "But if there's no one to return the book to, why return it at all?"

"Because we really don't want to keep it," said Neoma.

"Excuse me!" said a nervous voice. They all turned to see a library assistant, an awkward-looking boy with the face and russet fur of an Irish setter, stumble out of an archway across the atrium. His arms were laden with books. "I took these biographies down to the east storage room but it was already full, so I was wondering—"

"Get them out of here, Jim-Jim!" shouted Gertrude. "Quickly!"

Startled, Jim-Jim jumped and lost his grip on the books, which tumbled to the floor. "Oh no!" he yelped. "I'm sorry!"

Neoma snapped her fingers, and the two Lunar Guards who had accompanied Frederick snapped to attention. "Help him," she said. "Before—"

"It's too late," exclaimed Mr. Trellis. "Look!"

A black liquid was seeping from between the fallen books' pages and onto the floor. Suzy thought it must be ink, until it began evaporating into tendrils of smoke, which swirled and crawled through the air toward the desk.

"What's happening?" said Suzy's dad, dragging Suzy and her mom clear. The tendrils snaked toward the old black book and squirmed their way in between its pages. "What are those things?"

"They're words," said Frederick, with a weary resignation. "From the biographies that Jim-Jim was carrying." Jim-Jim gave a sorrowful whine and laid his ears flat against his head.

"I'm so sorry!" he moaned. "I didn't know you'd brought the book down already!"

Suzy broke free of her dad's grip and jogged over to the fallen biographies. She picked one up and leafed through the pages. Every single one of them was blank. She picked up a second volume and found the same thing.

"The other book drained them," said Wilmot, looking over her shoulder. "It sucked the words right off their pages."

Frederick nodded gravely. "It started as soon as the loan period expired, and we can't find any way to stop it."

Suzy looked at the piles of blank books heaped up around the atrium. "You mean all those books...?"

Frederick nodded. "We lost almost a million volumes before we even realized what was happening."

Suzy thought of the thousands of miles of bookshelves that filled the tower, and the countless words that had rested on them. The book had drained almost every single one of them, and without the help of the Express and her crew, it would probably finish off whatever was left.

The written records of whole worlds, scrubbed clean in a matter of hours.

"Why is this happening?" she asked, tossing the empty biography down and returning to the desk.

"We assume it's a curse placed on the book by the original owners to stop us hanging on to it," said Neoma. "They might have been happy to let us borrow it for a few hundred thousand years, but it seems they're serious about getting it back."

"Except that nobody knows how to find them," said Suzy flatly.

"Surely there's something in your records that can help?" said Wilmot. "Or a label in the book, perhaps." He tried to pry the cover open, but the metal clasp held it shut.

"You're wasting your time," said Frederick. "It's sealed with magic. There isn't even a key."

Suzy's dad put his hand up. "Sorry, but how do people read it if you can't open it?"

"They don't," said Frederick. "As far as we know, it's the only book in the tower that's never been read. We hardly know anything about it at all, really, except its title and where it came from."

Suzy frowned. "But that's the only thing we *do* need to know, isn't it?"

"Knowing what you're looking for and actually finding it are two different things," said Neoma.

"I'm sure it's nothing we can't solve if we put our minds to it," said Wilmot. "Now tell me, where exactly do we need to take this book?"

Before Frederick could reply, another voice, as low and thin as the sigh of wind through an old cave, spoke. "Take me back to Hydroborea."

Everyone froze. Suzy felt the hairs on her arms bristle.

63

"Did that book just speak?" her mom whispered.

"Yes," said Neoma, her face hardening. "Yes, it did." She stood up and unholstered her pistol. "What are you?" she demanded, addressing the book.

"I am overdue," the book intoned. "Take me back to Hydroborea."

"Hydroborea?" said Wilmot in an awed whisper. "But that's impossible."

"We'll take you anywhere if it stops you from eating your way through our library," Neoma replied. "Just tell us how to get there." When the book did not reply, she prodded it with the muzzle of her pistol. "Hello? Are you listening?" She turned her furious gaze on Frederick. "You didn't tell me it could talk."

"Because I didn't know!" he shot back. "It's never done it before."

They were interrupted by Mr. Trellis, who slapped his hand down on the desk. "Wilmot, lad! Your satchel!"

Wilmot looked down and gave a cry of dismay at the thin coils of inky smoke working their way out from beneath the flap of his satchel. He tore it open and pulled out a handful of blank papers. "Oh no, my delivery forms!" he cried.

A second later, Suzy's mom leaped to her feet as though she had been stung. Black smoke curled out of her trouser pocket, and he reached in and pulled out her phone. The smoke was lifting away from the screen.

"What's it doing to my apps?" she said. "My messages! My emails!" She swiped desperately at the screen, but Suzy could see the icons melting away beneath her fingertips, leaving blank spaces behind in the phone's background wallpaper. Then even that was gone, leaving the screen white and empty.

"And my merchandise!" said Dorothy as the rack of T-shirts was sucked clean.

There was a hissing sound, like breath being drawn in through teeth, and the lines of black smoke arrowed toward the book. Neoma picked it up and held it at eye level.

"That's enough!" she barked. "Stop this."

"I cannot," said the book. "I have been asleep for so long and I am *hungry*. This is the penalty for an overdue return."

"Then you leave me no choice," said Neoma. She turned to the glass cylinder she had left on the desk, prized its lid open, and dropped the book inside. "Stand back, everyone," she ordered. "And cover your eyes."

"Wait!" said Frederick. "What about—?"

But it was too late. Neoma snapped the lid shut and pressed a big red button on the cylinder's top. Suzy just had time to shield her eyes before the cylinder lit up like a small sun. There was a fearsome roar of noise and Suzy's mom grabbed her so tightly it hurt.

"Get down!" cried her dad. Suzy felt him throw himself against them, knocking them off their feet as the atrium disappeared in a blinding flash.

5

TALE AS OLD AS TIME

For a few seconds, all Suzy could sense was the crushing weight of her parents on top of her and a faint ringing in her ears. The sound resolved itself into shouts and screams of consternation, echoing back and forth around the atrium.

She forced her way out from beneath her parents and blinked away the splodgy blur on her retinas to find that everything looked just as it had a few moments before, except for the glass cylinder on the reception desk, which was now full of a writhing mass of bright light, like bottled lightning.

"Mom? Dad? Are you all right?" she asked, helping

them both to their feet. They looked shocked and ashen-faced, but they both nodded.

"What sort of a library is this?" said Suzy's mom. "They're insane!"

"I think I agree with your mother," said Suzy's dad.

"Stop overreacting, you two," said Neoma, leaning against the reception desk as though nothing had happened. "I know what I'm doing."

Frederick emerged from behind the two Lunar Guards, his hair badly ruffled. "To be fair, Neoma, you could have given us a bit of warning. You're not supposed to operate a quantum shredder without full protective gear."

Wilmot, Mr. Trellis, Gertrude, and Dorothy popped up from behind one of the piles of blank books. "Is that what this is?" asked Wilmot, taking a few nervous steps toward the cylinder.

"Yes, it breaks down any object to the subatomic level," said Neoma. "I use it for all the boring paperwork I don't want to deal with." She hit the button on top of the shredder, and its glow began to fade.

"That's a pity," said Wilmot. "This would have been our most important delivery yet."

Suzy couldn't say that she felt the loss as keenly as he did. The voice from the book had unsettled her in a way she couldn't quite identify. It had been old and powerful, and it had made her feel very small in comparison. But as her heart rate slowed, she realized that her most persuasive argument for remaining a postie had just been vaporized. Worse, it had scared her parents half to death in the process. *So much for my plan to win them over,* she thought glumly. *They're never going to let me be a postie after this.*

"I am not boring."

Suzy flinched. The low, hollow voice came from inside the shredder, and everyone turned to stare at it as the last of its glow faded. The book was still inside it, completely unscathed.

"Impossible!" said Neoma, wrenching the lid open. She pulled the book out and shook it. "You're supposed to be a subatomic vapor by now."

"You said I was boring paperwork," said the book. "But I am not."

Neoma gripped the book so hard its leather creaked. "Then tell me what you really are," she demanded.

"I am overdue," the book replied. "Take me back to Hydroborea."

Wilmot stared at the book in wonder. "Is that really where you're from?" he asked.

"Yes," said the book.

"Gosh," said Wilmot. "That's fantastic."

"Why?" said Suzy. "Where's Hydroborea?"

"Oh, come on," said Frederick. "Don't tell me this is another stupidly obvious thing you've never heard of."

Suzy scowled at him. "Then why not help me learn, Mr. Expert?"

"Hydroborea," he said. "The lost city? You really don't know about it?"

Suzy folded her arms. "I'm listening."

Frederick sighed. "When the Impossible Places first came together as a union, the people built two towers—one a stronghold of knowledge and the other a stronghold of justice."

"You mean the Ivory and Obsidian Towers." Suzy rolled her eyes. "I'm not a complete beginner, Frederick."

"I know," he said. "But some of the stories say there used to be a third tower, built long before the Union was formed. The Gilded Tower. A stronghold of magic."

Suzy felt her brain fizz with sudden curiosity, but not wanting to give Frederick the satisfaction, she did her best to hide it. "And?"

"They say the tower was part of an ancient city called Hydroborea," said Frederick, "and that the people who lived there were the very first to discover magic, back in the dawn of time. They became the most powerful sorcerers who ever lived, and ushered in a golden age of peace and prosperity. They helped found the Union and shared their powers with the other Impossible Places."

"My mum used to tell me bedtime stories about Hydroborea," said Mr. Trellis with a wistful smile.

"Ours did, too, didn't she, Gert?" said Dorothy. "According to the stories, every Hydroborean house was made of solid gold, and there was so much magic in the air that the people only had to wish for something to make it real."

"Yes, and they made the sky above the city shine a thousand different colors," said Gertrude. "And not a drop of rain ever fell on their heads."

"It all sounds wonderful," said Suzy. "So what happened to it?"

Frederick turned his hands up and shrugged. "That depends on which story you want to believe," he said. "Some say there was a natural disaster. Others claim that the Hydroboreans let their magic get out of hand, and it overwhelmed them. But whatever happened, the city—and the world it was on—just disappeared without a trace one day. No one's seen or heard from Hydroborea in almost five hundred thousand years."

"Then how do you know it even exists anymore?" said Suzy.

"I don't," said Frederick. "No one does."

Suzy's mother spoke up. "You can't possibly expect Suzy to deliver the book to a city that isn't there. Do you even have a map?"

"We had lots of maps," said Frederick. "But the book ate them."

"They were very interesting," said the book. "So much changed while I slept. There are so many new places and pathways to explore, and yet Hydroborea is not among them."

Neoma scowled at it. "You mean you don't know where it is either?"

"I do not," said the book. "I was sent away from the city before it disappeared. Now you must find it again and take me there."

"Of course," said Neoma dryly. "But here's another question—why shouldn't I just have the crew of the Express drop you in the deepest, darkest hole they can find? That would solve our problem pretty quickly."

"Because the penalty for the overdue return will only be lifted once I am delivered to Hydroborea," said the book.

This made Frederick stand up straighter. "You mean you'll give back all the words you've taken?"

"Once the magic binding me is lifted," said the book. "And you only have one day in which to do so."

"Why?" said Suzy. "What happens after that?"

"The penalty becomes permanent," the book replied. "Your words will be mine to keep."

Frederick went even paler than usual.

"That settles it, then," said Neoma, turning to Wilmot. "I don't care what it takes; I need you to deliver this book. Can you do it?"

Wilmot drew himself up to his full height, which was a good two feet shorter than Neoma, and puffed his chest out. "We'll give you the absolute highest priority, most guaranteed service the Express can offer," he said solemnly. "It's called the Gold Stamp Special."

Gertrude, Dorothy, and Mr. Trellis all gasped.

"Wilmot, no!" said Gertrude.

"Think of the risks, lad!" said Mr. Trellis. "It's not worth it!"

Suzy looked from them to Wilmot in confusion and mounting alarm. "What are they talking about?" she whispered to Wilmot. "What risks?"

"Never mind that," said Neoma. "What does this Gold Stamp do that's so special?"

Wilmot wet his lips. "It dedicates the Express and her crew to your delivery, and your delivery alone, in perpetuity," he said. "In other words, we guarantee never to undertake any other delivery until yours has been successfully completed."

"Wait," said Suzy. "That means if we can't find Hydroborea…"

"Then we'll have to keep searching until we do," he replied, his face carefully impassive. "Yes, I know."

"But what if Hydroborea isn't out there to be found?" said Gertrude. "You could be searching for the rest of your lives!"

"Remember the Night Flier, my boy," said Mr. Trellis, shaking a finger at Wilmot. "When I was a lad, it was the fastest Postal Express train in the Union. The crew were national heroes. But they signed up for a Gold Stamp Special and spent the rest of their careers trying to deliver a grocery bill to the Grand High DJ of Discopolis, all because he'd enchanted his house to teleport away whenever anyone rang his doorbell."

Suzy thought she saw a flicker of doubt cloud Wilmot's eyes for a second. "I know," he said. "But this is an emergency. If Hydroborea still exists, we'll find it."

"Does it guarantee that the book never comes back here, whatever happens?" said Neoma.

"Yes," he replied.

She scowled and drummed her fingers against the butt of her plasma pistol. "All right," she said. "Do it. You've got one day to find Hydroborea, wherever it is, and return the book. Or spend the rest of your lives keeping it at a safe distance."

Suzy looked to Gertrude and Mr. Trellis for support, but they seemed every bit as shocked as she did.

Wilmot, meanwhile, appeared to be caught somewhere between terror and excitement. "Right," he said, forcing a nervous smile. "Um . . . I'm afraid the book ate all the words off my delivery form." He produced a blank sheet of gold paper from his satchel.

"Forget the paperwork," said Neoma. "Get it delivered and I'll sign anything you want once you get back."

Wilmot's eyes sparkled at the thought. "I suppose a verbal agreement would do until then," he said. "Oh, and the most important thing, of course." He delved back into his satchel and withdrew a small oblong of gold foil, roughly five inches long. "It's not a Gold Stamp Special without the special gold stamp," he chuckled. "It's supposed to have a picture of King Amylum on it, but I suppose that got sucked up, too."

"It did," said the book. "His image had an unusual taste, but I think I like it. Do you have any more?"

"I'm sorry, but these stamps are very rare," said Wilmot. "I just hope this one still works." He peeled the stamp's adhesive backing off while Neoma removed the book from the shredder and set it down on the desk. Very carefully—almost reverently—Wilmot applied the stamp to the upper right corner of the book's front cover.

Suzy moved to Wilmot's side and watched as the stamp's gold foil glinted in the light. Then, quick as a flash, the glint raced out beyond the edges of the stamp and across the book's cover before disappearing.

"What was that?" she asked.

"Magic," said the book. "But not my own. This is a new spell."

"A postal spell," said Wilmot proudly. "It's an anti-tampering field, connected to the delivery form. You are now the official responsibility of the Impossible Postal Service and will remain in our protection until the form is signed by the recipient."

"Whoever that turns out to be," said Frederick. "And isn't a protection spell a bit redundant? The book's already indestructible and nobody's been able to open it for the past few hundred millennia."

Wilmot sniffed. "It's just part of the service," he said defensively. "Plus, the stamp has a tracking spell that will allow Neoma to chart our progress wherever we go. With this!" He delved into his satchel again and withdrew a magnifying glass with a thick metallic handle. He pressed a button on its side, and a glowing image of the moon sprang to life inside the lens. "You adjust it like this," he said, twiddling a dial at the base of the handle. The image zoomed in until it displayed a representation of the Ivory Tower, and a gold speck glowed brightly halfway up its length. "That's us," he said, handing the device to Neoma. "Wherever we go, you'll be able to find us."

"Excellent," she said. "Now, if that's all taken care of, get that book out of my tower and never bring it back."

Suzy saw the haunted expression shared by Gertrude, Dorothy, Mr. Trellis, and her parents, and knew exactly what they were thinking: *What if none of us are ever allowed back?*

Five minutes later, Suzy, her parents, and Wilmot were hurrying back across the concourse of Center Point, with Frederick in tow. The book was stowed safely out of sight in Wilmot's satchel, but it wasn't enough to stop the destinations on the departure board, the nearby platform numbers, the wanted posters, and even the numerals on the face of the clock above the ticket office, from vaporizing. There were cries of consternation and alarm from the crowd as the vapor spiraled across the concourse and was vacuumed straight into the satchel.

"Oh dear," said Wilmot, flushing with embarrassment as people pointed and stared. "It's going to do this everywhere we go, isn't it? And we don't even know where to *start* looking for Hydroborea."

"Don't the stories give any clues?" asked Suzy.

"None," said Frederick. "That's the thing about lost cities. They're lost."

Suzy glowered at him. "If you're going to be this helpful, you might as well have stayed behind."

"But I'm afraid he's right," said Wilmot. "Whatever

happened to Hydroborea, it didn't leave a single trace behind. It vanished and took its whole world with it."

"Brilliant," said Suzy as they turned onto the platform where the Express was waiting. "So what about the place where its world *used* to be? Do we know that much at least?"

"Not really," said Frederick. "People have come up with lots of theories over the years, but all we know for certain is that it was somewhere in the void."

"Excuse me," said Suzy's mom. "I'm trying my best to make sense of this, I really am, but there's just too much to process. What's this 'void' you're talking about? Has Suzy told us about it before?" She nudged Suzy's dad, who shook his head.

Frederick gave an exasperated groan. "Honestly, doesn't anyone on your world learn anything useful?" He ignored the arch looks that Suzy's parents directed at him. "The void is negative space. A big empty nothing, separating one Impossible Place from the next."

"It's the reason we trolls built the rail network," said Wilmot. "The tunnels bypass the void by linking the Impossible Places directly. In the olden days, the only way to get from one to another was to sail across the void in a ship. It took ages."

Suzy's mind began to itch. She knew the feeling well— it meant she was wrestling with a problem but hadn't quite reached a solution yet. In this case, the mention of a ship had lodged in her imagination, and she set about building an idea around it.

While she thought, her father said, "This might be a silly question, but why not try asking the book?"

"Why didn't I think of that?" said Frederick. He leaned toward Wilmot's satchel and said, "Can you tell us where Hydroborea used to be?"

The book gave a sigh like wind through tree branches. "Not until the magic binding me is lifted," it said. "Until then, I can only absorb information. I may not dispense it."

"You mean you know, but you won't tell us," said Frederick. "Well that's just perfect."

They soon arrived at the *Belle*, and Stonker waved to them from the gangway.

"Hello!" he called as they climbed up to him. "We're ready to make way. Are you joining us again, Frederick?"

They had barely reached him before the letters on the nameplate mounted to the *Belle*'s boiler began to melt. Stonker watched in horror as the locomotive's name was sucked into Wilmot's satchel.

"What the blazes . . . ?"

"I'm sorry, Mr. Stonker," said Wilmot. "I'll explain everything, but we have to get underway immediately. We've got a Gold Stamp Special and it's time sensitive. We've only got twenty-four hours to make the delivery."

"Actually, it's more like ten," said Frederick. "The loan period expired about fourteen hours ago. We didn't realize for eight of them."

"A Gold Stamp Special!" cried Stonker. The ends of his mustache went rigid with shock. "A little warning would have been nice. Where are we taking it?" He looked around the collection of blank faces. "Well?"

And that's when the solution, or part of it, at least, slotted into place in Suzy's mind. "We have to go into the void," she announced.

"I beg your pardon?" said Stonker.

"We have to sail into the void," she said, "and find the place where Hydroborea and the Gilded Tower used to be."

"I don't know," said Wilmot. "There's an awful lot of void out there."

"I know it's not a great plan, but it's our only shot," said Suzy. "If we can find out where the city was, maybe we can find a clue as to where it's gone."

Frederick rubbed the back of his neck and grimaced. "I suppose we don't have any other options," he said. "But how are we going to get there? There aren't exactly train tracks in the void."

"We can always use the H.E.C.," said Wilmot. "It can go anywhere, and I've been looking forward to giving it a proper test run."

"Now hold on a moment," said Stonker. "You can't just go blasting off into the middle of nothingness. Crossing the void is like crossing a desert. It's littered with the remains of people who went in and never came out again."

Suzy's mom's face sharpened. "I don't think I like the sound of this, Suzy."

"It'll be fine, Mom," Suzy replied. "We just need someone who knows what they're doing."

"Like who?" said Frederick. "The last of the void sailors died centuries ago."

"Yes, they did," said Suzy. "And I know just the ones to talk to."

6

A TRAIN WITH AN OCEAN VIEW

An hour after leaving the Ivory Tower, the Express blasted out of the tunnel network and into the dazzling sunlight of the Topaz Narrows. Turquoise waters stretched to the horizon in every direction, broken here and there by the tips of coral reefs and small islets of gleaming white sand.

"Calum! Look at this!" Suzy's mom was on tiptoe at the cab window.

It had been a tense and largely silent journey from the tower, thanks to the presence of the book, which had already sucked the labels and numbers from the *Belle*'s controls. Luckily, Stonker was so familiar with them that it made little difference, but he and Ursel were both on edge as a consequence. Far more serious was its absorption of every last letter in the Sorting Carriage—the tendrils of ink had crept into the cab under the door, and no amount of pleading or arm waving from Wilmot could stop it. Now the mail on the shelves was as blank as the books in the Ivory Tower, and in roughly nine hours it, too, would be lost forever.

The book apparently had nothing to add to its earlier instructions and remained mercifully silent in Wilmot's delivery satchel, which he had hung on a coat hook by the front door while he paced around the cab impatiently.

So it was a relief to finally see daylight lancing in through the windows, and taste salt on the air.

"It's like the Bahamas!" said Suzy's dad, joining his wife at the window.

"Or Mauritius!" she replied. "Suzy, is this really where your friends live?"

"Yes," said Suzy. "Although 'live' is probably the wrong word." She opened the front door and stuck her head out, savoring the rush of warm air against her skin. The train tracks floated, apparently unsupported, on the surface of the water, and the *Belle*'s wheels threw up great curtains of spray in which rainbows glittered. It was good to be back.

"We'll be there soon," she heard Stonker call. "Time to get ready."

Leaving the satchel on the coat hook, Suzy, Wilmot, and Frederick stepped into the sorting carriage. Suzy's parents drifted after them, chattering animatedly about the possibility of a beach holiday, and Suzy felt a flicker of hope that the change of scenery might finally have put them at ease. At the rear of the carriage was another door that, when Wilmot opened it, led directly into the Hazardous Environment Carriage at the rear of the train.

"Why does it look like a caravan?" asked Calum as they all squeezed into the confined space.

"I'm not sure," Suzy said. "It's very different from the old one. This is my first time inside it."

She had expected the trolls to have worked their magic and made it larger than the exterior, so she was surprised to find that it was every bit as small and cramped as it appeared from the outside. It looked a lot like a normal caravan, albeit one designed by a mad scientist. The tiny kitchen worktop had been converted into a control console, covered in blinking lights and buttons. Pipes and wiring covered the walls, the windows and sunroof were riveted into their frames, and the small cubicle that Suzy guessed had once been a toilet now had the words WARNING! AIR LOCK stenciled in big red letters on its folding plastic door.

"Can you shut the door behind you, please?" asked Wilmot. "I'm afraid we can't dive while it's open."

There was a lot of shuffling and apologizing as everyone rearranged themselves, until Suzy's dad finally had room to close the door. Outside the windows, the curtain of spray had dropped to a choppy wake. Then, with a distant sigh of steam, the Express rolled to a stop.

"Going down," said Wilmot. He flicked a few switches on the control panel, and the H.E.C. jolted slightly. "Excuse me," he said, squeezing past Frederick and Suzy to the toilet door. He pulled it open.

Suzy looked over his shoulder and was a little alarmed to see the toilet still in place. Above it, from a peg on the wall, hung a diving suit. Suzy recognized it immediately: It was the same one she had worn the last time she had visited the Topaz Narrows. It was old and worn, its fabric repaired with patches and tape. It sported a spherical brass helmet with a long concertina-like canvas sleeve on the front, designed to accommodate a troll nose.

"Hey, Frederick," she said, nudging him in the ribs. "Do you remember when you were a snow globe and I put you in here?" She gave the nose sleeve a playful tweak.

"Don't remind me," he said, cringing. "No matter what happens to me in life, at least I'll never have to suffer through that again."

Suzy's dad leaned in past her and examined the toilet cubicle. "There's only one suit," he said. He tapped

Wilmot on the shoulder. "Suzy's not going out there on her own, is she?"

"Um, yes," said Wilmot. "According to regulations, there has to be at least one fully qualified operator on board the H.E.C. in case of emergencies. And I'm the only qualified operator on the crew, you see, so—"

"In case of what emergencies?" said Suzy's mom. "You can't send Suzy out there on her own. She doesn't even have her bronze swimming certificate yet!"

"Mom, please," said Suzy. "I've done this before, remember? There's nothing dangerous out there."

"You said that about the library," her mom replied.

"What about sharks?" her dad said. "Or sea monsters? Are sea monsters real?"

"Of course they are," said Frederick. "But you'd have to be really unlucky to bump into one out here. They almost never come into the reefs."

Suzy's dad's face dropped. "*Almost* never?"

Suzy nudged Frederick in the ribs and he finally shut up.

"I'll be ten minutes," she said, addressing her parents. "Nothing's going to happen, and you can even keep an eye on me. Look." She pointed to the window behind them, and they turned to see that the waves and sky had gone, replaced by towers of neon coral and shoals of brightly colored fish. While they had been talking, the

H.E.C. had started its descent to the seafloor, and it settled on the sand with the lightest of bumps.

"We've sunk!" said her dad.

"Actually, we've dived," said Suzy. "It's like sinking, but on purpose." She shared a knowing smile with Wilmot.

Suzy's mom still looked troubled, so Suzy gave her arm a squeeze.

"Please, Mom. We're running out of time. I have to do this."

Suzy's mom nodded. "I just don't like the thought of you out there by yourself, that's all."

"I won't be," said Suzy. "I'm visiting friends, remember?"

A few minutes later, Suzy was secured in the diving suit and sitting on the toilet.

"Are you sure this is right?" she asked, feeling rather self-conscious as her parents and Frederick stood outside the cubicle, staring at her. "It's not at all like the old air lock."

"Perfectly sure," came Wilmot's voice from just out of sight. "Just close the door and pull the flush."

Suzy wondered if she had heard him correctly. "If you say so." She waved to the others and pulled the folding door across. Her parents looked more worried than ever.

The door clicked shut, and she heard a faint hiss as a hidden air seal locked tight around it. She reached behind her and gripped the flush handle.

This feels ridiculous, she thought, and pulled it.

The toilet flushed, and the cubicle suddenly began filling with water. It sloshed in around her feet, climbing higher and higher. Within a few seconds, it had closed over her, and she heard its muted rush trembling against the outside of the helmet. A few seconds later, the cubicle was full.

Now what? she wondered, a second before the toilet lifted off beneath her, propelling her up and out through an opening where the ceiling had been just a moment before.

For a dizzying moment, she was looking down on the roof of the H.E.C. She could see the tops of her parents' heads through the plastic sunroof. Then she drifted down to land gently in the sand. She caught her breath, and had enough presence of mind to offer a thumbs-up to the nearest porthole. Her parents, on the other side of the glass, waved back enthusiastically.

The trolls had made at least one welcome modification to the diving suit, she discovered. She no longer had to worry about connecting a cumbersome air hose to the H.E.C. Instead, she had a small oxygen tank on her back.

She could already see her destination up ahead—the dark hulk of a sunken galleon, partially embedded in the coral reef. The answers she needed were inside it. At least, she hoped they were.

With a last wave to the others, she turned and started toward it.

7

S·U·N·K

Suzy arrived at the ragged hole torn in the side of the shipwreck and peered into the darkened interior. A barnacle-encrusted nameplate on the prow was still barely legible: LA ROUQUINE.

"Hello?" she called into the darkness. "Is anyone there? It's Suzy, from the Express. Can I come in?"

A pale, shifting light flickered into being deep inside the wreck. It was weak and shapeless, but grew steadily brighter and more defined as it drifted toward the opening. Other lights joined it, until Suzy was faced with a row of five spectral human forms. They were all men, grizzled and bearded, and dressed in old-fashioned frock coats and tricorn hats. From the waist down, they were nothing but wisps of light, trailing back into the wreck. They bobbed like glowing balloons, and they all smiled with genuine pleasure.

"Suzy Smith!" said the tallest of them. "What a delight to see you again, my girl! What brings you to the final resting place of the Society of Adventure and Discovery? Has our message in a bottle washed ashore again so soon?"

"Hello, Chief," said Suzy. "No, I'm actually here because I need your help."

This set the ghosts chattering excitedly to one another.

"Then we are at your disposal, my dear," said the Chief, removing his hat with a flourish. "Don't tarry out there a moment longer. Pray, enter and enjoy our hospitality. Gavin! A chantey!"

Suzy held up a hand. "That's very kind, but I'm in a real hurry. Can the chantey wait for next time?"

Gavin, who had produced a ghostly accordion from somewhere, looked dejected. "And I was going to do the one about the cross-eyed lobster," he said. "It's my favorite."

"I'm sorry," said Suzy. "But Wilmot and I are in the middle of an urgent delivery, and we need your expertise."

The Chief looked taken aback. "What expertise would that be?" he said. "We're a few centuries out of date, you know."

"That's exactly why I'm here," said Suzy. "You used to

sail across the void between worlds on your explorations, didn't you?"

"Ah, yes, indeed," said the Chief. "La Rouquine was the finest void ship ever to put out of the Western Fenlands. We took her all over the Union, and beyond." He patted a fallen spar. Or rather, he tried to pat it, but his hand passed straight through.

"That's the expertise I need," said Suzy. "We've got a delivery that has to go through the void."

The ghosts all glowed a little brighter at these words.

"She's on a voyage of discovery!" said one of them. "Just like in days of yore!"

"Who's yore?" said another.

"Yore mom!"

The group cackled with laughter.

"Lads, please," said the Chief. "There are young ears present, and we're meant to be professionals." He cleared his throat and turned back to Suzy. "Forgive them, Suzy. After all these long centuries together, it's easy to forget the social niceties. So which empty stretch of beyond are you setting sail for?"

Suzy gathered herself. "Hydroborea."

There was a collective gasp from the ghosts.

"The lost city!" said Gavin. "Arrr, there's many an explorer has set out in search of its store of lost knowledge."

"They say mastery of all magic is the reward for any that finds it," said another.

"Eternal life and minty fresh breath is what I heard," said a third.

"I'm not looking for any of those things," said Suzy. "I just need to deliver a book there. And I hope that if I can find the place where Hydroborea's world *used* to be, I might be able to track down where it's gone."

The Chief stroked his beard in thought. "'Tis a bold and ambitious quest, to be certain," he said. "But in all my years as an explorer, I never heard of anyone who achieved it."

Suzy felt the hope she had been gathering start to fade. "No one at all?" she said.

"Alas, no," he replied. "Those that returned did so empty-handed."

"Can you at least tell me where to start looking?"

The Chief considered for a moment. "I think I might, at that. Because, in addition to Adventure and Discovery, we are also the Society of Useless Navigational Knowledge." He winked at her. "We've got dozens more where that came from. Neville? Fetch the map."

"Aye, Chief!" Neville, a hunched old man with an eye patch, drifted across to a chest that was half-buried in the sand. Suzy watched, intrigued, as he reached down and made to open the lid. Except the lid he opened was as ghostly as he was. The chest itself remained closed, but she saw a spectral blue outline overlay it. Neville reached into this ghostly double of the chest and drew out an equally ghostly roll of parchment. He drifted back to the group and handed it almost reverently to the Chief.

"How did you do that?" asked Suzy.

"We're not the only ghosts in here, y'know," said the Chief. "La Rouquine might have sailed her last journey, but she still remembers her glory days, don't you?" He addressed the barnacle-encrusted timbers as though they could hear him. "She's what sustains us," he said, unfurling the map. "Everything that went down with her that fateful night is still here, in spectral form. Including this." He presented her with the parchment. "An old adventurer's map that we liberated from a skeleton in the lightning mines of Thunder Mesa. It helped us steer through many a strange course in the void. Feast your eyes."

Suzy brought her face as close to the map as she could, leaning so far forward that its glowing blue canvas passed through her visor and into the helmet's interior.

The map was gossamer-thin and peppered with holes, but she could still make out the circle of the moon in the center, and a collection of oddly shaped ribbons streaming out from it toward the edges. They snaked and intertwined, and it was only when she looked closely that she saw place names and landscape features marked on them.

"Are these the Impossible Places?" she said. "Is this what they really look like?"

"Not really," said the Chief. "They're a bit rough and wonky, even by the standards of our day, but it's the void in between them that matters, and, on that front, whoever drew this knew what they were doing. There's none more accurate. And have you noticed this?" He pointed to a darkish blotch that sat in an empty space between several ribbons of land. It was marked with a cross and labeled with a line of spidery handwriting. Suzy had to squint to read it.

Hydroborea once was here.

"That's it!" said Suzy. "That's where we need to go! You've found it!"

"Hold your seahorses," said the Chief. "Marking it on a map is one thing. Steering a safe course to it is another. Did you not see this?" He indicated the dark stain surrounding the cross. "The great void storm. A swirling maelstrom of pure nothingness that'll chew up the strongest vessel and spit out the debris faster than you can say, 'Whoops, we're all going to die.' It takes an expert sailor to find a path through."

Suzy regarded the dark blotch with a sense of foreboding. As much as she trusted Wilmot to pilot the H.E.C., she didn't think he counted as an expert sailor. "I'm afraid we don't have any choice," she said. "We have to go. Isn't there any advice you can give us?"

"Advice won't help you in the teeth of a storm, lassie," said one of the ghosts. "Only a sharp eye and a brave hand on the tiller."

"I'm afraid Frank's right," said the Chief. "Fearless and true you may be, but that storm has been the doom of many a fine ship and her crew." He gave her a sad sort of smile. "If you're wise, you'll take my advice and seek adventure elsewhere."

Suzy watched him roll the map up, and clenched her fists. "You don't think we can make it," she said.

"It's not for a lack of heart," said the Chief. "Simply a lack of experience."

"We couldn't live with ourselves if we knew we'd sent you to an untimely death," said Gavin.

"You don't have to live with yourselves," said Suzy. "You're dead." The ghosts all winced, and Suzy was vaguely aware that she had been terribly rude, but she was now too angry to stop herself. "I'm tired of being told what I can and can't handle," she said.

"What knave has been telling you that?" said the Chief.

"My parents," said Suzy. "And they haven't been telling me, exactly, but they've been implying it. A lot."

"My parents said that running away to sea would be the death of me," said Gavin. "I proved them wrong every day, until I proved them right. So I probably win, all things considered."

Suzy stubbed the toe of her diving boot into the sand. "It's still not fair," she said.

"Life isn't fair, my dear," said the Chief kindly. "Nor is death, for that matter. Or parents. But they've known you since before you knew yourself, so if you're smart, you'll listen to them. That's what experience is for."

He drifted back toward the chest, map in hand.

"That's it," she said. "Experience."

"I beg your pardon?" said the Chief.

"You know how to navigate the storm," said Suzy. "So why don't you come with us?"

A look of pain and sorrow crossed the Chief's face. "I would love nothing more than to go adventuring again. We all would. Alas, we are tied to our old bones and the ship's timbers. If we stray too far from either, we'll cease to be."

Suzy's brow knotted. "How far exactly?"

"Ten feet or so at best," said the Chief. "Gavin here got as far as the first outcrop of coral once, before he started to fade."

"It took weeks of training," boasted Gavin. "My five-year plan is to reach the second outcrop of coral."

"Madness, I tells ye," said Neville. "You're dreaming too big."

"So you're trapped," she said. "You're prisoners here."

"We prefer to think of ourselves as permanent residents," said the Chief.

Suzy looked around the wreck. Her mind was itching again. "You say you're tied to the wreck," she said. "But how much of it are you tied to?"

The ghosts looked at one another in confusion.

Suzy reached up to a length of broken timber overhead, took a firm hold of the end, and twisted. A chunk of wood broke off in her hand. "Would this be enough?" she asked hurriedly. She could feel the minutes slipping away, and it was starting to make her anxious.

"For what?" asked the Chief.

"To take you with me," she replied. "We need to get to the center of that storm right away, and you're the only one who can get us there."

"Me?" said the Chief, surprised. "But I've never left LA ROUQUINE."

"Which is why we're going to take a bit of LA ROUQUINE with us," she replied. Without waiting for his reply, she turned and stomped out of the wreck, across the sand to the first outcrop of coral. "This is where Gavin got to, right?" she called.

The ghosts clustered in the hole in the ship's hull.

"Aye, that's the spot!" said Gavin. "None of the others got close."

"I want the Chief to try," said Suzy. "Come out and meet me."

The Chief bobbed up and down nervously. "I don't know," he said. "It's quite a long way."

"It's barely thirty feet," Suzy replied. "And if you start to fade, you can go straight back." She planted her feet in the sand, held up the chunk of timber, and waited.

The Chief looked longingly out at the reef and clasped his hands together.

"Go on, Chief," said Neville. "Nothing ventured, and all that."

"We'll all be cheering for you," said Gavin. "What if she's right?"

The Chief licked his lips, which, given that they were underwater, seemed a bit unnecessary, Suzy thought.

"All right," he said. "If you insist." He drifted out of La Rouquine and into the daylight. It shone through him so clearly that he became almost invisible: a faint outline moving against the deep blue. But Suzy saw the spectral trail leading back into the wreck, tethering him to it, and to his remains. The farther he got from the ship, the more his trail stretched, like elastic. It grew thinner, and the Chief's glow began to dim.

"I'm not sure I've got it in me," he said, his voice

strained. "The spirit is willing, but the flesh decomposed some centuries ago." He slowed and stopped. "I'm sorry, Suzy. It was a fine idea. It just wasn't meant to be."

Suzy took a step toward him to offer some words of comfort, and a curious thing happened. A strand of the Chief's trail peeled away, drifting aimlessly for a moment, before being drawn decisively toward the piece of timber in Suzy's hand. It made contact, and just for a second, she saw the faint outline of the wood's ghostly counterpart. At the same time, the Chief's glow returned, and he seemed to stand—or rather, float—a little taller again. With renewed confidence, he crossed the last few yards to Suzy and floated alongside her.

"You did it!" she said. "It works!"

The Chief turned to his shipmates, his smile glowing like a lightbulb. "Lads!" he said. "This changes everything!"

"Yes, it does," said Suzy, with a satisfied smile. "Now, where did you leave your skull?"

Suzy dropped back into the toilet cubicle and pressed the flush. The hatch in the roof closed, and with the same gurgling rush as before, the water drained away. When the last drop was gone, Suzy removed her cumbersome helmet and unfastened the door. Her parents were waiting for her, and pounced.

"You're back!" said Amandine.

"Are you all right?" asked Calum.

"I'm absolutely fine," Suzy said. "I told you I would be."

Her parents looked at her suspiciously.

"And there were no sea monsters?" asked Amandine.

"Or sharks?" asked Calum.

"None at all," said Suzy. "Just me, the fish, and some ghosts."

"How was the Chief?" said Wilmot. "I keep meaning to drop in and visit, but I've been so busy."

Suzy smiled. "Why don't you ask him yourself?" She pulled a skull out of her delivery pouch and held it up for everyone to see. The chunk of wood rattled around inside its empty brain case, and its eye sockets glowed a spectral blue.

"Hello there!" said the skull, in the Chief's voice. "Permission to come aboard!"

8

THE END OF THE WORLD

Everyone gathered around the table in the *Belle*'s navigation room as the Chief unrolled the phantom map. His glowing form trailed from the eye sockets of his skull, which Suzy still held.

"As I was explaining to young Suzy here," he said, "the great void storm has long been rumored to be the original site of Hydroborea's world. Some sailors claim the storm was caused by whatever magical calamity befell the city."

Stonker reached out and traced a line from the storm to one of the ribbons of land that represented the Impossible Places. His finger passed straight through the map to the table beneath it.

"It's not too far from the rim of the Topaz Narrows," he said.

"The Topaz Narrows have a rim?" asked Suzy.

"Didn't you know?" said Frederick. "They're a flat world. Like a dinner plate."

"Now I've heard everything," said Suzy's mom.

Wilmot was still scrutinizing the map. "Are you sure you can navigate us through the storm, Chief?" he said. "It looks quite big."

"It's huge, lad," said the Chief. "A veritable monster. If I were still living, I wouldn't dare try it."

Wilmot swallowed. "Oh," he said in a very small voice. But then he drew himself up and straightened his cap. "But a delivery is a delivery," he said. "Come rain, shine, or void storm, the Impossible Postal Express will deliver."

"That's the spirit," said the Chief.

"And you'll have me there to help you," said Suzy. "We'll find a way through." She was vaguely aware of her parents drifting away from the table, but she was too distracted to pay them much attention.

"Thank you, Suzy," said Wilmot. "I suppose we'd better get ready."

"Yes, indeed," said Stonker. "Prep the H.E.C. for a rolling launch, please, Postmaster. We can get you airborne without even having to slow down." He turned to Ursel.

103

"Let's get some steam up. We'll be at the rim in no time at all."

"Frrrrolf." Ursel nodded and lumbered after him to the door.

"Ah, to be adventuring again!" said the Chief. "I never thought I'd not live to see the day." He looked out of the mullioned windows that wrapped around the front half of the navigation room and smiled. "To see the sunlight again, and hear the gulls cry. I wish the lads were here."

"We can always bring them up, too, once you're back," said Frederick. "And now that we know how to do it, you can go anywhere you want to."

"A capital idea," said the Chief. "Perhaps our exploring days aren't over just yet." He rolled the map up, stuffed it into his jacket, and retreated back into his skull. Suzy slipped it into her satchel and turned to check on her parents. She found them huddled together in the corner, conversing in sharp whispers.

"Mom? Dad? Are you coming down to see us off?"

They looked around sharply, as if she had caught them doing something they knew they shouldn't have been.

"We'll be right there, sweetheart," said her father. "You go ahead and we'll catch you up." He took Suzy's mom by the elbow and drew her away to the window, where they turned their backs on the room and carried on whispering.

Suzy lingered for a moment. She had seen her parents argue before, but this looked different. They didn't just look angry, they looked scared. When neither of them acknowledged her, she turned and followed the others downstairs.

❧

The Express was quickly underway again, and while Ursel and Stonker were hard at work, Wilmot retrieved his satchel containing the book from the coat hook by the front door and made his way to the H.E.C. with Suzy and Frederick in tow.

Suzy placed the Chief's skull on a shelf above the control console. "Will you be all right up here?" she asked.

"This will do nicely, thank you," the Chief replied, his skull pulsing with blue light as he spoke.

Wilmot started making adjustments to the control console, but as he did so, the labels on the switches and levers began evaporating beneath his fingers. "Oh no!" he cried, trying to grab at them as they coiled through the air into his satchel. "Come back! I need you!"

It was useless, of course, and within a few seconds, the controls were all blank.

"That's going to make things more complicated," said Frederick. "Can you remember how everything works?"

Wilmot's hands hovered uncertainly over the console. "More or less," he said. "I think." He closed his eyes and, a little hesitantly, reached out and flicked a few switches. There was a hum of power from beneath the floor. "There. As long as I don't confuse the life-support systems with the self-destruct, we'll probably be fine."

"You'd better not mention that bit to my parents," said Suzy. "They're nervous enough as it is."

"I'm glad you noticed." Suzy turned with a start and found her parents standing in the doorway to the sorting carriage. Her father looked uncomfortable. Her mother looked determined.

"Mom!" Suzy exclaimed. "How long have you been standing there?"

"Just long enough," her mom replied. She and Suzy's dad stepped into the H.E.C. and shut the door behind them. "Are you ready to go?"

"Yes," said Suzy. "Wilmot's just getting the H.E.C. warmed up."

Her mom shook her head. "I mean are you ready to go home? We're leaving."

Suzy stared at her in shock. "What? No!"

"Yes, Suzanne," said her mom. "Your father and I have talked it through, and we both agree that we don't want you going on this delivery. It's too dangerous."

"But I have to!" said Suzy. "You know how important

106

this is. If we don't complete the delivery, the Express is as good as finished, and so is the Ivory Tower. There could be chaos!" Her mother seemed unmoved, so Suzy looked past her to her father. "Dad, please!"

He grimaced and rubbed the back of his neck. "I'm really sorry, sweetheart," he said. "We're both very proud of you, and everything you've been doing here. And the Impossible Places are wonderful. But…"

"But what?" said Suzy. She felt strangely numb, as though none of this were really happening.

"But your mother's right," he said. "This is all just a bit much. We'd be happier keeping you at home for the time being."

The numbness began to fade, replaced with a scorching anger. "You're just going along with this because you don't want Mom to think you're a soft touch," she said. Her dad looked hurt.

"Don't speak to your father like that, young lady," said her mom. "We reached this decision together."

"When?" said Suzy. "Just now in the navigation room? Is that what you were talking about?"

"You wanted to show us that you were safe on board this train," said Suzy's mom, " but so far we've had to deal with angry crowds, a haunted book, almost being blasted to atoms, scuba diving with dead people, and now you're talking about throwing yourself headfirst into a storm as if it's the most normal thing in the world. So we're putting an end to it."

"No!" Suzy knew she was shouting—she could see the embarrassment written all over Wilmot's face—but she was too angry to stop herself. "This isn't fair!"

"Get changed and give Wilmot your uniform back, please, Suzanne," her mom said. "He's still welcome to come and visit you once in a while."

"Wait, you mean you're taking me home for *good*?"

"Not necessarily," said her dad hurriedly.

"Yes, necessarily," said her mom. "It's for the best."

Suzy's dad started in surprise and opened his mouth. Then, after a moment's thought, he shut it again.

"Wilmot!" Suzy rounded on her friend. "Tell them. Tell them I have to stay and help you!"

Wilmot blushed scarlet. "I don't know, Suzy," he said. "I really want you to come, you know I do. But they're your parents."

She stared at him with mounting horror. "Not you, too!"

He shuffled his feet and looked hopefully up at Suzy's mom. "Is there any way I can convince you to reconsider?"

"None," Suzy's mom replied.

Wilmot's ears drooped. "I'm really sorry, Suzy. But it would be wrong of me to take you without their permission."

Suzy was too shocked and hurt to respond.

"You see?" said Suzy's mom. "Wilmot's taking this seriously, and so should you. We all just want what's best for you." This only made Wilmot look even more wretched, and he turned away to fuss with the control console.

"Well, I think it's a terrible idea," said Frederick. "If it wasn't for Suzy, I'd probably still be stuck inside a snow globe and the Impossible Places would be ruled by a giant killer robot. You two have got no idea what you're doing."

"We're not going to discuss it any further," said Suzy's mom. "Come on, Suzy." She held out her hand. Suzy watched it dissolve through a sudden veil of tears. She tried to blink them away, but they welled up and spilled down her cheeks. Hot with anger and embarrassment, she swatted her mother's hand aside and pushed past her parents.

"Suzy, wait!" Wilmot called after her, but she didn't stop. She threw open the door and fled through the sorting carriage into the cab, almost colliding with Ursel.

"Rrrrownf?" the bear asked.

Suzy couldn't speak. She put her head in her hands and ran past Ursel to the stairs.

"Suzy?" said Stonker. "What the devil's wrong, my girl?"

She didn't look back, but pounded up the stairs two at a time.

"Is she all right?" she heard Stonker say. "Should I go after her?"

"No," came her father's voice. "Let her be. She just needs some time."

She almost turned and screamed down the stairs, *I just need to be a postie!* But she was already through the door into the navigation room, and slammed it shut behind her. She leaned against it and took a deep, shuddering breath. Then the dam inside her finally burst, and she let the tears come freely.

Part of her felt ashamed to be crying, but she was too hurt and angry to care. After everything she had done, everything she had been through, it was all over.

She had no idea how long she stayed like that, but by the time the tears slowed and she was able to breathe clearly again, the shadows in the room had lengthened as the sun dipped lower in the sky.

Not knowing what else to do, she crossed to the windows and looked out. The huge bulk of the *Belle de Loin*'s boiler lay in front of her, juddering and steaming, and the twin curtains of spray rose up on either side of the wheels again as the locomotive charged across the waves. From this vantage point, Suzy could just see over them to the dazzling waters beyond. She felt a sudden need to remember as much about this place as possible while she still had the chance, and fixated on every little detail as it rushed past. The black tips on the wings of the seagulls coasting alongside the train. A chain of islands in the middle distance, each boasting a lone palm tree. The sweeping curve of the horizon.

Suzy blinked the last of her tears away and looked again. Sweeping curve? That couldn't be right. Horizons were supposed to be flat.

But it wasn't anymore. Instead of a straight line, the horizon had taken on a definite curve. She raced from one side of the navigation room to the other, and saw that the curve extended to both left and right, sweeping back out of sight behind the train. And it was getting closer.

Because this world is round and flat like a dinner plate, she thought. *And we're almost at the edge already!*

The realization struck her like a blow, and she forgot her self-pity in an instant. In its place, she felt a cold, hard determination—she couldn't let her time as a postie end like this. She wouldn't leave her friends behind. She had to do something.

But she was running out of time.

Moving quickly, she unfastened one of the side windows and leaned her weight against it, forcing it open against the rush of the train's slipstream. She stuck her head out and looked down. A narrow ledge ran along the base of the windows, all the way to the rear of the cab. It was glistening wet and warped with age, but looked just wide enough for her to get a toehold.

With a last, regretful look back at the door to the stairs, Suzy climbed onto the windowsill and swung herself out.

The wind struck her full in the side and would have hurled her straight into the sea if she hadn't still had a tight grip on the window frame. She braced herself, straining every muscle until she was certain of her footing. Then, with painful care, she reached up with one hand and took hold of the wonky guttering that jutted out above her. The cab's second story was slightly larger than the first, and it overhung the panoramic windows by almost two feet. By leaning backward, Suzy could keep a grip on it as she shimmied her feet along the slippery ledge toward the rear of the cab.

Salt spray settled on her face and clothes, and her knuckles glowed white with strain. There was nothing she could do when the wind finally plucked her cap from her head and sent it whirling away out of sight. Against her better judgment, she glanced down and saw the *Belle*'s drive wheels whirring away in a noisy blur below her.

What am I doing? she thought. *This is crazy.*

But then she imagined climbing back into the safety of the navigation room and returning home with her parents. There would be school on Monday. Homework and dinner and television in the evenings. And long, empty weekends wondering where the Express was and what the crew might be doing... Would they ever find Hydroborea, or would they be doomed to search endlessly, never delivering another package as long as they lived? If she turned back now, she would never know.

She tightened her grip on the guttering and, ignoring the stabbing pain in her hands and shoulders, inched her way to the rear of the cab. She swung herself around the corner of the building, where, finally sheltered from the battering winds, she lowered herself from the ledge onto a windowsill, being careful not to trample the begonias in their window box.

She peered in through the glass and saw Ursel tossing bananas into the fire, while Stonker worked the controls. Her parents were deep in conversation—or possibly an argument, it was hard to tell—by the front door. And Frederick was standing in the middle of the room, looking straight at her.

She froze for a moment, then raised a trembling finger to her lips.

Frederick blinked and looked around to make sure none of the others had seen them. Then he smiled and gave her a conspiratorial wink.

Suzy smiled back at him. "Thank you!" she mouthed. Frederick gave her a discreet thumbs-up and turned away.

Suzy didn't waste another second, but turned and leaped across the gap between the *Belle* and the tender, landing on the mound of fusion bananas piled inside it. She hurried across them toward the sorting car, stifling a yelp as they sparked with energy and spat tiny yellow lightning bolts to snap at her heels. The rim of the world was clearly visible on either side of her now, and she could hear the low roar of falling water beyond the hiss and rattle of the Express. At the far end of the tender she took a running jump and caught the edge of the sorting car's roof before pulling herself up and over. The roof was wet with spray, and her sneakers slipped as she ran on, but then she saw the H.E.C. up ahead. She was almost there.

Before she could reach it, the railway line curved sharply to hug the edge of the world. She looked down and almost screamed in shock. On one side of the train was the Topaz Narrows, with all its life and color and beauty. On the other was an endless curve of foaming white water, falling away into bottomless space below her. It was the end of the world and the start of the void, and the Express was hurtling along a gleaming thread of track between the two.

Suzy's stomach dropped through the floor and a feeling of vertigo threatened to overwhelm her. She pictured herself slipping off the roof and falling forever...

The high-pitched whine of the H.E.C.'s rocket boosters powering up cut through her thoughts, and she suddenly remembered Stonker's instruction to Wilmot in the navigation room. What had he called it? A "rolling launch." The thought had barely formed in her mind before she realized that the H.E.C. was gradually falling behind the rest of the train. They were going to launch the H.E.C. at full speed and had uncoupled it already! The gap between the sorting car and the H.E.C. was barely more than three feet, but it was steadily widening. If she didn't move now, it would be too late.

She ran. The wind was at her back, and it felt like a great hand had scooped her up and hurled her forward. She made it to the end of the sorting carriage in a few seconds and jumped, flailing her arms and legs, and letting the wind fill the folds of her coat like a sail. For an instant, she felt weightless. Then she crashed down hard on the sloping roof of the H.E.C., a second before its rocket boosters flared into life and it blasted upward into the sky.

Suzy held her breath. The invisible hand wasn't at her back now; it was pressing down on her like a rock, pinning her to the roof. She looked over her shoulder and saw the Express, already small and toylike with distance, racing away along the shining lines of silver that hugged the lip of the Topaz Narrows. The H.E.C. was rising on a pillar of fire into the strange twilight zone between tropical sky and profound darkness. It was breathtaking, and Suzy might even have taken a few seconds to appreciate it if the H.E.C. hadn't then begun to tilt underneath her as it banked toward the void.

She slid toward the edge of the roof but caught the raised edge of the sunroof just in time to save herself. She hammered on it with her free hand.

"Help!" she shouted. "Wilmot! Let me in!"

To her surprise, the translucent head of the Chief rose through the roof. He saw her, and started.

"Oh my!" he said. "What are you doing out here?"

"Trying to get in!" she yelled back. "Hurry!"

He dropped back inside, and there were an agonizing few seconds in which nothing happened. Suzy's hands cramped with the effort of holding on. The H.E.C. continued toward the void, leaving the mighty disk of the Topaz Narrows behind it. They were out beyond the edge of the world now, with nothing but blankness all around them. The air began to cool.

Then, without warning, the sunroof popped open. Unfortunately for Suzy, it opened away from her, wresting her fingers loose.

"Heeeeelp!" she cried as she slid helplessly down the slope of the roof toward oblivion.

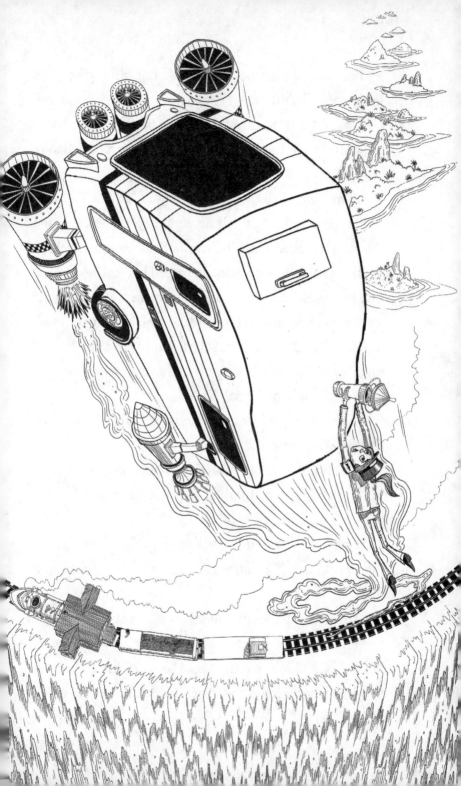

The loop of a satchel strap landed in front of her, and she grabbed it, stopping her slide just as her legs shot out over the edge of the roof. Wilmot's head popped out of the sunroof. He was gripping the satchel with both hands.

"Hold on!" he shouted.

"I am!" she cried.

He pulled back with all his might on the satchel, and the strap creaked with the strain. Suzy stopped kicking wildly against empty space and braced her feet against the side of the H.E.C. Then, one painful step at a time, she walked her way up onto the roof, at which point Wilmot's weight yanked her in through the sunroof. They landed together in a bruised and gasping heap on the floor.

"You did it!" she cried. "Thank you."

"That's all right," Wilmot groaned. "Would you mind shutting the sunroof?"

She climbed onto a fold-down table attached to the wall, reached up, and pulled the sunroof closed. "I can't believe I made it," she said.

"I was offering moral support," said the Chief, hovering beside her. "I'm afraid it's the best I can do these days."

"You're doing plenty," said Suzy. "Thank you."

Wilmot was visibly less relaxed. He was trying to pace, but the H.E.C. was so small that he had little choice but to turn in a circle on the spot. "I don't know, Suzy," he said, worrying at his fingernails. "It's not that I don't want you on this delivery, I really do, but what about your parents? They must be frantic."

"Let me worry about my parents," said Suzy. "They can be as angry as they like once I get home, but I'm going to prove them wrong. This plan was my idea, remember. I want to be part of it."

"Perhaps we should turn back," he said. "As your Postmaster, I'm responsible for your safety."

"And as posties, we're both responsible for delivering this book," said Suzy.

"The girl is right," said the book from inside Wilmot's satchel. "Return me to my rightful place in Hydroborea."

"We've got less than a day left if we want it to give back all the words it ate at the Ivory Tower," said Suzy. "This delivery is more important than anything else right now, including my parents. Besides, if you take me back, they'll never let me be a postie again. They think I can't look after myself."

"I just found you clinging to the roof," said the Chief.

"And I'm fine," she said, trying to look nonchalant. "You took off a little earlier than I expected, that's all. We have to carry on."

Wilmot shuffled from foot to foot, trying to make his mind up. "I suppose so," he said, although he didn't sound happy about it. "But assuming we make it back from this, I insist on taking you straight home and offering your parents a full apology."

Suzy folded her arms. "Fine," she said. "Not that they deserve one. And who knows? If we pull this off, maybe they'll change their minds."

Even as she said it, she knew it wasn't true—if she made it home, her parents were going to be anything but proud of her. She'd just run away! The enormity of it hit her as the darkness of the void pressed against the windows. Being grounded for a few weeks was going to feel like a piece of cake compared to whatever punishment she'd have to face when she got back. They were going to ground her for life.

What if this really is my last delivery? she thought as the H.E.C. roared into the void.

9

One of Our Posties
Is Missing

Everyone in the *Belle*'s cab felt the slight jolt of the H.E.C. uncoupling from the sorting car, and heard the distant roar of its rockets fading into the distance. Frederick, who had made his way outside onto the loco-motive's gangway, watched the column of fire rising into the sky far behind them.

"Good luck, you three," he said to himself. Then, doing his best to look composed, he stepped back inside. "That's it," he said. "Liftoff."

Stonker gave a satisfied nod, although his expression was stern. "A perfect rolling launch. Let's hope everything else goes as smoothly. The Postmaster's taking a big risk stepping into the unknown like this."

"I know," said Frederick. "But he wanted to go. And he's in good company."

"Grrrrolf," said Ursel as she tossed another bunch of bananas into the fireplace.

"Quite," said Stonker. "The Chief's a nice chap, but he managed to sink his ship, himself, and his whole crew."

Frederick felt a prickle of anxiety. "I'm sure he'll be fine in the void, though," he said. "There's much less to bump into." He picked a book off a nearby shelf, but of course, it was blank. He closed it with a snap and put it down. "So what do we do now? Just sit around and wait to hear from them?"

"More or less," said Stonker. "If they make it through the storm and back, the Postmaster can call us on his phone and we'll come out and collect them. There's no telling how long they might be, of course, so in the meantime, we'll take Suzy and Mr. and Mrs. Smith home, and collect Fletch."

"Thank you," said Suzy's mom tersely. "That's very kind of you."

Frederick noticed that she and Suzy's dad had retreated to opposite corners of the cab, where they were taking turns leveling accusing glares at each other.

"Yes, we really appreciate it," said Suzy's dad, still scowling at his wife. "I'm just sorry we're leaving you so abruptly. It wasn't exactly what we planned."

"We didn't plan any of this," said Suzy's mom. "But one of us doesn't know when to say no."

"We both agreed to come."

"Only because I knew you were bound to give Suzy whatever she wanted," Suzy's mom snapped back. "You always do."

Suzy's dad looked hurt. "That's not true. I agreed we should take her home, but you never said it would be permanent."

"Do you want her coming back to do this all again next week?" Suzy's mom replied. "It's not safe, Calum. It'll never be safe. This is our chance to put a stop to it before something dreadful happens."

Frederick watched their argument with growing satisfaction. He was quite looking forward to seeing their reaction when they discovered that Suzy had got the better of them.

"At least we can earn it in the safety of our own home, without having to worry about where she is or whether she's in danger," Suzy's mom went on. "Or would you rather watch her blast off in an old caravan, never knowing if she'll ever come back?"

"Such is the life of a postal troll, madam," said Stonker. "Bravery, duty, and the occasional jam sandwich. It's what the Postmaster lives for."

"Yes, well," said Suzy's mom. "That's not the life we want for Suzy. I'm sorry."

"If it's Suzy's life, maybe you should let her decide what to do with it," said Frederick. He fought back a knowing little smile as Suzy's parents glowered at him and didn't even flinch when Ursel growled in frustration.

"Grunf!" she barked.

"Ursel has a point," said Stonker. "Perhaps it would be wise to go upstairs and check on Suzy. I'm sure she'd appreciate some parental reassurance."

Suzy's mom sighed so deeply she seemed to deflate. "You're right, of course," she said. "Calum?"

"Yes, let's," Suzy's dad said. "Maybe talking it through will help."

They crossed the cab and made their way upstairs together. Frederick chuckled as he watched them go.

The shafts of sunlight angling in through the windows of the cab's seaward side began to shift as the track curved more sharply, heading away from the rim and back toward the center of the Topaz Narrows.

"We'll be at the tunnel mouth in a little while," said Stonker. "If you want to make yourself useful, you can put the kettle on. And please stop antagonizing Mr. and Mrs. Smith."

With a single claw, Ursel lifted a large brass kettle down from a hook on the wall and handed it to Frederick. It was so heavy that it almost pulled him over.

"Fine, but I don't see why they should stop Suzy from doing what she's good at," he muttered as he lugged it to the sink.

"We don't have to like their decision, but we do have to abide by it," said Stonker. "They're her parents, after all."

"And what did parents ever know about anything?" Frederick asked.

"I wouldn't know," said Stonker flatly. "But you've not got long before you have to say good-bye to Suzy permanently, so spend the time wisely."

Oh, I don't think we've seen the last of Suzy, Frederick thought. He filled the kettle and had just succeeded in manhandling it over to the fireplace, when the door to the stairs burst open and Suzy's parents almost fell into the room.

"She's gone!" said Suzy's mom.

"I beg your pardon?" said Stonker.

"Suzy," said Suzy's dad. "She's not there. We looked everywhere."

"And there's a window open!" said Suzy's dad.

Stonker's eyebrows shot up his forehead, and the tips of his mustache bristled. "You don't think ...," he began.

"That she fell overboard!" said Suzy's mom. "We have to go back and look for her. She could be drowning!"

"Or what if she fell over the edge of the world?" said Suzy's dad.

Stonker threw himself at the brake lever, and the *Belle*'s drive wheels let out a pained screech. The sudden deceleration almost threw them all to the floor.

"Frrrrowlf!" said Ursel.

"Yes, we'll go back," said Stonker. "If Suzy's gone overboard, we'll find her. Ursel here's an excellent swimmer."

"Fromf." Ursel nodded.

Frederick watched them busy themselves with the controls, while Suzy's parents clung to one another helplessly. He had been ready to enjoy watching them panic, but now that it was actually happening, he realized it was just making him feel guilty. Suzy's parents both looked scared and pale, and their eyes shimmered with tears. Stonker and Ursel, meanwhile, were stony-faced and grimly determined. This wasn't half as much fun as he had imagined it would be, and reluctantly, he realized he was going to have to do something about it.

"Call off the search," he said. "Suzy's not drowning,

126

and she hasn't gone over the edge of the world. At least, not in the way you're thinking."

The others all looked at him sharply.

"What are you talking about?" said Stonker.

"She's not on the train," said Suzy's dad.

"I know," said Frederick. His resolve was beginning to crumble under their hard stares, and he backed unconsciously away from them. "I never said she was still on the train."

"Then where is she?" demanded Suzy's mom, her voice pinched.

Frederick backed into the wall. "I'll tell you," he said. "But you're not going to like it."

10

THE COLOR OF NOTHING

Suzy stared out of the H.E.C.'s window into the void. She was captivated. Its darkness wasn't that of outer space or of the tunnels between the Impossible Places. It felt deeper somehow, more endless. And it had edges.

Suzy had no idea how such a thing could be possible, but she could see them—a jagged web of sharp angles bisecting the darkness, as though the void were an enormous three-dimensional puzzle made up of interlocking tiles. And perhaps it was just her perspective shifting as the H.E.C. sailed through them, but the tiles seemed to tilt and slide against one another until they formed new shapes through which she glimpsed flashes of reality— snowcapped mountains, a forest of walking trees, thunder dragons dueling in the skies above Cloud Forge...Each shape was a window into a different world, but as quickly as they formed, they broke up again, and the images vanished.

After a while, she found it quite hard to look at and turned instead to the small folding table on which the Chief had unrolled the phantom map. Wilmot was trying to take some measurements from it with a pair of compasses, but they kept passing straight through it.

"Even if you could make any marks on it," said Suzy, "the book would just suck them straight up."

Wilmot sighed and put his compasses away. "Good point," he said. "Chief? Have you got any suggestions?"

The Chief laughed. "The best way through the void is to navigate by sight."

"How?" said Suzy. "Everything out there keeps moving."

"So it does, my dear. But it's not entirely random, and there are patterns to be found, if you know how to look for them. Excuse me a moment while I check the stern." He rose up until his head and shoulders passed through the ceiling. Suzy scrambled by Wilmot and peered out of the rear window. The kaleidoscope of the void aligned into a fractured vision of blue waters and golden sands for a few seconds before the Chief descended again.

"As I thought, the Topaz Narrows are still visible

behind us," he said. "We can use them as a reference to chart our heading."

Wilmot hunkered down over the map. "We blasted off from this point here," he said, jabbing a fingertip through the spectral fabric. "And we need to be heading for this." He jabbed a second finger down through the dark stain of the void storm. The Chief peered over his shoulder, then bobbed back up through the roof. They watched his body turn this way and that for a minute before he rejoined them.

"Take us three degrees starboard, Postmaster," he said. "And lower our angle of descent a little. That should get us there."

With a grin, Wilmot turned to the controls and began altering their course. "I'll take us up to maximum speed," he said. "We've no time to waste."

The engines throbbed beneath the floor, and the Chief drifted to Wilmot's side. "Thundering typhoons, is that our speed?" he exclaimed, watching the speedometer's needle creep around the dial. "Why, that's twenty times faster than La Rouquine's best effort."

"The H.E.C. is top of the range," said Wilmot proudly. "It should only take us an hour to reach the void storm. From there, we'll have a little less than seven hours left to find Hydroborea."

"The wonders of technology," said the Chief. "I've got

130

so much to catch up on, but may I say what a pleasure it is to be voyaging again." He glowed a little brighter as the warmth of his smile spread through his body. "We're alone out here now, but in my day, you could look out from the helm and see the void speckled with hundreds of lights, like tiny stars. All the ships and flotillas making their way along the trade routes." His glow flickered. "How I miss it."

Suzy looked out into the void again and tried to picture it. In her imagination, at least, it looked very beautiful. "Do you think we'll actually make it?" she asked.

Wilmot raised his eyebrows. "To the center of the void storm?" He thought for a moment. "Yes," he said. "We have to. The future of the Express and the Ivory Tower both depend on it."

"And what do you think we'll actually find there?"

"That," he said, "is a really good question."

Time passed slowly. Seven hours hardly felt long enough to find a city that had been lost for thousands of years, and Suzy quickly grew restless. She began to wish she'd brought a book with her but then remembered that, even if she had, its pages would all be blank by now, and she'd still be left with nothing to distract her. Plus, she'd have ruined a perfectly good book.

131

Wilmot, meanwhile, had removed *The Book of Power* from his satchel and, along with the Chief, was plying it with questions. The book wasn't being especially cooperative.

"So, who wrote you?" asked Wilmot.

"I have many authors," the book replied.

"Are you a work of fiction or nonfiction?" the Chief asked.

"I am both," said the book. "And more."

Wilmot cupped his chin in his hand. "And what exactly do you do with all these words you suck up? Are they your food?"

"They add to my power," said the book. "It is the stuff of which I am made."

"Magical power, I'll wager," said the Chief. "Forged in the Gilded Tower by the great magicians of old." When the book didn't answer, he said, "Tell us, were you really there in the first days of Hydroborea, before the Union was formed?"

"I was," said the book.

Wilmot gasped and sat forward. "And are all the legends true?"

"Some of them," said the book.

"Are the buildings really made of gold?" Wilmot asked. "Is the sky a thousand different colors? Does it never rain?" His eagerness was contagious, and Suzy slid into the seat behind him, not wanting to miss a word. A moment passed in silence.

"Well, don't leave us in suspense," said the Chief. "A good book is supposed to be entertaining, y'know."

"I *am* a good book," the book replied, somewhat testily. "But I cannot share my contents until I am unbound."

The Chief puffed his cheeks out. "Well," he said. "I look forward to discovering your fine city and its people."

"Wait a minute," said Suzy. "How can you discover a city if there are already people living there?"

"Why, because it's completely unknown, of course. Uncharted."

"But not to the people who live there," she pointed out. "They know exactly where it is."

"Well, of course they do," said the Chief. "But are they actually looking for it?"

Suzy thought about this for a moment. "I suppose not."

"Which means they can't very well discover it, can they?" said the Chief.

Suzy shook her head. "Are you sure this is how discovery works?"

"My dear young thing, if we explorers weren't allowed to discover things that people already knew about, we'd never discover anything at all. And then who would explain all the far-flung corners of reality to you?"

Suzy frowned. "The people who live there?"

133

The Chief chuckled. "Such a quaint idea."

Suzy still wasn't convinced and was about to say so when she spotted the winking light on the console. She nudged Wilmot. "Is that a good or bad light?" she asked.

Wilmot handed her the book and bustled over to the console. He frowned. "I'm not sure," he said. "It's either the proximity alert, which means we're approaching the void storm, or it's a reminder to change the windshield wiper fluid."

At that moment, the H.E.C. was rocked by a powerful shudder that sent them all reeling.

"We're approaching the void storm," he said.

They all rushed to the front window, and Suzy gasped—the storm was a blizzard of black glass shards. Razor-sharp fragments of nothingness swirled together in a furious maelstrom so gargantuan, she couldn't see the edges of it. Black lightning flared where the shards crashed together, imprinting broken pictures of a hundred different worlds on Suzy's eyes.

Another blow struck the H.E.C. and she felt a rush of excitement, followed quickly by one of fear. They had made it this far, but the storm looked every bit as fearsome as the Chief had predicted. The H.E.C. suddenly felt very small and vulnerable.

Wilmot's hands danced over the controls. "I'll do my

best to hold us steady," he said. "Chief? What do we do now?"

The H.E.C. lurched to one side, throwing Suzy and Wilmot to the floor. Only the Chief, floating freely in the air, remained upright. Suzy's stomach plunged, and she realized they were caught in the storm's grip. They were being spun helplessly out of control.

The Chief rubbed his hands together in anticipation. "Stand ready, crew. Man the tiller and lower the topsail."

"We don't have a topsail!" said Wilmot, fighting to regain his feet as the H.E.C. pitched and yawed beneath them.

"Oh." The Chief stroked his beard. "Well, point us into the wind at any rate. We won't get far as long as it's broadsiding us like this."

Wilmot adjusted the controls and brought the nose of the H.E.C. around. Their dreadful rolling motion evened out and was replaced by a violent shaking that made Suzy's vision blur.

"Is this better or worse?" she shouted over the noise.

"Possibly both," the Chief replied. "We're pushing back at last, but we'll have to hope this vessel can hold together long enough to get us through. The storm's hitting us with everything it's got."

Indeed it was. Suzy could hear the H.E.C. creak and

groan all around her, and the ceiling light flared and dimmed.

At the same moment, something big flashed outside the window, so close they almost collided with it. It went by too quickly for Suzy to get more than a glimpse, but she got a fleeting impression of broken timbers and ragged canvas.

"What was that?" she cried.

"What was what?" said Wilmot, his attention still fixed on the controls.

Before Suzy could formulate an answer, another shape tumbled past outside, spinning like a pinwheel, but this time she saw it clearly. It was an old-fashioned sailing ship, its mast broken and its wooden ribs exposed. Suzy pressed her face to the window and watched the storm sweep it away. "They're old void ships," she said. "Like *La Rouquine.*"

"Old wrecks like *La Rouquine,*" the Chief said, joining her at the window. More shipwrecks appeared in the maelstrom, tossed and tumbled like broken toys. "These are the last resting places of all the brave explorers who came before us. And we need to push harder unless we want to share their fate."

"We're at full power already!" said Wilmot. "I don't want to overload the engines."

Sparks burst from the wiring on the walls, and a gout

of steam erupted from between the cushions of the pull-out sofa.

I'm so glad I wasn't sitting there, thought Suzy. She cupped her hands around her mouth and shouted to Wilmot, "I don't think we can last much longer! Just do it!"

Wilmot steeled himself and twisted a dial all the way over into the red. The H.E.C. bucked like a mule, and the groaning sounds increased. It sounded as though a rain of sledge hammers was striking the hull. The Chief shot up and stuck his head through the ceiling.

"That's it, Wilmot," he said, returning a moment later. "Keep nudging us to port and batten down the hatches. It's about to get really bad."

Wilmot's mouth dropped open. "You mean this *isn't* really bad?" he said.

"Oh, my dear boy, you've seen nothing yet!" the Chief replied. "We're in the teeth of the monster. We either beat it, or it devours us. There's no backing out now."

A look of fear flitted over Wilmot's face, but it was gone in an instant. "Right," he said. "Hold tight, everyone." He set his jaw and made another small adjustment to the controls. A second later, the H.E.C. suffered a blow that sent it tumbling end over end. Suzy didn't have time to process what was happening before she hit the ceiling. Then she was rolling away again, across the back wall, the floor, the front window. She collided with Wilmot, and

137

something hard struck her shoulder. It was the Chief's skull, and she grabbed it out of the air.

"Wilmot, what's happening?" she shouted. If he replied, she didn't hear him, as the H.E.C. flipped again and she fell the full length of the caravan, landing on her back on the rear window and striking her head. Everything went dark, and for a terrifying moment, she thought the end had come, until she realized the light fitting had blown. The caravan was now lit only by bursts of sparks, the madly blinking lights of the console panel, and the glow of the Chief.

"We're almost there," the Chief shouted. "Just a little farther!"

"All our systems are critical!" Wilmot shouted back. "They won't take much more!"

As if in confirmation, smoke began issuing from the cabinet beneath the control console, filling the H.E.C. with the stink of burning plastic. It caught in the back of Suzy's throat, making her retch, and Wilmot doubled over, his eyes streaming.

Suzy lurched to his side, trying to help, when a piercing white light cut through the blur of tears and smoke. It came from outside the H.E.C., and the Chief raised his voice in triumph.

"We've done it!" he cried. "We're at the eye of the storm. Well done, shipmates!"

Suzy wiped the tears from her eyes and saw that he was right. They had entered a pocket of stable void at the heart of the tempest, and running through it, like the twist of color in the middle of a marble, was a jagged fork of frozen lightning that pulsed and flared like a living thing.

Wilmot relaxed his grip on the console as the H.E.C. stabilized. "What is that?" he said.

"I don't know," said Suzy. "But it's beautiful."

"It is a fracture in reality," said the Chief. "A tear in the fabric of existence itself. They're extremely rare. They can only happen in the void, and I've never seen one anywhere near this size before." He put his hands on his hips as he admired the phenomenon. "Why, it's big enough to swallow an armada. Or a city! Or—"

"Or a world?" Suzy said. She picked the book up with both hands and held it at eye level. "We've come all this way, so you might as well tell us," she said. "Is this where Hydroborea used to be?"

The book was silent.

"Come on!" she said, shaking it in frustration. "We're risking our lives to help you, so why not help us for once? Are we in the right place?"

The book gave a long, weary sigh that sounded like the rustling of pages. "Yes," it said. "This is where my world once stood."

Despite the smoke and the stench, Suzy smiled. "Thank you," she said. "Now we know where to go next."

"We do?" said Wilmot.

"Yes," she replied. "Through there." She pointed out the front window at the fracture. "Whatever happened to Hydroborea, I bet we'll find it wherever that thing leads."

Wilmot reviewed the console's warning lights uneasily. "I don't know if we can," he said. "The H.E.C.'s already taken as much punishment as it can handle."

"Can it survive the trip back out through the storm?" asked the Chief.

Wilmot's ears drooped. He shook his head.

"Then we don't have any choice," said Suzy. "We take our chances in the fracture."

Wilmot took a moment to straighten his lapels and brush a few flecks of smut from the peak of his cap. "All right," he said. "Hold tight and keep everything crossed. We're going in." He flicked a few switches, there was another belch of smoke from beneath the console, and the H.E.C. leaped forward again, rushing toward the fracture.

Suzy wedged herself into the seat beside the table, keeping a firm grip on both the book and the Chief's skull as the blinding light filled the caravan. It was so bright it seemed to shine right through the walls, as though they were made of glass. Suzy scrunched her eyes shut, but the light shone straight through her as well. She felt as if she barely existed at all.

And with the light came images—a tower of gold rising above a slate-gray sea, magic arcing from it like the beam of a lighthouse, busy streets beneath a sky of shining rainbow colors. The taste of salty sea air.

This wasn't just her imagination, Suzy realized. The images had the weight and feel of memory behind them. But not her own memory. Hydroborea's.

Something stirred with a rustle like old paper, and with a start, she realized that she was not alone. Something else was there in the memory with her. She couldn't see it clearly, but she got the impression of something big and ancient and very, very powerful looking down on her with ink-black eyes.

"This is the world I left behind," it said, and its voice was that of the book.

Fascination and fear churned inside Suzy. "What are you?" she whispered.

"I am overdue," the thing replied. "Return me to Hydroborea. You have sixteen and a half hours remaining."

Then the H.E.C. plunged into the fracture, the memory faded, and there was nothing but light.

11
NOTHING TO SEE HERE

Suzy couldn't tell how long they traveled through the fracture in reality. She wasn't even sure that time existed there at all. There was just the all-pervading light, and when it suddenly snapped off, she found herself lying on the linoleum floor of the H.E.C. She tried to move, but her body responded by firing jagged bolts of pain through her head and down into her limbs. She groaned.

The H.E.C. was dark and still. Moonlight angled in through the windows, as cold and ghostly as the Chief, who hovered anxiously over her.

"Welcome back to the land of the living," he said. "Are you hurt?"

Suzy sat up, wincing. "Nothing serious," she said. "Wilmot? Are you all right?"

"I think so." He appeared as a dark silhouette against the moonlight, and patted himself down. "I'm a little battered, but everything still seems to be attached."

He helped Suzy to her feet, only for her to immediately lose her balance again as the H.E.C. rolled and shifted underfoot. At first, she put it down to dizziness, but then she realized that the caravan really was bobbing about. It made her feel a little queasy.

"They say any landing you can walk away from is a success," said Wilmot, dusting himself off.

Suzy staggered to the rear window and looked out. "What about ones you can swim away from?" she asked. Wilmot and the Chief joined her, and together they looked out on an endless expanse of ocean, dotted here and there with jagged islands that glittered a ghostly white in the moonlight. "Icebergs," said Suzy. "Where are we?"

"This is Hydroborea's world," said the book, from the floor underneath the folding table. Suzy picked it up.

"It is?" She hurried to the rear window, but there was nothing to see but more ocean. "Then where is it? Are we close?"

"I do not know," said the book. "This is where the city once stood. It should be here."

"You mean we came all this way, and Hydroborea's still missing?" said Suzy.

"Correct," said the book. "Return me to Hydroborea."

Suzy considered shutting the book in the air lock where she wouldn't have to listen to it, but she mastered the urge. As it said in Chapter 2 of *The Knowledge*, "A postie always treats their deliveries with respect." Even if they were really annoying.

"Fine," she said. "We'll just keep looking. At least we know we're on the right world now. It's got to be somewhere nearby."

Wilmot made a little noise in his throat. He had returned to the control console while Suzy talked to the book, and now he looked at her with foreboding. "I'm afraid we won't be going anywhere," he said. "Pushing through the fracture overloaded the engine's molecular bifurcator. It's completely burned out. We've got no power left."

The discomfort in Suzy's stomach intensified, but it had little to do with seasickness. "I can't have brought us all this way for nothing," she said weakly.

Wilmot gave her a sympathetic smile. "I'm sorry, Suzy," he said. "It was a really good plan. But it looks like the stories are true—the city must have destroyed itself completely. There's no trace of it left."

Suzy sat down heavily on the pullout sofa. Its cushions

were torn and the stuffing was leaking out, but she hardly noticed. She was too preoccupied with the sickly mix of guilt and anxiety crawling through her veins. "So now what do we do?" she croaked.

"I'm afraid there's nothing we *can* do," said Wilmot. "We're adrift, there's no sign of land, and without power we're going to stay here until we starve."

His words settled like cold weights in the pit of her stomach. "Can we fix the engines?"

Wilmot shook his head. "The molecular bifurcator's beyond repair, and we haven't got a backup. Even if we did, I'm a Postmaster, not an engineer. I wouldn't know how to replace it."

Even through the gloom, she saw the look of concern on his face. "I'm sorry," he said. "I wish I could do more."

Suzy put a hand on his arm. "This isn't your fault," she said. Because it was all *her* fault, she knew. Her plan had ended in disaster, and she couldn't see any way of fixing it. They were going to drift here, lost and alone, until the H.E.C. became just another empty wreck. She wondered if she and Wilmot would become ghosts, like the Chief and his crew. She couldn't tell if that would be better or worse than just dying.

Imagine haunting this place forever, a treacherous little voice in her mind said. *Stuck in a broken caravan with nowhere to go and nothing to do. You should have listened to your parents.*

Her parents!

They broke into her thoughts again like a wrecking ball. She hadn't even said good-bye to them. What were they going to think when she never came home? This new thought wasn't just painful; it was terrifying, and her eyes pricked with unexpected tears.

"Suzy?" Wilmot was at her side. "Are you all right?"

With a concerted effort, she blinked the tears back and nodded. "Don't worry about me," she said. "Let's just concentrate on finding a way out of here."

"But how?" he said. "Everything's dead."

"Except us," she replied. And then, to the Chief, "Present company excepted."

He doffed his hat to her.

"Much obliged. You know, being lost at sea is something of a specialty of mine, and I can't help noticing that neither of you have taken our bearings yet."

"Er, no," said Wilmot. "How do we do that?"

"With a clear sky and a keen eye, of course," said the Chief. "Follow me and we'll do a little stargazing." He rose up through the ceiling. Wilmot hopped up onto the table and opened the sunroof. Suzy gave him a boost, and he disappeared through it.

"G-gosh, it's cold!" Wilmot exclaimed, reaching down to help Suzy up. The air bit into her like a thousand tiny knives as she emerged onto the roof.

"It's not just c-cold, it's f-freezing!" she said, the words bursting out of her in a cloud of steam. She pulled her great-coat tightly around herself, but it did little to help. The skin of her face and hands already felt tight and raw, and she could see tiny ice crystals forming on her eyelashes.

There were no stars to be seen, but the sky was alive with dancing light: Curtains of pink, green, and blue shifted and billowed, as though blown by invisible winds.

"An aurora!" said Suzy. "W-we have these on Earth. They're caused by ionized p-particles from the s-sun entering the upper atmosphere. People call them the n-northern lights. I've always w-wanted to see them."

"To be sure, it's a fine display," said the Chief, who, Suzy realized, didn't feel the cold one bit.

"But s-still no s-sign of H-Hydroborea," said Wilmot, his whole body shaking with the cold now.

Suzy tore her gaze away from the aurora, climbed unsteadily to her feet, and turned a complete circle. He was right—the ocean seemed to go on forever, and there was nothing but broken flotillas of ice all the way to the horizon. "But it m-must be s-somewhere," she said. "Otherwise wh-why would the b-book have b-brought us here?"

"I d-d-don't know," Wilmot replied. "B-but at least w-we're out of the v-v-void. That's s-something."

"Yes, but without p-power, we're s-still stuck here,"

said Suzy. "And we're running out of t-time to deliver the b-book." She cupped her hands over her mouth and breathed through them, trying to coax some feeling back into her numb fingers.

"This is probably a bit of a long shot," said the Chief, pointing over her shoulder, "but perhaps that beastie over there can give us directions."

Suzy looked behind her, straight into a luminous green eye the size of a bowling ball. It was attached to the end of a muscular black tentacle that rose out of the water and towered over the H.E.C. Wilmot yelped and almost fell overboard, but Suzy caught him by the collar.

A second tentacle broke the surface, its lidless eye fixed on them. Suzy saw rows of circular mouths down the tentacle's length, each lined with rows of needle-sharp teeth. A third tentacle rose into view, and a fourth, and a fifth, until the H.E.C. was surrounded.

"Avast!" exclaimed the Chief. "Make no sudden moves. It's sizing us up."

"A-and th-then what?" stammered Wilmot.

"It'll either leave us in peace," said the Chief. "Or ..."

The tentacles twitched. Suzy just had time to react before one of them lashed down toward her. She grabbed Wilmot and rolled aside as it swept straight through the Chief and struck the roof, making the H.E.C. tilt alarmingly.

"Hold on!" shouted Suzy, grabbing the rim of the open sunroof with one hand and tightening her grip on Wilmot's collar with the other.

More tentacles erupted from the sea, churning the waters around the H.E.C. into foam.

"I th-think," said Suzy, "we're in t-trouble."

"It's a whopper all right," said the Chief. "Man the harpoons!"

"We d-don't have any!" wailed Wilmot.

Another tentacle lunged toward them, but Suzy was ready for it. Using all her strength, she pulled herself in through the sunroof, dragging Wilmot with her. The tentacle struck the roof and secured itself with a quick series of slurping noises. The H.E.C. rocked again, tossing Suzy off balance as she fought to climb onto the table and pull the sunroof shut.

She steadied herself and reached up for the catch, only to find herself face-to-eyeball with the creature. She froze, horrified, as the tentacle snaked in through the opening, looking her over from head to foot. The countless sucker-mouths slavered and slurped, dripping thick slime onto the linoleum.

Then a burst of white fog erupted from over Suzy's shoulder, straight into the eye.

"Leave her alone!" shouted Wilmot, wielding a small brass fire extinguisher. He unleashed another blast of vapor, filling the cabin of the H.E.C. When it dispersed a second later, the tentacle had retreated out of sight.

Suzy wasted no time, but jumped and pulled the sunroof shut, fastening the catch securely. The moment she had done so, another tentacle slammed down across it.

"Thanks," she gasped.

"Don't thank me yet," said Wilmot.

The H.E.C. shook as yet more tentacles struck. Suzy and Wilmot huddled together in the middle of the cabin as the view through the windows was obscured by the thick, fleshy protuberances, and a couple of the big green eyes were pressed against the glass, staring in at them.

"Chief!" Suzy shouted. "What's going on out there?"

The Chief descended through the ceiling.

"It's fascinating!" he said. "The beast is wrapping us in its clutches."

"Is that fascinating?" asked Wilmot. "Because I'd have thought it's mostly terrifying."

"My apologies," said the Chief. "But it's been many a century since I was last assailed by a sea monster, and the experience doesn't quite hold the mortal terror that it once did."

"Speak for yourself," said Wilmot as the H.E.C. tilted wildly in the creature's grip.

Suzy grabbed at the table to stop herself from falling

flat. "What about your phone?" she said. "We can call for help!"

Wilmot went wide-eyed. "Why didn't I think of that?" he said. "But will it even work this far from the Union? What if there's no signal?"

"There's only one way to find out," said Suzy. "Quickly! Call the Express."

"Right!" Fighting to keep his balance, he pulled the phone from his pocket and dialed the number. His face fell. "It's not dialing out," he said.

Suzy deflated.

"Wait!" she said. "It's powered by movement, and you're standing still. Hurry! Start moving!"

Wilmot started jogging on the spot. "Still nothing," he said.

Suzy's mind raced. Then she grabbed the Chief's skull, folded up the table, opened the door to the air lock, and squeezed inside. "There," she said. "That's as much room as we can give you. See if it's enough."

"Oh, good thinking," said the Chief, who hadn't bothered to move along with his skull, and still hovered in the middle of the H.E.C. "Don't mind me. I'm incorporeal, y'know."

Wilmot nodded eagerly and began jogging from one end of the H.E.C. to the other. It only took him a few steps in each direction, and he had to pass back and forth through the Chief as he did so. But then, as he turned to retrace his steps for the fifth time, the tips of his ears pricked up. "It's dialing!" he said.

Frederick leaned against the handrail of the *Belle*'s gangway and watched the shadows of the palm trees lengthen as the sun dipped toward the rim of the Topaz Narrows. The Express had left the main line and now stood on a siding in the shelter of a coral atoll, beside a scattering of weather-beaten fishing boats bobbing at anchor. The *Belle*'s boiler ticked as it cooled, and the crest of every wave was crowned with golden light. All was calm and peaceful. Apart from Suzy's mom's voice, which reached him from the cab's open doorway.

"Don't you dare put me on hold again! I demand to speak to your supervisor. To your supervisor's supervisor! To—" There was a moment's silence, followed by a scream of frustration that startled a few roosting seagulls out of the nearby trees.

Frederick sighed. He had retreated to the gangway to escape the angry exchanges that his confession had unleashed, but he had been out here for more than an hour now and things clearly weren't improving.

Why do they insist on being so stupid about all this? he

wondered. But he kept the thought to himself as he tip-toed to the cab and poked his head inside.

Suzy's mom stood at the hearth, the receiver of the cab's old-fashioned rotary dial phone clamped to her ear with both hands and her face set in a determined scowl. Suzy's dad, meanwhile, flitted nervously about the room, wringing his hands and muttering to himself under his breath.

Maybe we should just go home and call the police," he said. "Or the air ambulance service. Or NASA! Yes, maybe they can send a rocket or something..."

Frederick cleared his throat. "You're not still on hold to the Central Post Office, are you?" he asked.

Suzy's mom flared her nostrils. "Someone tell that boy that I'm not talking to him," she declared.

"Yes, she is," said Stonker, who was slumped in an armchair in the far corner. Ursel lay on the floor beside him, and they both looked thoroughly bored. "We've tried telling her it's no use. Even if she gets through to the Postmaster General himself, he won't be able to do anything."

"Well, somebody has to do *something*," said Suzy's mom. "I'm not going to rest until we get Suzy back, even if I have to take the matter all the way to the top. Calum and I can't be the only ones who care about her safety." She aimed a hard look over her shoulder at Frederick as she said this, and he felt a prickle of resentment in response.

"I'm not in charge of Suzy," he retorted. "She wanted to go. I just didn't stop her."

"Well, you should have," said Suzy's dad. "You let her put herself in danger."

"Suzy's always putting herself in danger," said Frederick. "And then she gets herself out of it again. It's what she does best."

"She's out there in a flying caravan," said Suzy's dad, "heading for a killer storm, guided by the ghost of a man who didn't survive his last voyage."

Frederick opened his mouth to respond, but his answer stuck in his mouth, half-formed. Before he could finish it, Suzy's mom jerked the receiver away from her ear and shook it.

"Hello?" she shouted into it. "Are you still there? Hello?" Her face reddened with anger and she slammed the phone down. "They hung up on me!"

"Gronf," said Ursel, lifting her head off the floor.

"Yes, it's probably just a fault on the line," said Stonker. "Perhaps they'll call you back."

"Not if I call them back first," said Suzy's mom. Stonker and Ursel rolled their eyes as she reached for the phone again, but it rang before she had even touched it.

"Gosh," said Stonker. "I wasn't actually expecting it to happen."

Suzy's mom snatched up the receiver. "And I should think so, too," she said into it. "If you think you're going to get rid of me that easily, then you…" She trailed off and her mouth dropped open in shock. "Wilmot?" she said quietly. "Is that you?"

"Grolf!" Ursel was on her feet in an instant and crossed the cab in a single bound, quickly followed by Stonker. She reached out a claw and hit the speakerphone button on the phone's cradle as Frederick slipped inside and hovered beside Suzy's dad, who finally stopped his pacing.

At first there was nothing but static. Then, tinny and broken, came a voice.

"Hello?" it said. "Mr. Stonker? Ursel? Is that you? Can you hear me?"

"It's the Postmaster!" exclaimed Stonker. He shouted into the phone, "Postmaster, we understand you've got Suzy with you. Is that correct? Are you both all right?"

There was more static, then Wilmot's voice again. He sounded out of breath. "Hello? Can anyone hear me? It's a bad connection. I don't know if anyone's even receiving this. I'm not getting anything at this end." His voice was half-swamped by a series of loud bangs and thumps.

"We can hear you, Wilmot!" said Suzy's mom. "What about Suzy? Are you both safe?"

Wilmot's voice faded in and out, swamped by interference. "Suzy," they heard him say. "I don't think this is working."

"Keep trying!" came Suzy's voice, very faintly. Suzy's parents clung to one another.

"Suzy!" cried Suzy's mom. "We're here, darling!"

There was a pause, and then Wilmot spoke again.

"Mr. Stonker. Ursel. If either of you can hear me, we made it to Hydroborea's world, but we're under attack from some sort of sea monster, our molecular bifurcator's burned out, and we've lost power. We need help, urgently. Please send someone!"

"We hear you, my boy!" said Stonker. "Keep your chin up. We'll get you out of there just as quickly as we can."

And then, through the crackling fizz of the line, they heard Suzy's voice again.

"It's pulling us under!"

There was a squeal of interference and the line went dead.

Frederick and the others clustered impatiently around the phone as Stonker dialed Wilmot's number. When there was no response, he did it a second time, and a third, but once again, the phone just rang and rang. At last he hung up and shook his head. "They're not answering."

"What happened to them?" said Suzy's mom. "What are we going to do?" She looked around frantically, and her eyes met Frederick's. "You! You must know someone who can help."

Frederick felt his cheeks burning. "Not really," he said. "Neoma and the other library staff already have one crisis to deal with, and Lady Crepuscula's out hunting for Aybek and Tenebrae somewhere." He was fully aware of how inadequate he sounded, which only made his blush deepen. "I didn't think it would turn out like this, all right?"

"There's no use apportioning blame right now," said Stonker. "We need to decide a course of action."

"But what can we do?" asked Suzy's dad.

Ursel reared up behind him. "Hrrrrunf grrrrunk," she grunted.

"Quite right," said Stonker. "We mustn't waste time looking for help elsewhere. We'll have to go after them ourselves."

"Through the void storm?" said Frederick.

"Precisely," said Stonker. "It won't be an easy journey, so let's think about this logically. What are the facts?"

"We know the H.E.C. is disabled," said Suzy's mom. "They need a new . . . what was it called?"

"Rrrolf," said Ursel.

"Yes, a molecular bifurcator," said Stonker. "It processes the H.E.C.'s fuel. A vital part, and not an easy one to replace."

"Easy or not, we'll have to do it," said Frederick. "Otherwise the H.E.C. is going to be trapped out there forever."

"But a new molecular whatsit isn't going to do any good if we can't get it to them," said Suzy's dad. "How are we going to do that?"

Frederick chewed on his lower lip. "We'll obviously need some kind of ship to get us there," he said.

"But if we can do that," said Suzy's mom, "why do we need a new bifurcator at all? Why don't we just bring Suzy, Wilmot, and the Chief aboard the new ship and all escape together?"

"Because the bifurcator gives us two chances," said Frederick. "What happens if our ship gets damaged, just like the H.E.C.? Then we'll *all* be trapped, the book will never get delivered, and the Union will spiral into a Dark Age. But if we take a new bifurcator with us, we know that, even if something goes wrong, we'll at least be able to get the H.E.C. working again."

"The boy has a point," said Stonker. "Our first order of business has to be getting a new bifurcator. Ursel, do you know where we could find one?"

"Frunk," said Ursel, shaking her head. "Grrronk."

"Ah, good point," said Stonker. "Fletch is the chap to ask. He can rustle up any spare part you care to think of. I'll set a course back to your house."

"Can't we just phone him?" asked Suzy's mom.

"I'm afraid Fletch doesn't hold with mobile phones," said Stonker. "Won't touch the things."

"He doesn't need to," said Suzy's mom. "He's still at our house. We can just call our home phone."

"Good thinking!" said Suzy's dad. He took the phone off the mantelpiece and hastily dialed the number. The phone rang for a long time before being picked up.

"'Ello?" said Fletch's voice. "Who's this?"

"Fletch!" said Suzy's dad. "It's Calum Smith. Suzy's father."

There was a pause on the line, during which they could all hear the unmistakable sound of running water. A *lot* of running water. In fact, it sounded to Frederick as though Fletch was taking the call from behind a waterfall.

"Is, er...is everything all right there?" asked Suzy's dad, clearly thinking along similar lines.

"More or less," said Fletch a little stiffly. There was a loud crash in the background on his end of the line. "Watcha want?"

Suzy's dad visibly fought the urge to ask what was happening. "It's quite a long story, actually. You see, it all started at the Ivory Tower..."

Frederick realized he couldn't stand to hear Suzy's dad recount the whole misadventure from the start, so he marched over and snatched the phone from him.

"Fletch? It's Frederick. We need your help. Suzy and Wilmot went to another world in the H.E.C. and they're stuck. We need a molecular bifurcator to help get them back again. Where can we find one?"

"Tricky," said Fletch. "There used to be half a dozen scrap dealers in Trollville who could've got you one no trouble at all, but since the quakes, nobody's got the parts." He sucked his breath in through his teeth. "There might be somewhere else, mind."

"Where?" said Frederick.

"You ever been to a city called Propellendorf?"

"No," said Frederick. "Never."

"I have!" said Stonker. "Capital idea, Fletch."

"I make no promises," said Fletch. "But talk to the right people an' you can find almost anythin' in Propellendorf."

"All we have to do is find it," said Stonker. "I'll get onto rail traffic control straightaway and see if they can give me the city's current coordinates."

"*Current* coordinates?" said Suzy's dad. "I don't understand."

"Propellendorf moves around," said Frederick.

160

"Of course it does," said Suzy's mom flatly. "Why wouldn't it?"

"You said we need to talk to the right people, Fletch," said Frederick. "Can you give us some names? We're in a big hurry."

"Well, let's see…" There was a sound like falling masonry down the line. "There's One-Eyed Talyesin, although he's not been the same since he walked into that turbine last summer. Terrible thing, that lack of depth perception. Or you could try Anna Poon, if she's in town. She might still be out prospectin' in Autopolis, mind you."

"We don't have time for this," said Suzy's mom. "Can't we just take Fletch with us?"

"I thought you wanted this boggart dealt with," said Fletch.

"The boggart can wait," said Suzy's dad. "Suzy and Wilmot can't."

Stonker tugged at the ends of his mustache. "I'm afraid they're right, Fletch. Time is of the essence, and you could save us a great deal of searching."

"Yeah, I s'pose," said Fletch. "Where are you right now?"

"Frrrrarf," said Ursel.

"Blimey," Fletch replied. "It'll take you ages to reach

161

me from there. Just send me the coordinates for Propellendorf when you get 'em and I'll make my own way."

"How?" asked Stonker. "We didn't leave you any transport."

"Ways and means, Stonks. I've got a few favors I can call in."

"As long as you're sure," said Stonker. "We'll see you at Propellendorf, but please hurry. The future of the Impossible Places depends on the Postmaster and Suzy. And right now, they're depending on us."

The H.E.C. tilted alarmingly, throwing Suzy out of the air lock and onto the pullout sofa. A second later, Wilmot landed beside her, upside down.

The hull groaned as the creature squeezed it tight. Through the gaps between the mass of flesh covering the windows, Suzy saw that they were already several yards underwater.

"It's taking us down to the depths to feast at its leisure, no doubt," said the Chief. "A true adventurer's death."

Suzy wished she could order him back into his skull, but his glow was now the only light in the cabin as the waters around them darkened.

"Nobody panic," said Wilmot, regaining his feet. "I know this isn't ideal, but I don't think the creature can break through the hull." He fussed nervously with his cap. "At least, I hope not."

"A void storm, a reality fracture, and now a sea monster," said Suzy. "At least things can't get any worse." But as soon as she had said it, a new, horrible idea occurred to her. "Wilmot?" she said slowly. "How long will our air last?"

The sudden look of horror on his face was all the answer she needed. "Oh," he said. "Oh dear." His eyes darted around the cabin, making a quick calculation. "Without power to the oxygen generators, we've got less than an hour of breathable air left."

"If it's any consolation, I don't need my share," said the Chief. "A little ghostly humor to lighten the mood there. I hope you don't mind."

Suzy did mind but was too terrified to say anything as her future prospects had just been narrowed down to drowning, asphyxiation, or being eaten alive. She and Wilmot clung together as the creature dragged the H.E.C. down into the frozen darkness.

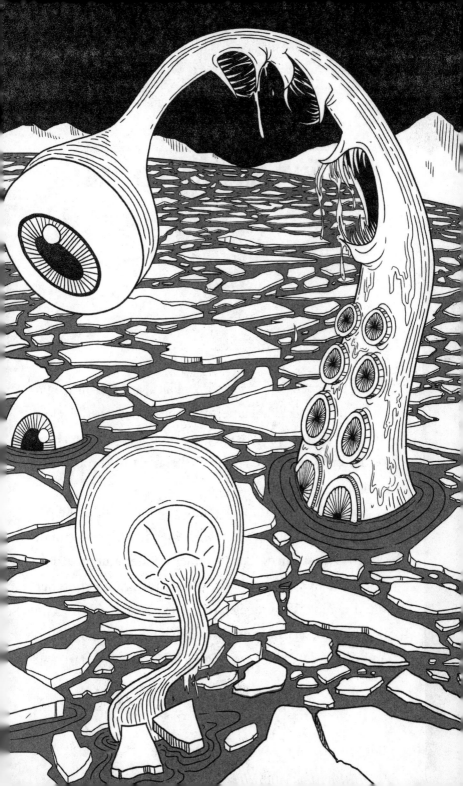

12

THAT SINKING FEELING

The ocean depths were inky black, and the only light
in the H.E.C. came from the Chief's pallid glow
and a sickly phosphorescence given off by the lidless eyes
of the creature, which were still staring in through the
windows.

Suzy tried not to meet their gaze but couldn't help a
shudder of discomfort. It felt as though she and Wilmot
were being studied, like specimens under a microscope.
But through her fear, she felt that infuriating itch in her
mind again. "How deep are we now?" she asked. The
beast had been dragging them down for several minutes,
and the H.E.C.'s hull was giving off a series of alarming

pops and creaks as the weight of water outside grew ever greater.

"I don't know," said Wilmot. "The instruments are still dead. Chief, can you see anything outside?"

The Chief obligingly drifted up through the H.E.C.'s ceiling, returning a moment later with a shake of his head. "We're too deep to see the surface," he announced. "I'd wager we're at five hundred fathoms at least." His glow flared. "I know! I'll see if I can spot the bottom." He flipped over and stuck his head through the floor. It only took a few seconds for him to pop back up like a cork, his face a picture of astonishment.

"Did you see it?" asked Wilmot.

"I saw something all right," said the Chief. "But I've no idea what."

"I think I can see something, too!" said Wilmot. He pointed to the front window. It was still angled downward, and through the small gaps between the tentacles and the eyes, Suzy saw something new: a faint light in the darkness far below them.

She pressed herself against the glass, trying to suppress her revulsion at the close proximity to the squirming creature, and looked out. Sure enough, a light had dawned on the seafloor, which spread out below them like a vast plain covered in dirty gray snow. But there was something else down there, too. A monolithic shape, as tall and wide as a mountain, although Suzy knew immediately that it couldn't be anything of the sort.

"It looks like a gigantic snail shell!" she said.

"Gosh!" breathed Wilmot beside her. "I think you're right."

The shell might have been gold once, but was now pitted and tarnished with age. Its ridged slopes rose in a tightening spiral toward the summit, on which a tall spire stood, its tip glowing fitfully, like a guttering candle. Suzy caught her breath. She knew that spire—she had seen it in her vision as they entered the reality fracture. Could this really be it? "Hydroborea," she whispered to herself.

The light from the tower shone in through the windows as the creature dragged them down toward the base of the shell. There, half-buried in sediment, Suzy saw a circular opening, wide enough to hold several jumbo jets, wingtip to wingtip. The creature headed straight toward it.

"This must be the beastie's lair," said the Chief. "Where it no doubt feeds. I'd just like to offer you both my sincerest condolences. And if you're lucky enough to come back as ghosts, it would be my pleasure to help you both settle into the afterlife."

Suzy flinched. If she died down here, her parents would never know what had happened. The thought was

so awful she could barely stand it, and she shrank back from the windows as the creature dragged them into the opening. The interior of the shell was clearly hollow and deep, because the creature didn't slow for almost a minute. Then it jerked the H.E.C. violently, pitching Suzy and Wilmot onto the floor again. The tentacles slithered and scraped across the hull.

"This is it!" cried Wilmot, as darkness closed around them once again. "I'm going to die with undelivered post!"

Suzy screwed her eyes shut and waited for the creature's killing blow. It didn't come.

When Suzy opened her eyes again, she saw that the tentacles had vanished from the windows. More than that, they were no longer underwater—droplets ran down the outside of the glass, and the floor bobbed gently underfoot once more.

"What happened?" she whispered. "Where did the creature go?"

"I don't know," said Wilmot. "Chief, would you mind taking a look outside for us?"

"Good idea, m'boy," said the Chief. "I'll see if the beastie's lurking in wait." He bobbed up through the ceiling but was only gone for a moment before he returned, grinning from ear to ear. "The coast is clear," he said. "I think you'd better come up and see this. And don't forget my skull, will you?" He shot back outside.

Suzy stuffed his skull into her satchel while Wilmot unfastened the sunroof. Then, standing together on the folding table, they climbed out onto the roof and looked around.

It was dark and raining, but the Chief's glow was enough to show them that the H.E.C. had surfaced in the middle of a flooded street, deep inside the mountainous shell. Ruined buildings lay half-submerged all around them, their walls encrusted with barnacles. The street climbed uphill away from the water, curving out of sight into the downpour. Water gushed in curtains off the rooftops and foamed over the pavements. No lights shone anywhere. The whole street looked abandoned.

"Where are we?" Suzy wondered aloud.

The letters of a street sign attached to one of the nearby buildings melted into smoke and were absorbed by the book.

"Coelocanth Drive," it announced. "In the seventh ward of the Lowertwist district. We are in Hydroborea."

Wilmot was so surprised that he opened his satchel and addressed the book directly. "Are you sure?" he asked, being careful to shield it from the rain. "What's it doing at the bottom of the ocean?"

"I do not know," said the book. "Nevertheless, this is Hydroborea. We have arrived."

Suzy pushed her sodden hair out of her face and

looked around the ruins with a newfound sense of wonder. "We did it!" she said. "We actually did it. We found the lost city."

"Discovered it, my dear," said the Chief. "Or should I say, as the first of our little expedition to set eyes on the place, *I* discovered it." He toyed with his beard. "It's nice to know I've still got the knack after all these years."

"But *what* have we discovered?" said Wilmot. "This is supposed to be the most magical city in existence." He pulled his standard-issue Impossible Postal Service clockwork flashlight from his coat pocket, wound the key sticking out of the bottom, and flicked the switch. The flashlight's powerful light cut through the darkness, and Wilmot played it over their surroundings.

The crumbling buildings must have been like miniature palaces once, Suzy realized. They were tall and ornate, decorated like wedding cakes with twists and flourishes of intricately sculpted stone. Flakes of brightly colored paint still clung to some of their facades, but their windows were broken and empty. There was no life left in them.

"What happened here?" asked Suzy. As she spoke, a few drops of rainwater ran into her mouth and she recoiled. It was freezing cold and very salty.

"This isn't rain," she said, spitting the taste away. "It's seawater!"

Wilmot wiped the moisture from his face and pointed the flashlight straight up. High above the rooftops, barely illuminated by the beam, they saw the interior curve of the great shell. It was smooth and pearlescent, shimmering with subtle rainbow colors, but it was also riddled with cracks, through which fine jets of water sprayed.

"The city is leaking," said Wilmot.

"The city is *drowning*!" said Suzy, and checked her pocket watch. "We've got a little less than six hours left before the book digests all the words it's taken. We need to find someone to sign the delivery form."

There was a splash in te waters behind them, and Wilmot swung the flashlight around to reveal one of the creature's tentacles sticking out of the lagoon, its glowing eye watching them like a periscope. Suzy tensed, but the creature made no move toward them. It seemed more curious than aggressive.

"Why's that beastie lost its appetite all of a sudden?" asked the Chief. "It could have eaten us twice over by now."

"Maybe it's friendly after all," said Suzy, who didn't want to tempt fate by examining the question too closely.

"It is a kraken," said the book. "A servant creature of Hydroborea. It can be made to follow simple instructions."

"You knew it came from Hydroborea all along?" said Suzy. "Why didn't you tell us?"

"Because I knew you would find out when it brought us here," said the book.

The eye continued to watch them from the middle of the lagoon.

"It seemed to be waiting for us," said Suzy. "Do you think someone knew we were coming and ordered it to bring us here?"

"Maybe," said Wilmot.

"But then why aren't they here to meet us?" He shone the flashlight around the street, but it was still devoid of life.

"Whatever the answer, we'll certainly never find it by sitting here," said the Chief. "Rule number one of discovery—when in doubt, be nosy."

"Good idea," said Wilmot. "But first we need to get onto solid ground." He turned his flashlight uphill, where the street emerged from the water. "I've got just the thing." He ducked back into the H.E.C. and reemerged a minute later with something that looked like a cross between a fishing rod and a leaf blower. The rod was fashioned from a length of pipe with an oversized fish-hook at the end, while the reel was attached to a small piston engine.

"My dad showed me how to use one of these," said Wilmot cheerily. "But I've never tried it myself. You'd better stand back." He stood up, swaying a little, and pulled the piston engine's rip cord. The engine chugged to life, making the whole contraption vibrate, and Wilmot fought to keep it steady as he angled it back over his shoulder. "It's all about a nice, clean overhand cast," he said. Then he snapped his wrist forward, there was a loud *bang!* and the fishhook blasted out of the end of the rod, trailing a shimmering silver thread behind it. It struck a wrought iron balcony on a mansion house just above the waterline, and caught. Wilmot gave the line a tug, and the hook held fast.

"Excellent shot!" said the Chief.

"Thank you!" Wilmot grinned. "I wish my dad could have seen it." He began turning the fishing reel, the line went taut, and the H.E.C. was slowly pulled to the water's edge. When they heard the caravan's belly scrape the road surface, Wilmot stopped winding them in and pressed a button on the rod's side. At once, the line of silver thread twitched as though it were alive, the hook unfastened itself from the balcony, and the line spooled itself back onto the reel.

"You're a natural," said Suzy as they both climbed down from the roof onto the ground. "That spire we saw on top of the city must be the Gilded Tower.

"It is," said the book.

"And we're practically at the bottom," said Suzy. "It's going to be quite a climb."

"Think of all the discovering we can do along the way," said the Chief, hovering between them.

"I just hope we can discover a way out of here when we're finished," said Suzy. "Because right now, we're trapped."

"We'll do our best," said Wilmot, winding his flashlight. "But our delivery comes first. Everyone at home is depending on us."

"Right," said Suzy. She wiped her soaking hair out of her eyes again. "I just wish we'd brought an umbrella."

13

THE ONLY WAY IS UP

The Express left the tunnel with a *whoosh!* and daylight flooded into the cab again. Frederick, who had been sitting on the kitchen worktop trying to keep a lid on his impatience, sprang into action and hurried to the front door. To his annoyance, Suzy's parents hurried with him.

"Where on earth are we?" asked Suzy's mom as the three of them stepped out onto the *Belle*'s gangway.

The Express was racing through an undulating landscape of sand dunes, stained all the colors of the rainbow, as if someone had upended gigantic pots of ink across them. The colors spread out in rings from shards of crystal that jutted out of the sand here and there, pointing toward the azure sky.

"I think I've heard of this place," said Frederick. "It's the Tie-Dye Desert."

Suzy's dad shielded his eyes with his hand and squinted out across the dunes. "Is that because of all the colors?" he said.

"Yes," said Frederick. "You see those big crystal things? They absorb the light from the sun and break it into its component colors, which soak into the sand."

"It's incredible," said Suzy's mom, who had been steadily regaining her composure since the Express had got underway again in the Topaz Narrows. Frederick supposed she felt better now that they were actually doing something about Suzy's situation. "But why are we here? I thought we were looking for a city."

"The city of Propellendorf," said Stonker, sticking his head out of the front door. "We're almost there. Now get back inside, all of you, and hold on to something. We've got a tricky maneuver ahead of us."

"But where is it?" said Suzy's dad. "I can't see anything but sand."

"Because you're looking in the wrong place," said Stonker.

He jabbed a finger at the sky. A gigantic, angular shape

had appeared over the horizon and was riding through the air high above the dunes. It was too far away for Frederick to make out many details, but he saw that it was crowned with several tall spires, all topped with whirling rotor blades.

"That thing's Propellendorf?" said Suzy's mom.

"The greatest of the sky cities," said Stonker. "It's only going to cross our path for a moment, so our timing's got to be spot-on. Now hurry up and get inside." He ushered them all back into the cab and slammed the door.

"Our timing for what?" asked Frederick as Stonker made a quick assessment of the controls.

"Our ascent, of course," said Stonker. "Propellendorf doesn't land to pick people up. We're going to have to catch it as it flies by."

"You mean the Express can fly, too?" said Suzy's dad.

Ursel caught Stonker's eye. Stonker chewed his lip. "Not exactly," he said. "But it can be persuaded to fall upward. Probably."

Frederick's mouth dropped open. "Oh no," he said. "No way! Not the Negotiable Gravity."

"It's against regulations to use it like this," said Stonker. "But this is an emergency."

"What?" said Suzy's mom. "What's he talking about, Frederick?"

"He's going to reverse the effect of gravity on the Express," said Frederick, stumbling to the sink and gripping the taps with both hands. "Instead of pulling us down, it's going to pull us up toward Propellendorf." The idea was already making him queasy. Suzy's attempt to do something similar, by making the Express fall sideways across the gap between Center Point Station and the Ivory Tower, had only just worked, but the results hadn't been pretty.

"Brace yourselves, everyone," said Stonker, taking hold of a large dial. "Ursel? Disengage the safety locks."

Ursel hammered at a section of the controls with a wrench until a large red light started blinking.

"Is this a good idea?" asked Suzy's dad. "It sounds dangerous."

"Of course it's dangerous," said Frederick. "So hold on!"

Suzy's parents lunged for the nearest door and took hold of the handle together.

"Ready...," said Stonker, his voice clipped. "Steady..."

The Express raced on through the dunes. Through the front windows, Frederick saw the great shadow of Propellendorf sweep across the track ahead of them.

"Now!" shouted Stonker, and turned the dial one hundred and eighty degrees.

Frederick's stomach did a little flip as his feet left the floor. He clung to the taps as gravity shifted and pulled him up toward the ceiling. Suzy's parents screamed as they, too, flipped upside down. Stonker and Ursel gripped the controls, fighting to stay right side up.

"It's working!" said Stonker. The ends of his mustache had risen to point upward and looked like an enormous hairy grin.

Outside the windows, the Tie-Dye Desert dropped away below them. The Express had lifted clear of the rails and was rising straight up into the sky.

If we miss Propellendorf, we'll just keep falling upward into nothing, thought Frederick, and he immediately regretted it. The idea of tumbling helplessly until they left the world behind them, or, even worse, of the Negotiable Gravity overloading and the Express plunging back to solid ground, terrified him.

He was only a second away from screwing his eyes shut and screaming along with Suzy's parents when he saw Propellendorf through the window, and his terror was momentarily bested by wonder. It was a gleaming machine of a city, with four mighty spires at its corners. Each spire was crowned with triple-decker rotor blades several hundred yards across, whirling so quickly they were little more than a blur. Runways jutted like tongues from the city's sides, and swarms of small aircraft buzzed around it like flies.

It all rushed closer and closer until they were in the city's shadow, its huge underbelly blotting out the sky above them—vents and pipework and bundles of cargo suspended in netting.

"We're going to make it!" shouted Stonker.

"We're going to crash!" Frederick replied.

He shut his eyes, and the Express hit the city, not with the sickening crunch he had expected, but with a loud wet *splat!* The jolt was still enough to dislodge his grip on the taps, and he fell, flailing, to the ceiling, where he landed among the clutter of pots and pans. A second later, Stonker, Ursel, and Suzy's parents landed beside him.

They lay in dazed silence for a moment, until Suzy's dad spoke.

"Um . . . what's that orange stuff?"

Frederick looked and saw that a viscous tangerine substance was dribbling down the outside of the windows. At the same time, a sweet, hot-peppery smell invaded the cab.

"Hrunf," said Ursel, sniffing the air and sneezing.

"Squashed magma berries, apparently," said Stonker. "We can thank them for the soft landing."

Frederick gave a shaky laugh. "You call that soft?"

"We've had worse," said Stonker.

"Never mind that," said Suzy's mom. "Let's find Fletch and that bifurcator while there's still time. Suzy's and Wilmot's lives depend on it."

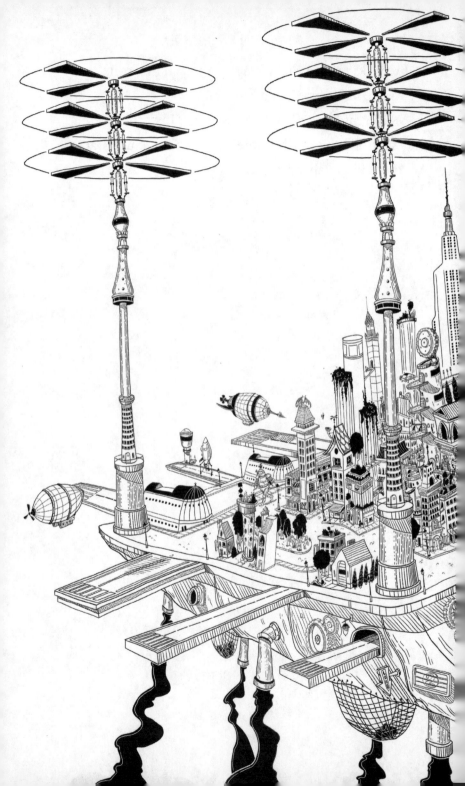

14

WELCOME TO THE NEIGHBORHOOD

Suzy, Wilmot, and the Chief trudged uphill through the curling streets of Hydroborea until they'd left the floodwaters below them. It was hard going—the salty rain was incessant, and Suzy and Wilmot were soon drenched to the skin. The ground was slippery underfoot, and every building they passed was dark and empty. Things that looked like streetlights lined the pavement—glass bowls mounted on columns of sculpted coral—but the coral was bleached and dead, and the glass broken. Wilmot's flashlight cut a dazzling wedge from the darkness ahead.

Suzy's spirits dipped with every squelching step. *So much for the birthplace of magic*, she thought. *It's totally dead.*

And that means there'll be no one to take the book back, which means we can't complete our delivery, which means the crew will never be able to deliver anything again. Not that it matters, because the whole Union is going to fall apart without the Ivory Tower to hold it together. And to think a few hours ago I was just worried about having my friends over for dinner.

"Cheer up, you two," said the Chief. "I've just discovered something else. Look." He pointed across the street to a shop decorated with jewel-like mosaic tiles and a striped awning, now badly tattered. The words FRESH CORAL GROWN TO ORDER were still visible on it before the book sucked them up, although when she approached the windows, Suzy saw that the coral arranged in the plant pots behind the glass was dead and gray.

"How does this help us?" she asked.

"I was talking about the poster," said the Chief, pointing. Sure enough, a simple red-bordered poster had been pasted inside one of the windows. In bold black letters it said:

OBEY FROGMAGGOG!
(Or else.)

"What d'you suppose that means?" wondered Wilmot.

"I'm not sure," said Suzy. "But I don't like the sound of it."

The words on the poster evaporated and were drawn

into Wilmot's satchel. He sighed. "I don't suppose you can shed any light on this?" he asked the book.

"Obey Frogmaggog," the book answered. "Or else."

"Very helpful," said Suzy. "But who is Frogmaggog?"

"I do not know," said the book, its voice muffled by the satchel. "Hydroborea is not as it once was."

You can say that again, thought Suzy. She pictured the old ruins she had seen on television and in books at home: the Roman Forum, the Parthenon in Athens, the Aztec pyramids in Mexico... Once-great civilizations that had crumbled and faded. Had the same thing happened to Hydroborea?

She pulled her sodden coat tighter around herself and shivered.

Wilmot's flashlight flickered and died as if in sympathy. He had begun winding it again, when Suzy realized that the darkness hadn't reasserted itself completely— there was a faint but steady glow emanating from behind the houses farther up the street.

"Look!" she said, pointing. "What's that?"

"I don't know," said Wilmot. "But it's worth a look."

They hurried on with renewed enthusiasm. The light grew clearer as they climbed, and faint sounds began to filter through the hiss of the rain—Suzy heard footsteps, voices, and the steady background hum of a city going about its business.

"There really is someone else here!" she said, her soaking clothes and numb fingers suddenly forgotten.

"I think it's this way," said the Chief, pointing to a narrow alleyway between two of the vacant mansions. Suzy clasped Wilmot's hand and together they plunged into it. The alley was thick with shadows, but the light at the end of it was almost dazzling. When they reached it, Suzy let out a little gasp of delight.

The alley opened into a small plaza, ringed with glowing streetlights and busy with people. They looked roughly human in size and shape, although they walked with a curious waddling gait and were so wrapped up in waterproof jackets and boots that it was impossible to make out their features clearly. The bits of their skin that Suzy could see were so white they practically glowed.

Her gaze was drawn to the streetlights. Their coral supports were a riot of colors, and their glass bowls were full of water in which shoals of tiny neon fish swirled and danced, their bodies emitting a fiery glow. The light they cast fell like dappled sunshine across the square and turned every raindrop into a flaring golden spark. Suzy let it play across her face and immediately felt a little warmer.

The houses overlooking the square were clearly inhabited, and although their facades were cracked and faded, they looked clean and well cared for.

The city's not completely abandoned, she thought. *We've got five hours left before our delivery deadline. We can still do this!*

"Extra, extra!" shouted a warbling voice from across the square. "No problems in Hydroborea, Frogmaggog confirms. Golden age of magic continues. Read all about it in today's *Daily Snail*!" The voice came from inside a newspaper stall on a street corner opposite the alley, and as one, the Hydroboreans all stopped whatever they were doing and made toward it. Their behavior seemed eerily coordinated, but as they lined up in front of the stall, it gave Suzy her first proper look at them.

Their faces were smooth and simplistic—big, blue-ringed eyes, two small holes for a nose, and wide mouths that stretched almost from ear to ear. Or rather, would have done, if the Hydroboreans had had ears at all. Instead, they sported fern-shaped fronds on the sides of their heads, and the sight of them triggered a connection in Suzy's mind—her school biology textbook, and the term they had spent studying amphibians.

"They're newts!" Suzy whispered. "Or something a bit like newts. I think."

"Fascinating!" the Chief declared. "I've not seen anything quite like them before. Have you, Postmaster?"

"Never," said Wilmot. "I'm sure we're going to look just as strange to them, which means we have to be even

190

more diplomatic than usual. Remember chapter five of *The Knowledge*: 'When on a delivery, always give a good first impression.'"

"Allow me to make the introductions," said the Chief. "I've done this sort of thing before, remember." He straightened his hat and cleared his throat in preparation.

"We'll all say hello together," said Wilmot, putting his flashlight back in his pocket. "But perhaps you'd better stay inside your skull to begin with. We don't want to overwhelm them."

"Taking the low-key approach, eh?" said the Chief. "Good thinking." He retreated back inside his skull. Suzy wasn't sure that a talking skull with glowing eye sockets was any less overwhelming than an actual ghost, but she chose not to comment as she removed the skull from her satchel.

"Just make sure you hold me where I can see what's going on," he said. Suzy tucked the skull under her arm.

"Now, remember," said Wilmot. "The most urgent thing is getting to the tower. Someone here must be able to help us."

As they started across the square, the newspaper seller began hawking his wares again.

"Get your list of today's arrests and executions! Today's mandatory news bulletin, ladies and gents! One copy per citizen! Fines for noncompliance!"

Suzy wavered. "Um, Wilmot?" she said. "Maybe we need to think about this more carefully."

But it was too late. The newspaper seller saw them approaching and clapped a hand to his forehead. He seemed too astonished to speak, so just pointed a trembling finger at them. The Hydroboreans standing in the queue turned, and a ripple of disquiet ran through them.

"Hello," said Wilmot, doffing his cap. "We're very sorry to bother you all, but we've just arrived from the Impossible Places and—"

"*Outworlders!*" the newspaper seller screeched. "They're here to steal our magic!"

Wilmot laughed nervously. "I promise you, we're not going to steal anything. We're just here to . . ." He trailed off as he saw the ribbons of ink rising from the newspapers on the stall and swirling into his satchel. "Oh, honestly!" he said, lifting the satchel's flap and admonishing the book. "Is this really the time?"

"I must have words," said the book. "And these words are . . . unexpected." Its voice caused a few Hydroboreans to shuffle back in fear, but for the first time Suzy thought it sounded uncertain. "They speak of a golden age, but they are full of fear and anger."

"You see?" shrieked the newspaper seller, brandishing

a newly blank paper. "They're stealing the words right off our pages!"

"Thieves!" someone shouted.

"They don't want us to read the truth!" cried another.

The queue dissolved as the Hydroboreans advanced on Wilmot and Suzy.

"We don't want you here," said one of them. "Hydroborea's closed."

"That's right. Why don't you go back where you came from?"

"Please, if you'll just listen to me...," said Wilmot, but he and Suzy were already surrounded.

"We've been warned about your sort," said an elderly female Hydroborean wearing a big floppy rain hat and a sour expression. "You've got no magic of your own, so you sneak in here to help yourselves to some of ours. Well, we're not having it!"

There was a chorus of agreement from the others.

"That's not true at all!" said Suzy, her face prickling with anger. "We've got plenty of magic. We're actually here to give some of yours back."

"So you've stolen some already!" said a Hydroborean man sheltering under a striped umbrella.

"No!" Suzy shot back. "Why won't any of you listen?"

"Fear not, my dear," said the Chief from inside his skull.

"I've seen this sort of behavior before. It's culture shock. The poor blighters just need putting at their ease."

Before Suzy or Wilmot could stop him, the Chief unfurled like a glowing ribbon and hovered above the crowd. "Hello. There. Hydro. Borea!" he shouted, very slowly. "We. Come. In. Peace! We. Are. Looking. For. Your. Tower. Of. Magic!" He did an exaggerated mime of shielding his eyes with his hand and searching for something.

The mob, which had been stunned into silence by his sudden appearance, drew a collective breath. Then they scattered, pushing and shoving at one another as they fled the square and disappeared into the surrounding streets.

"Somebody call the Watch Frogs!" warbled the newspaper seller as he pulled down the shutters on the kiosk and sealed himself inside.

"Wait!" Wilmot called, but it was fruitless. The square was already empty.

"This happened to me once in the underground rain forests of Mychopia," said the Chief. "If it's anything like last time, they'll be back in a minute with a sacrificial walrus and an offer to crown us all king."

But as the sound of the Hydroboreans' footsteps retreated, the glow of the streetlights guttered and faded from gold to bloodred, plunging the whole square into an eerie semidarkness. Then a new sound reached them through the rain—a deep, wailing scream that made Suzy's skin crawl. It rose and fell like a lamentation, growing steadily louder. It was joined by a second wail, and a third. They were sirens of some sort, and they were getting closer.

"I don't think they're bringing us a walrus," said Suzy.

"If they're the authorities, maybe they'll be able to help," said Wilmot, looking almost as uncertain as he sounded.

"Or maybe they'll think we're here to steal their magic, too," said Suzy. "Whoever's in charge of this place, they don't sound friendly, and we can't deliver the book if we're in prison. Or worse."

Wilmot pressed his lips together into a thin line. "You're right," he said. "We'll just have to reach the tower by ourselves. The delivery comes first."

"Then let's hurry up and get out of here," said Suzy.

The sirens were getting louder by the second, approaching from a broad avenue that curled uphill from the square. Suzy and Wilmot set off at a run, diving into a much narrower, parallel street. Gothic townhouses loomed over them on either side, their carved stone porches and soaring gateways firmly shut. Every streetlight they passed turned bloodred, changing the street into a nightmarish jumble of shadows in which the Chief's glow stood out like a beacon.

"Hide!" Suzy hissed at him.

The Chief nodded and spiraled like water down a drain back into his skull. An instant later, they heard something arrive in the square with a squeal of brakes. Its siren cut off abruptly, and there came a *thud-thud-thud* of boots hitting the ground.

Suzy and Wilmot pressed themselves into the meager cover of a doorway and looked back down the street to see the beams of flashlights sweeping the square.

"Fan out!" shouted a fat, wet belch of a voice. "They can't have got far!"

The voice belonged to a short, squat frog-like creature wearing black leather armor over a chain-mail vest and carrying a three-pronged trident. His skin was smooth and shiny, and he had yellow eyes the size of tennis balls set in the top of his domed head. He wasn't alone—half a dozen more Watch Frogs spread out across the square, crossing it in great bounding leaps.

"They look fast," Wilmot whispered. "I don't think we can outrun them."

He and Suzy ducked back into the shadows as the Watch Frog shone his flashlight up the street.

"But they haven't seen us yet," Suzy whispered back. "We can still get away if we're careful." The flashlight beams played across the buildings, swept over their heads, and moved on. "Go!" Suzy hissed.

They slipped out of cover and stole uphill, keeping low and heading for the dark recess of an arched doorway.

They almost made it.

When they were barely three feet away, a glare of headlights cut through the rain in the street up ahead, accompanied by the scream of another siren. Suzy threw up her hands to shield her eyes, but Wilmot caught her by the arm and dragged her into the archway, which housed a pair of heavy wooden doors.

"I saw them!" a voice cried. "Two suspects heading uphill from Plankton Plaza. Block the street!"

"What do we do now?" said Wilmot. "We're trapped!"

Suzy pressed her back against the doors as the Watch Frogs' shadows advanced across the houses opposite, stretched and distorted by the headlights until they resembled figures in a nightmare. There were more shouts from the direction of the plaza now as well. Her heart crawled up into her throat. They were out of options.

Then the world tipped on its side as the door opened behind her and she toppled backward through it.

"Quick!" said a girl's voice. "Get in and be quiet!" A webbed hand reached down and Suzy took it, allowing herself to be pulled to her feet. She saw a flash of big Hydroborean eyes in the gloom as her rescuer reached past her, pulled Wilmot inside, and eased the door shut a second before the sounds of pursuit arrived outside.

"I'm sure I saw someone, Commander!" a voice shouted. "They were here."

Someone tested the door. Suzy held her breath as its big iron handle rattled, but their rescuer held it firm with both hands, trembling with the effort.

"Not unless they can walk through locked doors, they weren't," came the reply. "Continue the sweep, Check every door. His Greatness wants these outworlders found, and quickly."

"Yes, Commander!" There was the sound of several pairs of boots stamping to attention and then leaping away toward Plankton Plaza.

The mysterious rescuer waited until the noises had receded to a safe distance before releasing her grip on the handle and turning to Suzy and Wilmot with an enormous grin.

"Well!" she said. "That was close, wasn't it?"

She was a Hydroborean girl, roughly Suzy's height, with a round, youthful face that smiled at them. A simple smock was visible beneath it, and she wore large Wellington boots on her feet.

"Very close," said Suzy, still fighting to regain control of her racing pulse. "Thank you."

"Yes, indeed," said Wilmot. "I don't know what we would have done without you."

The girl's eyes darted back and forth between them, sparkling with excitement. "Wow," she said. "Look at you two. Genuine outworlders! I knew something big must be happening when the red alert kicked in, but oh boy! This is going to make such a great front page."

Suzy, who didn't quite understand what the girl was talking about, wiped the soaking hair from her eyes and looked around. They were in the entrance to a tiny residential courtyard, overlooked by three stories of open-sided landings. Anemone-like flowers bloomed in an old stone planter in the middle, and fishbowl lanterns on the walls glowed the same ghastly red as the streetlights outside.

"Let's get straight down to business," said the girl. She produced a notepad and pen from her pocket and hunched over to shield them from the rain. "I want to know who you are, what you are, and what inspired you to risk everything and come to Hydroborea." She poised her pen over the pad. "Assuming you're happy to speak on the record, of course."

"I'm sorry," said Wilmot, "but would you mind telling us who *you* are first?"

The girl guffawed. "Sorry, I completely forgot. I'm Ina—founder, editor, lead reporter, and unpaid intern for the *Daily Scuttle*."

"Is that the newspaper we saw being sold in the plaza?" asked Suzy.

"Ugh, please," said Ina. "That's the *Snail*, the mandatory propaganda rag. The *Scuttle* is totally independent, exposing the truths that Frogmaggog and his cronies don't want people to hear." She gave a sheepish chuckle. "Actually, it was just my school newsletter until a few months ago, but the headmaster shut it down when I broke the story about the kelp cakes in the school cafeteria actually being made from ground-up blobfish. Totally vegan unfriendly! That's when I decided to go independent and cover the stories that really matter. Like the flooding, which doesn't officially exist, and the magic shortage, which nobody's supposed to know about even though everyone totally does. And now you!" She beamed at them again, but then her eyes widened. "Oh no! I've got to hold tonight's front page. This story is way more important than the new rationing restrictions!"

She bounded away across the courtyard. A door under a porch had the words WELCOME TO FLOUNDER HEIGHTS written on it, but Ina ignored it in favor of one of the ground-floor windows. "Keep up!" she called in a stage whisper. "I need you!" She slid the window open and hopped inside.

"Do you think we should go with her?" asked Wilmot.

"She sounds like a terribly enterprising young lady," said the Chief from inside his skull.

"I don't think we have much choice," said Suzy. "It's not safe on the streets, and someone's bound to spot us if we stay out here much longer."

Crouching low, they hurried to the window and followed Ina inside. They found themselves in a makeshift bedroom-cum-kitchen that, like the rest of Hydroborea, had clearly been very grand once upon a time. The high ceiling boasted a tarnished golden chandelier in the form of an octopus, but most of the fishbowls wrapped in its tentacles were missing, while the remainder gave out a weak, jaundiced glow.

They still offered enough light for Suzy to see the two beds standing against opposite walls, the dilapidated wardrobe overflowing with clothes, and the small writing desk. Someone had also marked a chalk line down the middle of the floor, dividing the room in two.

The opposite half was scrupulously tidy, while the one in which they were standing was covered with discarded clothes, papers, and unwashed plates and mugs.

"Sorry it's a bit cramped," said Ina, kicking the worst of the mess under her bed. "I lived here by myself for a while after my parents died, but everyone's had to double up since Frogmaggog closed down the Lowertwist district."

Straddling the line in the middle of the room was a machine that looked like a treasure chest with an old clothes mangle attached to the front. It buzzed and shook and made wet bubbling noises, while the rollers of the mangle turned and ejected double pages of newsprint every few seconds. They dropped neatly into a pile on the tidy half of the floor and Suzy saw the banner of the *Daily Scuttle* above the headline FLOODS CONTINUE, and a smaller article, IS FROGMAGGOG LOSING HIS GRIP ON MAGIC?

Ina shut the bedroom window and drew the curtains, then crossed to the machine and thumped it on the side. The rollers stopped. Then she opened up the lid to reveal a bed set with hundreds of tiny metal blocks, each carved with a raised letter or punctuation mark. A jar labeled SQUINK!—BUDGET SQUID INK was screwed into a socket alongside them.

"Do you like my printing press?" she asked. "I built it myself."

"It's very impressive," said Wilmot, walking around it to examine it from all sides. "My people are great builders, but I've never had a talent for it myself. I've always been slightly envious of anyone who does."

Ina lowered the hood of her coat to reveal pink speckles across her cheeks, running to coral-pink fronds. She turned to the pile of printed news sheets. "I suppose I can still distribute these," she said. "But I'll need to start printing a new edition as quickly as possible. There have never been any confirmed sightings of outworlders in Hydroborea before. At least not officially." She produced her notepad and pen again. "So, what are your names?"

"Suzy Smith," said Suzy.

"And I'm Wilmot Grunt," said Wilmot. "Pleased to meet you."

Ina scribbled these down, but stared at her pad in amazement as her notes lifted clear of the paper and twisted toward Wilmot's satchel.

"Oh no!" said Wilmot. "I should have thought about this." He turned to the stack of papers, but the newsprint was already running like wet paint.

"My latest edition!" said Ina as the words spiraled through the air. Then, putting her hands to her face in horror, "My movable typeface!" The letters carved into the little metal blocks inside the printing press were dissolving, leaving the blocks smooth and featureless. She grabbed at the swirling trails as the book sucked them in, but they slipped right through her webbed fingers. "No!" she cried. "Your bag's eating all my work!"

Suzy's hand went reflexively to the blank shape of her Impossible Postal Service badge. "I'm so sorry, Ina," she said. "We didn't mean for this to happen."

"Fascinating," said the book from inside Wilmot's satchel. "All this information directly contradicts that of my last meal. And yet both purport to be factual."

Ina gawked at Wilmot. "Your bag ate my work and now it's talking!"

"Again, we're really, really sorry," said Wilmot. "But it's not my bag, it's our delivery." He pulled the book out to show her. "It keeps eating information and we can't stop it."

Ina approached it with hands outstretched but hesitated to actually touch it. "*The Book of Power*," she said. "Is it magic?"

"Very magic," said Wilmot. "In fact, we think it was written by this city's founders."

"Among others," said the book. "Their ink is still on my pages."

"Excuse me." The Chief's voice broke into the conversation. "But is anyone going to do me the courtesy of an introduction?"

Ina pointed at Suzy's satchel. "That bag definitely talked," she said. "Or have you got two magic books?"

"Actually, it's a friend of ours," said Suzy. She patted her satchel. "Sorry, Chief. You can come out now."

The Chief emerged from the satchel in an expanding cloud of ectoplasm. Ina gave a squeak, half-afraid, half-excited. Seeing her, the Chief doffed his hat.

"A pleasure to make your acquaintance, young lady," he said. "They call me the Chief, and it is my great pleasure to announce that you are now officially discovered."

"I'm what?" said Ina, cocking her head to one side.

"It's a long story," said Suzy. "And we'll tell you everything you want to know, but the most important thing right now is the book. It's drained almost all the vital information from our biggest library, and it won't give it back until we return it to its rightful owners, and we've only got a handful of hours left to find them. Please." She put her hands together. "Will you help us?"

Ina looked from her ruined printing press, to the ghostly figure of the Chief, to the book, and then to Suzy and Wilmot. "I will," she said firmly. "But I've got some questions."

Suzy sagged with relief. "Anything," she said. "Ask away."

"First of all, what's a library?"

Suzy and Wilmot exchanged a look of surprise.

"It's a collection of books and information," said Wilmot. "You know. Stories, histories, poems, biographies. Things like that."

"And it's run by librarians, who know their way around it all and can help you find what you need," said Suzy. "Don't you have anything like that here?"

Ina shook her head, her eyes wide with astonishment. "No. Frogmaggog controls all the information in the city. We're only allowed to read what he tells us to."

"Then what about the *Daily Scuttle*?" asked Wilmot.

Ina's smile returned, more sheepish than before. "Yeah. The *Scuttle*'s just a tiny bit illegal," she said. "If anyone ever traces it back to me, I'm in big trouble."

"Aren't you afraid of getting caught?" said Suzy.

"Of course," said Ina. "But someone needs to tell people the truth, and I always cover my tracks. Trust me, this operation is completely foolproof."

And that was when the door burst open.

15
THE DELIVERY COMES FIRST

Suzy, Wilmot, the Chief, and Ina whirled round in a panic as the bedroom door swung open and crashed against the wall.

Suzy's first thought was that the Watch Frogs had found them, but standing in the doorway was a lanky Hydroborean youth with orange fronds, wearing a pair of ill-fitting dungarees and dripping water onto the floor. They stared at one another in surprise, before the youth raised a trembling hand to point at them.

"Ina!" he said. "It's them! Those are the outworlders the Watch Frogs are looking for!"

"Amlod, what are you doing here?" Ina snapped. "You're supposed to be at work."

Amlod blinked and seemed to forget his shock for a moment. "They sent us home because of the red alert," he said. "There are dangerous criminals on the loose. Except they're not on the loose. They're here!" He lunged forward and grabbed Ina by the hand. "Get away from my sister!" he shouted as he tried to drag her out of the door.

Suzy grabbed Ina's other hand and dug her heels in, pulling back against Amlod. "But we're not criminals!" she protested.

"And we're certainly not dangerous," said Wilmot, taking hold of Suzy and joining in the tug-of-war.

"I can't do much to help, I'm afraid," said the Chief, hovering above them. "But I want you both to know I'm with you in spirit." He chuckled. "Another little ghostly joke for you."

Ina grimaced. "Let go of me, all of you!" she shouted. Amlod was the first to release his hold, meaning that Ina was catapulted back into Suzy and Wilmot. The three of them crashed to the ground together.

"Thank you," said Ina pointedly as she got to her feet. "Now, if you've finished trying to tear me in half, perhaps we can sit down and talk about all this."

"Sorry," mumbled Suzy. "I thought he was going to fetch the Watch Frogs."

"I was," said Amlod. "I still am! You're wanted fugitives, here to take our magic."

208

Suzy threw her hands up. "Why does everyone think we're here to steal magic?" she said. "It makes no sense."

"Yes, it does," said Amlod. "Everyone knows that magic is extinct everywhere except in Hydroborea."

Suzy frowned at him, thinking he must be joking, but his expression was deadly earnest. "You can't really believe that, can you?" she said.

Ina's eyebrows shot up. "Are you saying it's not true?"

"It's not true at all," said Suzy. "There's loads of magic out there."

"That's right," said Wilmot. "I'm from a magical world myself, and there are hundreds of others."

Amlod shook his head vigorously. "There can't be. It's just one of the basic facts of life. The Gilded Tower is the source of all magic. The other worlds got jealous and kept trying to take it for themselves, so the city fathers hid Hydroborea where it could never be found. All the other worlds fell into chaos without our power to sustain them, so now Hydroborea soldiers on alone."

"Says who?" asked Suzy.

"Says everyone," Ina replied with a shrug. "Every teacher, every historian. It's even in our national anthem, 'Hydroborea, the Last Home of Magic.'" But as soon as she said this, her expression clouded.

"If you don't believe us, look at the Chief," said Suzy. "He's a ghost. Isn't that magical enough for you?"

"And in the unlikely event that it's not," said the Chief, "I've spent the last few years developing a rather amusing one-man musical revue which I'd be honored to perform for you. Although I will need the use of a halibut for the climax."

Amlod seemed overwhelmed. He gripped his fronds and kept shaking his head, although he didn't make any more moves toward the door. Ina, meanwhile, had lapsed into a thoughtful silence.

"What if they're right, Amlod?" she asked.

"Don't be silly, Ina. How could they be?"

She toyed with the end of one of her fronds.

"I don't know, but when a good journalist hears two conflicting stories, it's her job to keep snooping until she finds out which one is true."

"This is when a library really comes in handy," said Suzy. "It lets you look these things up."

Wilmot cleared his throat. "Until we can prove our story one way or the other, would it help if we explained why we're actually here?"

"I don't know," said Amlod. "Maybe?"

Ina stepped past him, shut the door, and put her back against it. "Yes, Amlod, it would," she said. "So sit down and listen."

A short while later, the explanations finished, Amlod was sitting on his bed looking stunned while Ina couldn't keep still.

"It's all so incredible!" she said, almost skipping around the room. "Whole worlds connected by these railway things. And your train! And the Ivory Tower! How many books did you say it had?"

"Frederick would have to tell you the exact number," said Suzy. "But I think it's a few hundred million."

Ina guffawed. "And anyone can just walk in and read them?" She put her hands to her head. "I'm trying to imagine it, and I just can't."

"Neither can I," muttered Amlod, although his protest sounded half-hearted. "And you say this book ate all the others?" He nodded to *The Book of Power*, which was cradled in Wilmot's lap.

"Almost all of them, yes," said Wilmot. "It sucked up the knowledge of whole cultures, and it won't give any of it back until we deliver it to someone who can lift the spell that's keeping it closed."

"And who's that?" said Ina.

"Good question," said Suzy. "No one's ever been able to open it so the spell must be super strong. Who's the most powerful magic user in Hydroborea?"

Ina and Amlod looked at one another in alarm. "Frogmaggog," said Ina.

"Obey Frogmaggog," intoned the book. "Or else."

Ina wrapped her arms around herself. "That's him," she said darkly.

"His name's come up a few times already," said Wilmot. "But who exactly is he?"

"You don't know about Frogmaggog?" said Amlod. "He's *Frogmaggog*! The great and terrible. Ruler of Hydroborea. Master of Magic."

"And he's your most powerful magician?" said the Chief.

"He's our *only* magician," said Ina. "Nobody else in Hydroborea is allowed to use magic on pain of death."

"Because Frogmaggog's the only one who's qualified," said Amlod. "He's an expert."

"If he's such an expert, why doesn't he use his powers to fix the city?" said Suzy. "There are leaks everywhere."

This prompted a little round of applause from Ina. "Thank you!" she said. "That's what I keep asking."

"Yes, and you really need to stop asking before someone reports you," said Amlod. "That sort of talk can get you arrested."

Ina folded her arms and put on a haughty expression. "If you ask me, I think Frogmaggog's hoarding all the magic for himself," she said. "He sits up there in his palace surrounded by luxury, while every year there's less and less magic to maintain the rest of the city. You've seen how bad it is out there. Things are falling apart."

Amlod shuffled uncomfortably. "I suppose the flooding does keep getting worse," he said, although he cast a wary glance in the direction of the door, as if he expected it to be kicked open by the Watch Frogs at any second.

"Whether he's a good ruler or not, it sounds like Frogmaggog is the only one who can unbind the book," said Suzy. "We need to get it to him right away, before it digests all the words it's stolen and we lose them forever. What's the quickest way to reach him?"

"That's easy," Ina replied. "Get arrested. The Watch Frogs take all their prisoners to Frogmaggog's throne room in the tower."

"And after all the trouble we went to avoiding them," said the Chief. "You were right, Wilmot, m'lad. We should have waited in the square and asked them for help."

"At least the answer's clear now," said Wilmot. "We can just hand ourselves in."

"No!" said Ina and Amlod together.

"That would be a really bad idea," said Ina. "Prisoners go into the tower but they don't come out again."

Suzy felt a chill that had nothing to do with her soaking uniform. "What happens to them?"

"Nobody knows," said Ina. "But it's nothing good."

"How wonderfully ominous," said the Chief.

Suzy thought of the piles of empty books littering the floors of the Ivory Tower. She thought of Frederick and her friends on the Express. She thought of her parents and wondered where they were at that moment. She felt their absence more keenly than ever. "I think we have to try," she said.

"But it's suicide!" said Ina.

Suzy felt her resolve start to crumble until Wilmot drew himself up beside her and flared his nostrils.

"A postie always does his duty, no matter what the danger," he said. "If we can save our friends and the Impossible Places, it'll be worth it, whatever happens."

Suzy nodded. "I'm with Wilmot," she said. "The delivery comes first."

Wilmot puffed up with pride. "You know, I really do have the best staff in the service," he said.

"That's the spirit," said the Chief, who glowed a little brighter. "Greet certain death with a smile. It worked for me."

Suzy did her best to smile. She had sounded brave. But she just wished she felt it.

❧

Suzy's courage still hadn't materialized five minutes later, as she crouched beside Wilmot, Ina, and Amlod in the shadows of a small colonnade on the edge of Plankton Plaza. There were only three Watch Frogs in sight now—Suzy guessed the others must be searching the surrounding streets and buildings. Two of them were interviewing the newspaper seller, who seemed to be reenacting the events of earlier through a series of grand gestures and melodramatic expressions. The third Watch Frog loitered beside a strange vehicle parked in the middle of the plaza.

It was a bizarre sort of unicycle, consisting of one large wheel, taller than Suzy, housed in a protective spiral shell that reached almost to the ground. The engine jutted out in front of it, topped with a driver's saddle and a pair of tall handlebars.

"That thing looks like a big snail," said Suzy.

"It's a Secure Cargo Unit," Ina replied. "A Watch Frog prison transport. They'll use it to take you to the palace. Look." She pointed at two open-topped trailers coupled behind the vehicle. The first featured two rows of seats back to back, presumably for a squad of Watch Frogs, but the second was full of wavering tentacles topped with eyeballs—a miniature kraken. "Once those get hold of you, they don't let go."

"So how exactly do you propose we go about this?" asked the Chief, who had retreated to his skull to remain inconspicuous.

Wilmot thought for a moment. "We'll go about it like good, honest posties," he said. "Are you both ready?"

"Of course," said the Chief. "What's the worst that could happen?"

Suzy bit back the various answers that rushed to suggest themselves, and instead did her best to look as determined as Wilmot. "I'm ready," she said. "Let's get this done while there's still time."

Wilmot straightened his cap and turned to Ina and Amlod. "Thanks for your help, both of you," he said. "You should get back home. We don't want them to catch you as well."

"That's exactly what I was thinking," said Amlod. "I still think you're all mad, but for whatever it's worth, good luck to you." He took Ina's hand and started to draw her away.

Ina tried her best to smile, but just looked troubled. "Are you sure this is a good idea?" she said.

"Not really," said Suzy, stepping out to join Wilmot. "But it's the only idea we've got. Now go, please!" She did her best to look brave for Ina as Amlod dragged her away up the street toward their home. "All right," she said to Wilmot. "Let's do this."

They straightened their uniforms, set their faces, and stepped out together into the red glow of the streetlights.

"Excuse me," Wilmot called. "I believe you're looking for us."

The Watch Frogs looked round and the newspaper seller leaped into the air.

"That's them!" he shouted, pointing. "The outworlders!"

As Suzy, Wilmot, and the Chief approached the middle of the plaza, the three Watch Frogs sprang high into the air, landing around them with their tridents drawn.

"Stay where you are," one of them croaked. "You're under arrest."

"Good," said Suzy. "We've got an urgent delivery for Frogmaggog, and we need you to take us to him as quickly as you can, please."

This clearly wasn't the reaction the Watch Frogs had been expecting. They looked at one another in dismay for a moment until one of them turned to the driver of the Secure Cargo Unit. "Call the others."

The driver put his head back, inflated his throat, and let out a low bellowing roar so loud that Suzy and Wilmot were forced to cover their ears. It was the noise of the sirens they had heard earlier, Suzy realized. She hadn't imagined it had come from the frogs themselves.

The call died away, and within seconds, Suzy heard the tramp of many boots as the rest of the squad rushed to the plaza from all directions. They leaped into view from the surrounding streets, covering thirty feet at a single bound. Soon, the circle of Watch Frogs surrounding them was two rows deep.

"I say, isn't this exciting?" said the Chief, emerging from his skull. "So many new experiences."

"Clear the way. Let me get a look at them." The circle parted, and a Watch Frog with a plume of seaweed on his helmet swaggered up to the trailer. "So this is what you look like," he said, his wide mouth turning down at the edges. "What hideous creatures you are." Suzy recognized his voice—this was the Commander who had almost caught them outside Ina's home.

"We'd like to see Frogmaggog, please," said Wilmot, who sounded remarkably composed, although Suzy noticed he rubbed nervously at the blank surface of his badge. She had to screw her mouth shut to avoid telling the Commander exactly what she thought of him and his insults.

"So you want an audience with His Greatness, do you?" the Commander smirked. "Well, you're going to get one, up close and personal. And then you're going to be very, very sorry."

The assembled Watch Frogs laughed. It was a low, drawn-out croaking sound that reignited Suzy's fear.

"Get them in the detention trailer," said the Commander. Two pairs of Watch Frogs stepped forward smartly, caught Suzy and Wilmot under the arms, dragged them to the trailer containing the kraken, and simply tossed them in. The tentacles coiled around their bodies and held them tight. Suzy tried wriggling, but it was useless. She tried to keep calm by reminding herself that this was all part of the plan.

"What about this one?" said the Commander. He indicated the Chief, who floated a few feet above the trailer, untroubled by the grasping tentacles, which slipped straight through his ghostly form.

"Oh, don't mind me," the Chief replied. "I'll come quietly."

Scowling, the Commander pushed his way to the trailer and made a brief but fruitless attempt to seize hold of the Chief himself. When he realized it was hopeless, he simply turned his back, put his hands on his hips, and declared, "The prisoners are secure. Cancel the red alert."

Suzy couldn't see what happened, but a few seconds later, the red glare of the streetlights faded from bloodred back to gold. Despite being trapped, the return of the warm dappled light came as a relief to Suzy. The flood of colors made the city feel slightly more real.

"S-Cargo Unit, move out on the double," the Commander croaked. "I'll present the prisoners to His Greatness myself."

The squad sprang straight up into the air and landed neatly in the seats in the trailer immediately behind the S-Cargo Unit. The driver vaulted clean over the top of the machine and out of Suzy's field of vision, but she heard the machine's engine rev a moment later. The Commander, meanwhile, hopped up onto the detention trailer between Suzy and Wilmot. Suzy was a little annoyed to see that the kraken didn't react to him in the slightest.

She was glad of the creature's tight embrace once the S-Cargo Unit surged forward, though. It roared in a victory lap around Plankton Plaza, the trailers whiplashing behind it. Suzy and Wilmot were facing backward, and she hated not being able to see where they were going. She heard the newspaper seller and the remaining Watch Frogs cheering. Then the vehicle roared away uphill, the Watch Frogs all giving the same rising and falling siren call.

Buildings flashed past, curious faces at every window. Then, just for an instant, Suzy saw Ina watching from the recesses of a narrow lane. Her eyes were wide and sorrowful, and she might have raised a hand in farewell but the S-Cargo Unit raced onward, around the curve of the street, and she was gone.

Suzy spluttered as they plowed through a particularly heavy sheet of rain. She hoped that Ina's predictions about Frogmaggog were wrong, but she knew, deep down, that they weren't. She, Wilmot, and the Chief were heading into mortal danger, and there was nothing she could do about it.

Wilmot was obviously thinking the same thing, because he turned his head to her and said, "Brave heart, Suzy. Very soon we'll have completed the most difficult delivery of our careers."

And maybe the last *delivery of our careers*, she couldn't help thinking.

16

PROPELLENDORF

The Express was safely inside one of the aircraft hangars built into the city's belly. It had taken two whole teams of deckhands and a little more creative use of the Negotiable Gravity to get them here, but now the train's gravity had been restored to normal, and it was safely parked between a sleek dirigible with flame decals and a flock of giant swans wearing diamond-encrusted saddles. The swans, which had been asleep until they were forced to make room, were less than happy with the arrangement and snapped at anyone who got too close. Which was why Frederick was watching them from the safety of the *Belle*'s gangway beside Propellendorf's Harbor Master.

"You lot certainly know how to make an entrance, I'll give you that," the Harbor Master said. He was a stocky man with a graying Afro, bright red overalls, a clipboard, and a square metallic pack on his back. "You destroyed two whole cargo nets of magma berries, dented the city's hull, *and* got a fine for illegal parking before any of you put a foot on deck. That's sort of impressive."

"Sorry about that," said Frederick. "We're in a bit of a hurry."

Below them, Stonker and Ursel were pacing around the train, examining the damage. There was plenty of it—the cab's roof was badly crumpled and had shed a lot of its tiles, the *Belle*'s chimney was cracked, and the windows of the sorting carriage were all broken. Added to which, the whole train was still coated in a layer of sticky orange magma-berry pulp.

"How's it looking down there?" called Frederick.

"Frowlf," Ursel replied.

"Ursel's right," said Stonker. "It's certainly not pretty, but all the essentials seem to be intact. The two of us can conduct some quick repairs while the rest of you hunt down a bifurcator."

"Are you sure we'll find one here?" asked Suzy's mom. She was on the hangar floor with Suzy's dad, admiring the swans. She kept just out of snapping length, so they glared at her imperiously instead.

"Propellendorf's the greatest free port in the Union, ma'am," said the Harbor Master. "If you can't find what you want here, it's not worth looking for."

"I hope you're right," said Frederick. "A lot depends on it."

Their attention was drawn by a strange squelching noise approaching from across the hangar. A moment later, Fletch appeared around the rear of the dirigible. He was soaking wet and left a trail of soggy boot prints behind him.

"You made it, then," he said. Then he saw the battered Express and drew his breath in through his teeth. "Blimey. What have you lot done to her this time?"

"It's not as bad as it looks," said Stonker.

"Grrrolf?" said Ursel.

"Yes, good point," said Stonker. "How did you get up here?"

"Got to the Tie-Dye Desert, then hitched a lift from a bloke with a griffin," said Fletch. "Simple, really."

"Wait a minute," said Suzy's mom. She looked Fletch over disapprovingly. "Why are you so wet?"

Fletch sniffed dismissively, but his eyes darted away from her. "Stepped in a puddle," he said.

"In the desert?" she demanded. Her eyes widened. "Wait! Was the puddle in our house? What have you done to our plumbing?"

"Nothin'!" Fletch protested. "I just had to make a few adjustments to get to the boggart, that's all. Everythin's still in one piece. More or less."

"Well, which is it?" asked Suzy's dad. "More or less?"

Fletch scowled. "More in some parts an' less in others. But it'll all be up an' runnin' by the time you get home. I left instructions for the kids to follow. There's no way they can mess it up."

"Kids?" Suzy's dad regarded Fletch with consternation. "What kids? What are you talking about?"

"Youth apprenticeship engineers," said Fletch. "Young trolls in trainin'. I volunteer with 'em sometimes an' thought they'd probably like a break from helpin' to rebuild Trollville, so they've agreed to finish the job while I'm here. Honestly, you're makin' a big fuss over nothin'."

Frederick was pleased to see Suzy's parents look a little embarrassed.

"Oh. Well. That's different," said Suzy's mom. "But you still shouldn't have left a group of troll children in our house, completely unsupervised."

"Don't worry," said Fletch. "They've got their probation officer with 'em."

"Their *what?*" said Suzy's mom.

Fletch was saved from having to answer by the Harbor Master, who cleared his throat. "As much as I'd love to stay for the reunion, I've got a Berserker dragon rider to deal with in hangar three." He scribbled his signature on a form on his clipboard, tore off a strip at the bottom, and handed it to Frederick. "Here's your docking permit," he said. "Try and stay out of trouble, yeah?" He winked at Frederick, then pressed a big red button on his belt and four mechanical dragonfly wings sprang out of the pack on his back. They flickered into motion, so fast they were just a blur, and he shot into the air. The hangar doors yawned open, revealing the inkblot patterns of the desert far below, and he flitted outside and out of sight.

"Bit flash, that," said Fletch, watching him leave. "I might pick some up myself while we're here."

Frederick tried to blot out the image of an airborne Fletch zooming about the place. "The Union's got enough problems to deal with," he said. "Let's get started."

A levitating platform carried Frederick, Fletch, and Suzy's parents from the hangar deck to the streets of Propellendorf, although "streets" didn't do them justice, Frederick decided. The city consisted of a series of aerial walkways and bridges, crisscrossing each other at various elevations. Slender streamlined buildings were threaded in between them, many of which boasted observation platforms and rooftop gardens. They were all overshadowed by the four towering spires at the city's corners, whose enormous lateral rotor blades provided a comforting background purr to the city, as well as a cool downdraft that cut through the hot desert air.

"Stay close an' let me do all the talkin'," said Fletch. "We'll have this bifurcator in no time."

They followed him to a row of mechanics' workshops grouped around a launchpad, on which a dart-like rocket steamed and hummed with energy. The workshops were filled to overflowing with boosters, fuel pumps, energy crystals, and any number of parts that Frederick couldn't even begin to identify, but almost half an hour later, it was clear that the one thing none of them had was a bifurcator.

"I just don't understand it," said Fletch. They had left the launchpad behind and paused at a busy intersection overlooking one of the city's main landing strips. "Even if we couldn't find a bifurcator, I'd have expected to find the parts for one by now." He puffed his cheeks out. "What can I say? Some days the parts are out there and some days they're not."

"You can't give up now!" said Suzy's mom. "Not when we've come all this way. What about Suzy? What about Wilmot and the Chief?"

"Don't forget the fate of civilization as we know it," Frederick added. "I'd quite like to do something about that as well."

"Gimme time to think, will you?" snapped Fletch. He

chewed distractedly on the corner of one thumbnail for a minute before finally shaking his head. "It's no good. Propellendorf just isn't givin' us the goods today. I say we get back on the Express and head somewhere else."

"But how long will that take?" said Suzy's dad. "Suzy needs our help right now."

"They're right, Fletch," said Frederick. "There has to be another answer."

Fletch folded his arms. "Go on, then, clever clogs."

"I don't know." Frederick screwed his eyes shut and thought hard. "If we can't find a bifurcator, then maybe . . ."

"Maybe what?" asked Suzy's mom.

Frederick rubbed his temples and did his best to ignore the noise of a gyrocopter taking off from the landing strip. Then an idea hit him. "Maybe we could build a new engine," he said excitedly. "A totally different one that doesn't even need a bifurcator at all. Could we do that?"

"You're a bright lad, but you're no engineer," said Fletch. "We could cobble an engine together, but it wouldn't be compatible with the H.E.C. The whole vehicle's designed around that bifurcator."

Frederick felt his newfound hope wither. "Why?" he said. "What does it do that's so important?"

"It bifurcates the molecules in the H.E.C.'s fuel," said Fletch. "Divides 'em into different types so the engine can use 'em more efficiently."

"And there's absolutely no way the H.E.C. will run without one?" said Suzy's dad.

"Not a chance," Fletch replied. "Which means the sooner we start lookin' somewhere else, the better. C'mon. Let's get back to the hangar decks."

Frederick trailed disconsolately after him, unwilling to let the question go. Surely there was something they hadn't thought of yet? He had the frustrating sense that an answer hovered tantalizingly within reach, if only he knew how to grasp it. Fletch was right to say that he was no engineer, but that shouldn't matter, because he was a librarian, and anything he didn't know, he could usually find out. He was *certain* that he'd read something about magical molecular filtering lately—some strange little snippet of information that he'd chanced across when looking for something else. If only he could remember what it was...

He wished he could call the Ivory Tower and ask Jim-Jim or one of the other library assistants to dig out a few likely volumes in the fuzzics-and-engineering section. Unfortunately, *The Book of Power* had wiped the magical science floors clean. But then, he hadn't spent any serious time on those floors for ages anyway, so he couldn't have read that little snippet there. If it hadn't been in a fuzzics book, where had he found it?

While he tried to remember the books he'd been

reading over the past few weeks, he looked over his shoulder to make sure that Suzy's parents were following, and saw them clutching one another's hands tightly as they walked.

At least they've stopped arguing, he thought, then realized it was probably because they were both still angry with him instead. But when he looked at them again, he didn't see any trace of anger in their faces—just worry. He tried to remember if he had ever seen his own parents look so concerned for somebody. For *him*. He couldn't think of a single instance.

He became so preoccupied with the thought that he almost walked straight into the back of Fletch, who had stopped abruptly in front of him.

"What's wrong?" Frederick asked.

Fletch said nothing but pointed at the large gray figure that loomed over the other pedestrians up ahead. It was a statue, more than six feet tall, carved to resemble a knight in armor, and it was wrestling clumsily with a roll of posters, a bucket of paste, and a brush.

"Oh no," said Frederick. "What's that thing doing here?"

Suzy's parents reached them and followed Frederick's nervous gaze to the statue.

"Wow," said Suzy's dad. "Is that one of those living statues Suzy told us about?"

Frederick nodded. "It's one of Lady Crepuscula's guards from the Obsidian Tower," he said. "But it's unusual to see them alone like this."

"Is it dangerous?" asked Suzy's mom, inching in front of Suzy's dad to shield him.

"That depends who you ask," said Fletch. "But I guarantee it won't be friendly. We're better off steering clear of it."

"I think it's putting up more of those Wanted posters," said Suzy's dad, peering over his wife's shoulder. "Like the ones we saw at the station."

Sure enough, the statue had stopped in front of a billboard mounted to the walkway's handrail and was pasting up copies of the Wanted posters featuring Aybek and Tenebrae.

"Does that mean Lady Crepuscula's here in Propellendorf?" asked Suzy's mom.

"Nah, she probably just sent this stone goon out to do the hard work for her," said Fletch. "This isn't exactly her sort of place."

"And what, pray tell, is my sort of place?" said a voice like cut glass behind them.

Frederick felt his spirits drop into his boots. Very slowly, he turned to meet the steely gaze of Lady Crepuscula. She was a small old woman in a heavy black-lace dress. She leaned on her silver cane and waited for

Frederick's answer with the barest hint of a self-satisfied smile on her face.

"Oh," said Frederick, going bright red. "Hello." When Lady Crepuscula didn't reply, he said, "What are you doing in Propellendorf?"

"My job, thank you very much," she said. "In case you'd forgotten, my reprobate brother and his feathered accomplice are still at large. Somebody has to find them before they cause any more trouble."

Frederick watched the statue at work with the posters. "Do you think they're here?" he asked.

"No," she replied, with obvious annoyance. "But so far they haven't been anywhere else I've looked either, and I'm running out of options. In fact, for all the success I've had in tracing them, they may as well have stopped existing altogether. Which I'd be perfectly happy with, incidentally." She glared at them all in turn. "What are you doing here?"

"It's a long story," said Fletch.

"Then don't tell me," she said. "Because I haven't got time. Given your track records, I'll simply assume there's been some sort of disaster that you're desperately trying to remedy." She took in their awkward expressions and nodded. "Yes, I thought so. I just hope you're not expecting me to ride in and save you all the last minute, because I have other things to do. Good day to you."

With a sharp nod, she turned and hobbled away toward her statue, swatting passersby aside with her cane as she went.

Frederick breathed a sigh of relief. "That could have gone a lot worse," he said.

"It could have gone a lot better," said Suzy's dad. "She wasn't even interested in helping us."

"Trust me, life's easier when she stays out of the way," said Fletch. "And I've never trusted those big stone idiots either." He shot a disdainful look at the statue, but only once its back was safely turned. "Why couldn't she have adopted kittens as her evil henchmen instead?" he grumbled.

Frederick tried to imagine Lady Crepuscula surrounded by gamboling kittens, but the image was so unnatural it refused to materialize. As their group started back toward the hangar, he idly wondered what sort of pet *would* be a natural fit for Lady Crepuscula. A poison-quilled terror turtle, perhaps? Giant grabantulas? One of the more disagreeable species of demon?

He stopped so suddenly that Suzy's parents almost walked into him.

"Careful," said Suzy's dad. Frederick hardly heard him. He finally had the answer he'd been racking his brain for.

"Fletch, wait!" he said. "I think we can fix the H.E.C.'s engine without a bifurcator."

Suzy's parents clasped hands. "Really?" said Suzy's mom.

"That's impossible," said Fletch. "How?"

"It's a bit of a long shot," said Frederick. "But does Propellendorf have any pet shops?"

17

THE MASTER OF MAGIC

The S-Cargo Unit climbed the mighty spiral of Hydroborea, cutting a V-shaped wake through the steady flow of water gushing down the streets. Suzy, held firm by the miniature kraken in the detention trailer, turned her face to one side in an attempt to keep the rain out of her eyes and wondered if she would ever be dry again. Every layer of her postal uniform was wet and clinging, her hair was a sodden mess. She tasted salt water whenever she swallowed.

If I live through this, she told herself, *I'm going to spend the rest of my life indoors, wrapped in a heated blanket drinking hot chocolate.*

Beside her, Wilmot appeared to be having an equally

miserable time. He was doing his best to maintain a dignified silence, but the effect was spoiled somewhat by the rain that kept dribbling down his nose and making him sneeze every few minutes.

At last Suzy couldn't take it anymore and raised her head to glare at the Watch Frog Commander, who was still standing over them in the trailer.

"Why is this taking so long?" she demanded. "Shouldn't we be there by now?"

"I wouldn't be in such a hurry if I were you," the Commander replied, barely glancing at her. "This is a one-way trip."

A sharper cold than the rain cut through Suzy, and she wished she had never spoken. They were rushing toward Frogmaggog's tower, and whatever fate awaited them within its walls.

"It'll be okay, Suzy," Wilmot whispered. "We'll get the job done. We'll save the Ivory Tower and the Express."

"That's the spirit," said the Chief, who was still hovering above them. "Never say die. Unless you already *have* died, of course."

The spiral of Hydroborea's great shell tightened and narrowed the higher up they went. Suzy got the impression that the streets were funneling into one another until at last they culminated in a single wide avenue. The buildings overlooking it were even more grandiose than their counterparts in the lower reaches of the city. Signs above their doors said things like BANK OF HYDROBOREA and MINISTRY OF NEWS, and the pavements outside were busy with frogs in fine robes and large colorful umbrellas, all of whom pointed and stared as the vehicle passed. There seemed to be no sign of their newt-like counterparts at all, and it was clear to Suzy which of the two species wielded power in the city.

She only had a moment to ponder this before the S-Cargo Unit drew to a halt. She couldn't see what had stopped them, but she heard a voice from somewhere up ahead call, "Who goes there?"

"This is Commander Kecker of Frog Team Four," the Commander called back. "We've captured the outworlders. His Greatness wants to interrogate them personally."

Suzy and Wilmot exchanged a nervous glance.

"He's expecting you," came the answer. "Proceed."

The Commander pulled a small silver conch shell from his belt and blew into it. Whatever note it produced was too high for Suzy to hear, but the kraken released its hold on them and curled up, as if stung.

"On your feet," Commander Kecker said. He jumped down into the road and leveled his trident as Suzy and Wilmot clambered down after him, rubbing the stiffness from their limbs. The other Watch Frogs sprang out of their seats and landed in a protective cordon around them. "Eyes front."

Suzy turned and got her first look at the Gilded Tower. Its gateway was a mammoth stone frog's head, five stories tall, its mouth wide open as if to swallow the avenue in front of it. Only the base of the tower was visible, of course. It rose in a tightly bound spiral of pink stone, carved into the likeness of a gigantic octopus tentacle with circular windows in the suckers. It met the roof of the city, and Suzy knew from her brief glimpse of it during their descent in the H.E.C. that it extended a long way above that, jutting up into the ocean.

A pair of red lacquered doors within the great stone mouth swung open with a crackle of magic, releasing a cloud of steam from inside the tower. It rolled over the group, carried on a breath of warm air that filled Suzy's nostrils with the scent of roses. The welcome heat did little to steady her nerves though.

"Are you okay?" she asked Wilmot.

"I think so," he said, rubbing at his badge again. "This is what we came here for, so remember chapter five of *The Knowledge*."

"Always make a good first impression," she said. He gave her a nervous smile, which snapped off abruptly when Kecker shoved him in the back with the butt of his trident.

"Quiet, both of you," Kecker ordered. "You'll only speak when addressed directly by His Greatness. Now, get moving." With another shove of his trident, Kecker and the Watch Frogs marched Suzy and Wilmot into the waiting maw of the gateway.

Once over the threshold, the steam settled on them as thick as a cloud bank, and Suzy couldn't see more than a couple of yards in any direction. The floor beneath her feet was pink marble shot through with veins of gold, however, and judging by the distant echoes of their footsteps, they were walking through a very large space indeed.

Water splashed somewhere up ahead.

The Watch Frogs clearly knew where they were going and didn't slacken their pace, even when Wilmot caught his foot on something and stumbled. The Commander grabbed him by the collar before he could fall, and shoved him forward. Meanwhile, the object that Wilmot had tripped on skidded across the floor and came to a halt in front of Suzy, who came to a sudden and complete stop.

It was a skull.

A Hydroborean newt skull, judging by its size and shape, but she didn't get time to examine it closely, as she received a push in the back.

"Keep moving," Kecker croaked.

They left the skull behind, but it was only a matter of seconds before Suzy saw another one in their path. And then a rib cage, followed by a frog skull. There were bones everywhere, Suzy realized with horror—a graveyard's worth, all picked clean and gleaming. She and Wilmot did their best to step over them until Kecker finally ordered them to a halt.

The slap and gurgle of water came again, much closer now.

"Your Greatness," Kecker called. "We have brought you the outworlders responsible for the disturbance in Plankton Plaza."

Suzy could just make out a vague shape in the mist ahead of them. She couldn't be certain, but it looked like a shining white wall, stretching high up above them. The sounds of water came from somewhere near its top.

"How many?" said a gelatinous voice, so deep and heavy that the floor trembled with every syllable.

"Three, Your Greatness."

The voice gave a rumbling growl, and a curtain of water crashed to the ground a few yards in front of the group, showering them with warm spray. "Show me."

Suzy and Wilmot joined hands as the Watch Frogs pushed them forward. At the same time, the mist parted and Suzy saw the huge shape for what it was—not a wall, but an old-fashioned claw-foot bathtub, taller than a double-decker bus. The steam rose from it in great clouds, and something shifted inside it with a wet squittering noise. A pair of gigantic hands appeared over the rim, displacing another curtain of water. They were webbed and pale, with long, flat fingers. A silver signet ring glinted on one of the fingers, inset with a lapis stone in the shape of a snail shell. A huge semi-spherical head followed. The creature was identical to the other Watch Frogs but easily ten times their size.

Kecker dropped to one knee. "Kneel before Frogmaggog, the Master of Magic," he ordered. Not daring to take their eyes off the titanic figure above them, Suzy and Wilmot did as instructed.

"Gosh, he's a big fellow, isn't he?" said the Chief, looking up at Frogmaggog with his hands on his hips. "Hello! Nice to discover you."

Frogmaggog's huge eyes swiveled independently of each other until they both came to rest on the three friends. He drew a fat, wormlike tongue across his lipless mouth. "What hideous specimens," he said. "Hydroborea is closed to inferiors like you. Why have you violated our borders?"

Suzy bridled at the words. Her first impulse was to answer back, but she remembered her promise to Wilmot outside the gateway: *good first impression.* The future of her friends and of the whole Union rested on this meeting,

241

and they were running out of time, so she held her tongue as Wilmot stepped forward and removed his cap.

"If you'll excuse the intrusion, Your Greatness," he said, "we don't intend to stay in Hydroborea at all and are only here on business. In fact, we came to see you."

"Naturally," said Frogmaggog. "I suppose you're going to beg me for some magic." He gave a deep-throated laugh that shook the throne room and turned Suzy's legs to jelly. The Watch

Frogs laughed along, although their humor sounded forced and nervous.

Wilmot swallowed audibly. "Actually, no," he said. "We're here to deliver a package to you, from the Impossible Places."

Frogmaggog's laughter stopped abruptly. "Liars!" he said. "The Impossible Places fell into ruin when we stopped them leeching our magic from us. Everybody knows that." He leaned forward out of the bath and pinned Wilmot to the spot with a furious glare. Suzy sprang to her friend's side while the Watch Frogs retreated a few steps.

"Hydroborea endures alone," said Frogmaggog. "Say it."

"Hey, you can't—" Suzy began, but shut her mouth when Wilmot elbowed her in the ribs.

"Say it!" Frogmaggog's eyes blazed, but Wilmot stood with his back straight and his chest out, and Suzy followed his lead. She couldn't let him down now.

"I'm very sorry, Your Greatness," said Wilmot, with only the slightest tremor in his voice. "But as a Postmaster, and as a proud troll, I won't say something that I know to be untrue."

A shocked silence descended upon the throne room. Frogmaggog narrowed his eyes.

"I decide what's true," he said coldly. "This city is the last stronghold of magic in a hostile universe, and I alone have the power to command it." The bulging expanse of his forehead creased into a frown. "So what have you brought me that I could possibly want?"

Very slowly and carefully, Wilmot removed *The Book of Power* from his satchel and held it up for Frogmaggog to see. "This was written by the founders of Hydroborea," he said. The Master of Magic's reaction was subtle, but Suzy saw it clearly—a brief shiver of excitement, which he quickly covered by sitting back in the bath.

"A book?" He gave a dismissive wave of his hand. "We don't need books here. I tell everyone what they need to know."

Before either Wilmot or Suzy could respond, the book spoke. "That explains why they know so very little." Its voice echoed around the throne room, drawing scandalized gasps from the Watch Frogs. Suzy and Wilmot cringed.

"Be quiet!" Suzy whispered out of the corner of her mouth. "He's the only one who can unbind you."

"It's got a point though, don't you think?" said the Chief. Suzy gave him a look that might have killed him if he hadn't already been dead.

But Frogmaggog seemed more intrigued than angered by this new curiosity. He extended a gigantic hand toward Wilmot, who, after a moment's hesitation, placed the book in his palm.

"You're either brave or foolish to speak to me like that, little book," said Frogmaggog, raising it to eye level.

"I am neither," the book replied. "But I am honest. Everything you have said so far about Hydroborea and the Impossible Places has been wrong."

Frogmaggog's scowl deepened. "And I suppose you know better, do you?"

"Much better," the book replied. "I was created here a long time ago, and the power on which this city was founded was placed in me for safekeeping."

"Lies!" said Frogmaggog. "Only I possess the power of Hydroborea."

"No, you do not," said the book. "You never have. Your ancient ancestors sought to destroy it, so it was sent with me to the Impossible Places, where I have guarded it ever since. Now I have brought it back, and if the spell that binds me is lifted, I can share it."

The color rose in Frogmaggog's face and he closed his fist around the book. "What is this insolence?" he hissed.

Wilmot's ears drooped. "It's, er... news to us, too," he said. "But the book clearly belongs in Hydroborea, so if you wouldn't mind signing this proof-of-delivery form..." He fumbled the blank gold sheet from his satchel. "Please? It's rather important."

Frogmaggog sneered, but Suzy could still see a trace of hunger in his eyes. Despite his anger, he wanted the book. "I'll take it," he said, "but only to protect my people from its lies." He reached for the delivery form, and Suzy's breath caught in her throat. This was it. One signature, and their friends and the Impossible Places would be safe.

"No," said the book.

Everything seemed to stop. Suzy was sure her heart froze for a second, and even Frogmaggog paused. He opened his hand again. The book was a tiny black speck on his palm.

"What do you mean, 'no'?" he demanded.

"I do not wish to be delivered to you," said the book. "You are not an adequate recipient."

Wilmot went pale. "Oh dear."

"Not adequate?" Frogmaggog's voice was a whisper of fury. "How dare you!"

"I have reflected on everything that I have learned since my return," the book went on quite calmly. "The city has fallen into disrepair, and the Gilded Tower no longer serves its true purpose. Worse, the stories that Hydroborea tells about itself are false. The city has forgotten its true self and is happy to believe the lies that you and your predecessors have invented for it. This is not acceptable."

Suzy sensed their achievement slipping out of reach. "But you can teach him," she called to the book. "You said yourself, you know better."

"The Master of Magic doesn't need teaching," said Frogmaggog.

"Which is why you are not fit to use my power," said the book. "And I will not allow you to unbind me."

"But Frogmaggog's the only one in Hydroborea with any magic," said Wilmot, who was looking increasingly flustered. "If he can't open you, who can?"

The book thought for a moment. "Ina," it decided. "Deliver me to Ina."

Suzy and Wilmot stared at one another in disbelief.

"Why didn't you tell us that when we were with her?" said Suzy.

"Because I wasn't sure then," the book replied. "It's a very big decision. It took a lot of thought."

Frogmaggog raised a finger for silence. "I don't know who this Ina person is," he said, "but she can't have you. You're mine."

Suzy turned to Wilmot. "What do we do now?" she whispered. "Is a delivery supposed to choose its own recipient like this?"

The question was clearly taxing Wilmot as well. "It's unorthodox," he whispered back. "But there's no rule against it."

"Then that means...," Suzy began.

Wilmot nodded gravely. "Leave it to me." He cleared his throat, set his jaw, and called up to Frogmaggog. "I'm sorry, Your Greatness, but in light of this new development, I'm going to have to ask you to return the book." He didn't flinch as the Master of Magic leaned over the edge of the bath and regarded him closely. "We're very sorry for the inconvenience."

Frogmaggog nodded in understanding. Then he opened his mouth, and his tongue lashed out like a whip. It struck Wilmot in the chest, yanked him off his feet, and carried him straight into Frogmaggog's open maw, which snapped shut again. It was all over in a second.

"Wilmot!" Suzy screamed. "What have you done? Spit him back out!"

Frogmaggog's mouth curled into a cruel grin. He swallowed noisily and let out a rumbling belch. "Your friend tasted better than he looked." He let out another belch, and something shot from his mouth, drifting down to land at Suzy's feet. It was the gold delivery form, badly creased and slick with slime.

Too horrified to speak, Suzy staggered back until she tripped over a heap of discarded bones and fell on her haunches.

"This is appalling behavior!" said the Chief, who still bobbed at her side. "You, sir, should be ashamed of yourself!"

Frogmaggog ignored them. He reached down into

the bath, removed the plug, and tossed it over the rim, where it swung back and forth on a length of thick silver chain. The throne room echoed with a deep-throated gurgle as the water began to drain away. "I'm going to dispose of this seditious book," he announced as he heaved his immense bulk out of the bath and stepped over Suzy, showering her with warm water. "Take the girl to the kitchens and tell my chef to prepare her for dinner. I don't want to be disturbed before then."

"Yes, Your Greatness," said Kecker. He bowed as Frog-maggog lumbered away into the thinning steam.

Suzy looked around in a daze. The enormity of what had just happened was too much for her, and she could feel her mind growing numb with shock. She had no idea what to do.

"Quick, Suzy," the Chief whispered. "While they're not looking."

It was only then that she realized Kecker and his men were still bowing low. Just for a second, nobody was watching her. She pushed herself to her feet and ran, stooping to snatch up the fallen delivery form as she passed it. She didn't know why she did it—she had no plan and no hope of escape, but when her feet carried her toward the bath and she saw the huge plug swinging toward her on the end of its chain, she leaped and grabbed hold of it.

"Get her!" shouted Commander Kecker. He sprang and almost caught her, but the chain's pendulum swing carried her just out of his reach. As Kecker landed on the floor and prepared to pounce again, Suzy stuffed the delivery form into her satchel and began climbing the chain toward the rim of the bath.

"What's happening back there, Commander?"

Suzy heard Frogmaggog's heavy footsteps returning. She scrambled upward and was halfway to the top when she felt the chain shake. She looked down and saw Kecker climbing after her, quickly followed by two more Watch Frogs.

"Keep climbing and don't look down," said the Chief, hovering at her ear.

Suzy put every scrap of effort into the climb. She reached the rim a few seconds ahead of Kecker and pulled herself over the top, getting unsteadily to her feet. Behind her was the fifty-foot drop to the throne-room floor. Before her lay the dwindling pool of bathwater, disappearing in a noisy whirlpool down the drain. And beyond that, staring at her in disgust from the other side of the bath, towered Frogmaggog. He still had the book clenched in his fist.

"Where do you think you're going?" he said.

Suzy wanted to say something, anything, back, but her anger was so big now that she couldn't get it out of her mouth. It lodged in her throat, leaving her in open-mouthed silence.

Frogmaggog reached for her. At the same instant, Kecker pulled himself over the rim of the bath behind her and made a grab for her legs.

Suzy closed her eyes and jumped forward, slipping through Frogmaggog's fingers and plunging into the steaming bathwater. It closed over her head, and before she could surface again, the pull of the whirlpool caught her. She didn't fight it but let it drag her toward the drain.

"Oh, I see," said the Chief. "Very cunning!"

"Stop her!" Frogmaggog's voice was indistinct through the rush of the escaping water. Suzy looked up and saw the dark shape of his hand reaching down, but he was too late—the whirlpool dragged Suzy into its heart, spinning her round on the spot before, all at once, she was sucked down the drain and everything went black.

18

THE HUNT BEGINS

Frogmaggog saw Suzy vanish down the drain an instant before his fingers closed on the spot where she had been. The last of the water followed her down with a burbling belch, as if adding one final insult to his defeat.

"Imbeciles!" He thumped the rim of the bathtub in frustration, almost causing Kecker to topple over the side. "Commander! You've let me down badly. Give me one good reason why I shouldn't eat you and your men on the spot."

Kecker turned a sickly shade of yellow and fell to his knees. "Forgive us, Your Greatness! I will personally follow her down the drain and get her back. You won't go hungry on my watch!"

"Too little, too late, Commander. If the girl doesn't drown, she could crawl out of the sewers almost anywhere."

"Then we'll search the city," said Kecker. "Street by street if we have to."

"And by the time you've found her, how many people will she have infected with her stories of the outside world?" said Frogmaggog. "Her *false* stories." His free hand strayed to the silver conch hanging from his belt, and he toyed nervously with it. "What will the people say when they realize she escaped me? A powerless outworlder defying the Master of Magic. That news will spread like a disease. The people will never fear me again!"

"What should we do, Your Greatness?" said Kecker. "Just give us an order."

Frogmaggog stared off into the swirling mist while he considered the question. "I want you to find this 'Ina,'" he said. "You say you caught the outworlders in Plankton Plaza?"

"That's right, Your Greatness. In the lowest ward of the Midtwist District."

"And did many people see them? Speak to them?"

"Quite a few, according to the reports," said Kecker.

Frogmaggog's mouth drew down into a sneer of distaste. "In that case, I want you to take ten squads of Watch Frogs and arrest everyone in the area."

Kecker blinked in surprise. "What... what exactly do you mean by 'everyone,' Your Greatness?"

"Everyone!" Frogmaggog shouted. "Empty every building, clear every street, arrest the whole ward if you have to. Ina's bound to be somewhere among them, and the lies told by the outworlders and their book are an infection that may already be spreading. We need to stop it before it contaminates the whole city."

"But that means hundreds of arrests, Your Greatness, and the dungeons are already overfull. Where will we put them all?"

"Bring them to me," said Frogmaggog. "It would be a shame to let so much nutrition go to waste."

Kecker looked up in horror. "*All* of them?"

As if in answer, the hideous tongue lashed out again and snatched up one of the Watch Frogs standing beside Kecker. The poor creature vanished into Frogmaggog's cavernous mouth with a scream.

"I'm always hungry, Commander," said Frogmaggog, his face darkening. "And there's room on the menu for you."

Kecker bowed so low that his face almost scraped the porcelain. "I will carry out your orders immediately, Your Greatness."

Frogmaggog stroked the rubbery mound of his biggest

chin. "And as for the girl and specter who escaped, this might be the time to see what my little pet can do," he mused. "Doesn't that sound like fun?"

Kecker knew better than to answer, and simply watched as Frogmaggog waved away the clouds of steam overhead to reveal an enormous crystal chandelier. Its thousands of crystal pieces were shaped like fish and floated freely in the air, moving slowly together in a great shoal around a large central bowl, in which schools of real fish glowed brightly. But something else hovered beneath it—a birdcage the size of a telephone booth, draped in a black shroud. Frogmaggog plucked the cage out of the air, set it on the rim of the bath beside him, and removed the shroud.

The creature inside shrank away from the light and shielded its eyes with a clawed hand. It was the size and shape of a large man, although a pair of wings sprouted from its shoulder blades. Their golden-brown feathers were matted and bent, and the jerkin and breeches covering the creature's powerful body hung in tatters. It wore a thick metal collar around its neck.

"Look at me," Frogmaggog ordered, flicking the cage with his forefinger.

With obvious reluctance the creature lowered its claw and turned its large yellow eyes on Frogmaggog. They were set in a flat, feathered face and burned with hatred.

"I have a job for you, little pet," said Frogmaggog.

The creature hissed. "I am not your pet," it said in a voice as rich and dark as woodsmoke. "I am Egolius Tenebrae, criminal mastermind, and I will not be kept here like this." His glare intensified as he looked deep into Frogmaggog's eyes.

The Master of Magic stared back for a moment, then laughed. "You're a dirty little outworlder and you'll do as I say," he replied. "And are you still trying to hypnotize me? I've told you before—your powers might work on the pitiful creatures of your own world, but we Hydroboreans are made of sterner stuff. We're immune."

Tenebrae hissed again, but lowered his eyes to the ground.

"That's better," said Frogmaggog. "I only spared your life because you claimed you could be useful, and now the time has come to see if you're right. You tell me you're a hunter. Well, I've got some prey for you."

"You mean the ghost and the outworlder girl," said Tenebrae. "I was listening. That girl's caused trouble for me before."

"Is that so?" said Frogmaggog. "Then this is your chance to get even. Find them, and make sure they never trouble either of us again."

"What's in it for me?" said Tenebrae.

"Apart from revenge?" Frogmaggog smirked. "I won't eat you. Yet."

"Is that all?" Tenebrae dragged his talons down the bars of his cage with a piercing metallic shriek that made Kecker and the remaining Watch Frog wince. "Once I'm out of this cage, why should I ever come back?"

"Because you won't have any choice," said Frogmaggog. "Haven't you wondered why I put that collar on you?"

Tenebrae picked at the band of metal around his neck. "It's another attempt to humiliate me," he said.

"Of course," said Frogmaggog. "But it also makes sure you behave. Like this."

He snapped his fingers, the collar sparked with magical energy, and Tenebrae disappeared in a flash of blue light. With a burbling laugh, Frogmaggog drew the cage lower so that Kecker and his Watch Frog could see into it. On the spot where Tenebrae had stood was a small blue hermit crab with a spotted shell, waggling its feelers in surprise. It turned in a slow, stumbling circle before raising its tiny pincers toward Frogmaggog and clacking them ineffectually.

The Master of Magic roared with laughter. "Isn't it ingenious?" he said, flashing the signet ring on his finger. "As long as I'm wearing this, all I have to do is click my fingers and I can turn you into anything I like." He snapped his fingers again, and with another flash of light, Tenebrae was restored to his true form, the collar still in place around his neck.

"You can't do this to me!" he said.

"I can and I will," Frogmaggog replied. "So deal with the girl and be quick about it, or I'll transform you permanently."

Tenebrae flew into a rage, hissing and clawing and rattling the bars of his tiny prison. Frogmaggog merely folded his arms and waited until Tenebrae slumped, exhausted, to the floor of the cage. "What will it be, outworlder?"

"Fine," Tenebrae growled. "I'll do it."

Frogmaggog gave a satisfied grunt and turned to Kecker.

"You have your orders, Commander. Why are you still here?"

Commander Kecker and his remaining Watch Frog both blanched and scurried down the plug chain to rejoin the rest of the squad.

"And as for you," said Frogmaggog, carrying Tenebrae's cage to one of the circular windows high in the wall, "I want proof that you've taken care of the girl."

"You'll have it," said Tenebrae.

"And be discreet," said Frogmaggog, pushing the window open. "I can't have the city knowing I'm using an outworlder to do my dirty work." He unfastened the cage, and Tenebrae sprang out onto the window ledge, taking a moment to stretch his wings. He tugged at the collar but it didn't budge.

"I'm going to make you pay for this one day," he said, looking back at Frogmaggog. Then he turned and leaped out of the window, disappearing over the rain-lashed city with a single snap of his wings.

19

FLUSHED WITH SUCCESS

Suzy fought for breath as she was swept along in a raging torrent of white water. She didn't have much chance to see where they were, but she could guess—Hydroborea's sewers.

"Chief?" she spluttered.

"I'm here," came the reply. "Don't worry."

At last the flood began to calm and she was able to keep her head above water without being swamped. She took a few choking breaths and looked around. Sure enough, the Chief was hovering alongside her, half in and half out of the water, and his glow was just bright enough to illuminate the large pipe down which they were being swept. She grabbed at the walls to try to slow herself but only succeeded in scraping her hands on the rough stone.

"We have to go back," she said. "We have to find a way to save Wilmot."

"My dear," said the Chief softly, "there's nothing we can do for him. He's gone."

She spat dirty water. "But he can't be!"

His glow dimmed. "I'm so sorry."

Suzy was speechless.

She knew he was right, but that didn't make it feel any better. She wasn't sure *anything* would ever make this feel any better. When the tears came, she didn't try to stop them.

Wilmot was gone. The book, too, and with it, any hope of retrieving the words it had stolen from the Ivory Tower. She and the Chief were trapped here. She would never make it home. She would never see her parents again, and her friends on the Express would never make another delivery. She had failed them all, and she didn't know how to fix it.

She wasn't any closer to an answer twenty minutes later, when her satchel caught on a rusty ladder set into the wall of the pipe, bringing her to an abrupt halt. Shards of cold light slipped in around the rim of a manhole above her.

"Where do you suppose we are?" she said.

"I'll take a little look, shall I?" said the Chief. He rose

up and stuck his head through the manhole cover, ducking down a moment later. "A little bit of good news," he said. "The coast's clear."

Suzy clambered out of the manhole and flopped onto her back in the middle of the street. There was no one to see her—the road was dark and the buildings around her were empty and crumbling. The sewer had carried her back to the abandoned Lowertwist district, not far from where they had left the H.E.C.

"There's not a soul about," said the Chief. "We can regroup and come up with a new strategy."

Suzy covered her face with her hands to shield it against the rain. "We *are* the group now, Chief," she said. "And there are no strategies left. This is it. We're finished."

"Nonsense," said the Chief. "Is that any way for a postie to talk? What would Wilmot say if he could see you now?"

Suzy screwed her eyes shut. She didn't want to think about Wilmot right now. It was too painful.

"He'd be doing his best, of course," the Chief continued. "Come rain, shine, or meteor shower, and all that."

"The Impossible Postal Express will deliver," Suzy muttered. She wiped the rain and tears from her eyes and sat up. "I know. And he'd probably find a way, but I'm not as good at this as he is." She swallowed a painful lump in her throat. "As he *was*."

"Neither was he when I first met him," said the Chief. "He was constantly out of his depth. And not just because he was standing on the seafloor of the Topaz Narrows." He chuckled. "Wilmot had such a legacy to live up to, you see. His father and grandfather were both exceptional posties in their own day, his mother was Postmistress General, and he was terrified of falling short. That's why he always tried so hard—because he could see the heights reached by those who had gone before him, and didn't want to let them down."

Suzy watched the rain ping and patter against the road as a peal of thunder sounded overhead. "This is the bit where you tell me I've got to live up to his standard now, isn't it?" she said.

The Chief smiled. "I always knew you were a bright girl," he said. "So, what's the first item on our to-do list?"

Suzy gave a weary sigh. "We need to get the book back from Frogmaggog and deliver it to Ina," she said. "But how? Walk back into the palace and tell him to hand it over?"

"I can't tell you *what* to do, I'm afraid," said the Chief. "But I have every confidence that you will find a way to do *something*. And maybe it will work, and maybe it won't, but at least we'll have hope. Why, if it weren't for you, I'd still be stuck on board La Rouquine with no chance of ever leaving."

His words went a very small way to lessening the painful lump of grief that had set up home in Suzy's chest. "Thanks." She dragged her hair out of her face and took a proper look around for the first time. "We should find cover. Frogmaggog's probably looking for us by now."

"Smart thinking," said the Chief. "Where do you suggest we go?"

She got to her feet, wincing as her various scrapes and bruises made themselves known. "Ina's place," she said. "She and Amlod are the only friendly faces we've met so far. And now that Frogmaggog knows about her, they're both in danger. We need to warn them."

The Chief's glow brightened again. "There you are, you see? I told you you'd come up with something. Let's get started."

Suzy nodded.

All she really wanted to do was curl up into a ball and sleep for a whole day, then wake up to discover that everything in her life had magically fixed itself. But she knew that life didn't work like that, and neither did magic. You could have the best spells in the business, but sooner or later you had to put in the legwork.

The Chief bobbed ahead of her as she set off uphill, her head bowed against the rain. Every drop struck her like a tiny hammer blow, and the runoff from the streets surged around her ankles. She checked her pocket watch—barely three hours until the delivery deadline. How was she ever going to do this?

There was a sudden crack of thunder high above them. The sound died away into a low rumble, which swept out across the rooftops before being lost in the steady drumbeat of the rain.

"Dreadful weather," said the Chief.

Suzy stopped, suddenly afraid. "This city doesn't have weather," she said. "It just has leaks." She shielded her eyes and peered up into the rain, but all she saw above the rooftops was a vague darkness.

"But if that wasn't thunder, what was it?" asked the Chief.

"I'm not sure," said Suzy. Then she remembered the groans and creaks that the H.E.C.'s hull had made as the ocean tightened its grip around it, and a new, horrifying idea occurred to her. "It's the city's shell," she said. "I think it's starting to buckle under the pressure."

"What does that mean?" said the Chief.

"It means we might have even less time than we realized," said Suzy. "We'd better hurry."

With the Chief's light to guide her, she set off uphill at a run.

20

A NEW PLAN

By the time Suzy found her way back to Plankton Plaza the streetlights had changed again, from their summery golden light to a soft dusky purple. This was apparently what passed for evening in Hydroborea, and Suzy found it a bit disorienting. Although she knew perfectly well that each of the Impossible Places kept their own time, her body clock was still tuned to home, where it was currently the middle of the night. At least the late hour and heavy rain had driven everyone indoors. Even the newspaper seller had packed up and gone home.

I suppose we didn't leave him anything to sell, Suzy thought.

"I'll lie low for a while, shall I?" said the Chief. He retreated into his skull as Suzy crawled out from underneath the netting in the alleyway and hurried across the Plaza onto Ina's street. Another low rumble of thunder sounded, dim and far away, as she flitted from one bit of cover to another.

"I really don't like the sound of that," she whispered.

"This city's at the bottom of an ocean. There are hundreds of thousands of tons of water outside, threatening to pour in. How long can the outer shell withstand that sort of pressure without the right magic to maintain it?"

"Hopefully a little bit longer," said the Chief. "I'd hate to leave one seafloor just to end up trapped on another."

They reached the archway leading to the courtyard of Ina's building. Suzy tested the big wooden doors, expecting them to be locked again, and was surprised when one of them swung open. She poked her head into the courtyard and looked around. Lights burned in every window, but there was nobody in sight. Crouching low, she hurried to Ina's window and knocked. It opened almost immediately, and Ina stuck her head out.

"I knew it!" she said, breaking into a huge grin. "I left the courtyard door unlocked in case you made it back. Come in, come in! I want to know everything!" She practically pulled Suzy off her feet and in through the window.

Amlod, who had been sitting on his bed, jumped to his feet.

"I don't believe it!" he said. "Did you see Frogmaggog? How did you get away?"

Suzy's relief at seeing them both again was almost overwhelmed by the sorrow that tried to force its way up her throat when she opened her mouth. She bit the feeling back, but Ina saw her pained expression and her own face clouded.

"Where's Wilmot?" she asked.

Suzy's eyes pricked with tears again. Sharing the news was like reliving it all over. "We met Frogmaggog," she said. "He took the book and he ... he ate Wilmot."

Amlod sat down heavily, but Ina's expression became unreadable. "He *eats* people?" she said, mystified.

Suzy nodded. "The Chief and I only just escaped, but the Watch Frogs are bound to be looking for us. We can't stay long."

Ina wrapped her arms around Suzy. They were surprisingly warm and dry for a newt, Suzy thought.

"We'll do everything we can to help you, won't we, Amlod?"

Amlod seemed ready to give the question some serious thought, until Ina gave him a sharp look. "Oh," he said. "Yes, of course."

"Thank you," said Suzy. "But there's something else. Something important."

"Wait!" Ina got out her notepad and pen. "Okay, I'm ready. Shoot."

Suzy took in her breath and gathered herself. "The book rejected Frogmaggog when we tried to hand it over. It wants to be delivered to you."

Ina had only scribbled a few words when she looked up abruptly. "Me?" she said. "What for?"

"I don't think it likes Frogmaggog any more than you do," said Suzy. "Whatever its powers are, it wants to share them with you instead."

Ina sat down heavily on her bed. "But I don't know how to use magic," she said. "How am I even supposed to unlock it?"

"I'm not sure, but I think it'll just unlock itself if you ask it to," said Suzy. "It *wants* to be opened, but only by the right person, which means we've got to get the two of you together as quickly as we can." Another lump, another swallow. "It's what Wilmot would do."

"But how?" asked Ina.

"I don't know yet," said Suzy. "The palace is a fortress. We can't force our way in, and if we hand ourselves over, Frogmaggog will eat us on sight. We need another plan, and fast. We've only got a few hours left to unbind the book before it keeps all the words it stole forever."

Ina looked perturbed, but before she could reply, there

was a loud crash from the courtyard as the doors to the street burst open.

"Secure the building!" shouted a voice that Suzy knew all too well: It belonged to Commander Kecker. The rapid tramp of Watch Frog boots poured into the courtyard, and they heard the front door to the building give way with a splintering of wood.

"Oh dear," said the Chief. "We can't seem to stay out of trouble today."

Amlod's fronds turned a sickly yellow with fear. "We're all going to get eaten!"

Outside the apartment door, the building rang with the sounds of the Watch Frogs' search: doors being kicked in, people shouting in confusion, glass shattering.

"Everyone is under arrest!" shouted Commander Kecker. "Leave the building and assemble in the street for processing. No exceptions!"

The sound of Watch Frog boots approached the bedroom door, which shook as someone pounded on it. "Open up in there!"

Ina's pink speckles paled. "We need to get out of here."

"Suzy hurried to the window and peeked through the curtain, but the courtyard was already filling with Hydroboreans as the Watch Frogs marched them, protesting and struggling, out to the street. "We're too late," she said. "They're everywhere."

"Open up or we'll smash it down," came the voice outside the door.

"Just a minute," Amlod shouted back. "I'm, er ... getting dressed." He turned to his sister and hissed, "Think of something!"

Ina tugged on the ends of her fronds in frustration, then caught her breath. "I've got an idea," she said, her face lighting up. "Are you scared of heights?"

"Why?" asked Suzy, but Ina had already thrown open the window and climbed out. At the same instant, the door to the room cracked under a vicious blow and would have burst in completely if not for Amlod, who threw himself against it.

"Go!" he said. "I'll hold them off."

"But—" Suzy started.

"Quickly!" Amlod gritted his teeth as the door began to splinter behind him. "If even half the stuff you've told me is true, then Ina needs that book, so go and get it!"

"He's right, Suzy," said the Chief from inside his skull. "There's no time to waste."

With a last pained look at Amlod, Suzy followed Ina out the window. She expected the clammy webbed hands of the Watch Frogs to seize her immediately, but the courtyard was in such chaos that, for a few seconds at least, nobody even noticed her.

"This way, Suzy!"

She looked up and saw Ina climbing an ornate drain-pipe toward the roof. She followed, her hands slipping on the wet metal, and had not got far before she heard the door to Ina's apartment give way with a crash. A few seconds later, the cry went up from below her: "It's the outworlder! Stop her!"

Suzy didn't look down but kept climbing, past land-ings on which people jostled and fought with the Watch Frogs, until she finally pulled herself, panting and shak-ing, onto the sloping scallop-shaped tiles of the roof.

"Where's Amlod?" Ina looked down over the edge and cried out in shock. Suzy did likewise, and saw Kecker climbing grimly after them.

"Amlod stayed behind to buy us time," said Suzy breathlessly. "We have to go, now!"

"No!" Ina looked stricken. "I can't leave him. He's all I've got!"

"Give yourselves up!" Kecker's voice reached them from below. "Surrender immediately!"

Suzy grabbed Ina's hand and squeezed it hard. "If we stay here, they'll catch us, too, and he'll have done it for nothing." She tried to pull Ina with her up the slope of the roof, but Ina resisted. For a horrible second, Suzy thought she was going to hand herself over to Kecker, until she began stamping on the top of the drainpipe, where it met the guttering.

"Don't just stand there, help me," Ina said.

Realization dawned in Suzy's mind and she joined Ina, kicking down hard on the guttering. It was old and rusty and began to separate from the roof just as Kecker's furious face rose into view.

"What are you doing?" he shouted. "Stop! That's an order!" He reached for them, but it was too late—the drainpipe peeled away from the wall, slowly at first, but then faster and faster, taking Kecker with it. Suzy took great satisfaction in the look of helpless fury on his face as he receded from them, toppling into the courtyard and landing in the central flower bed with a crash.

The pandemonium of the crowd lessened momentarily as everyone stopped to watch him. He staggered to his feet, his helmet askew, and spat a wad of plant mulch from his mouth. "Stop those two!" he said, pointing a shaking finger at Suzy and Ina. "They're enemies of Hydroborea!"

Suzy couldn't resist giving him a little wave good-bye. Before either of them could turn to leave, though, a new voice reached them from the crowd.

"Run, Ina!" It was Amlod, being dragged toward the gates by a couple of Watch Frogs.

Ina gasped. "Let him go!" she cried. "Somebody, please help him."

"Don't worry about me," he shouted, digging his heels

273

in as best he could. "Go and get the book. And if it has any power, use it to help us!" Then he was through the gates and hidden from sight.

"Amlod!" Ina cried.

Kecker signaled with his trident, and a group of Watch Frogs broke away from the crowd and began climbing the remaining drainpipes. Suzy pulled Ina away from the edge.

"We can't stay," she said.

"I know," Ina replied. Her face was set in a determined scowl. "We need to open the book. It's the only way to save everyone."

She gripped Suzy's hand and led Suzy up the roof into the gathering dusk.

21

WHERE THE MAGIC HAPPENS

The inside of Frogmaggog's stomach was hot, dark, and smelly. In fact, Wilmot noted, it felt a little like being sealed in a damp and spongy sleeping bag— not exactly fun, but not fatal either. At least, not so far.

I wonder if I'm causing him indigestion, he thought, and secretly hoped he was.

He was just wondering whether it would be even more uncomfortable for Frogmaggog if he tried jumping up and down, when the stomach walls enveloping him quivered. There was a gurgling rumble from all around him, a moment of pressure, and with a sudden rush, he was propelled up and out of Frogmaggog's gut. He sailed from the cavernous mouth, tumbled through the air, and landed on a cold, hard floor that knocked the wind out of him.

Wilmot waited for the fireworks inside his skull to clear, then warily opened his eyes.

Frogmaggog loomed over him, wiping a string of drool from his chins. "You're still with us, outworlder," he boomed. "Good. I wasn't sure which stomach you'd ended up in. I've got two of them, you see." He patted his great belly. "One for storage and one for digestion. I was aiming for storage, but I sometimes miss."

Wilmot sat up and looked about. They were no longer in the throne room, but a smaller, darker chamber of rough-hewn pink stone. The ceiling was low enough that Frogmaggog had to stoop to avoid scraping his head, and the space was lit by the flickering glow of pure magic. It leeched out from between the stones to form wavering balls of light that bobbed through the air, hissing and fizzing away into nothing. Their restless light glinted off an array of jars that filled the shelves lining the walls. Wilmot caught fleeting glimpses of their contents: a collection of bulbous eyeballs clustered together like frog spawn, wriggling wormlike creatures, bright red starfish, shark teeth, and countless other things that he couldn't even identify. He also saw that he and Frogmaggog weren't alone—a handful of Hydroboreans, both newts and frogs, cowered in the chamber's gloomier recesses, trying to look inconspicuous.

"Well?" said Frogmaggog. "Aren't you going to thank me?"

Wilmot got to his feet and straightened his uniform, doing his best to ignore how damp and sticky it was. "Quite the opposite," he said. "You have impeded two Impossible Postal operatives in the course of their duties and stolen an item of registered mail. These are criminal offenses that can result in a fine or even a custodial sentence. Now, I'm willing to let the matter drop if you will return the book and reunite me with my deputy postal operative so we can complete our delivery." He fixed Frogmaggog with what he hoped was a commanding look, although he couldn't stop the tips of his ears from trembling nervously.

Frogmaggog narrowed his eyes. "I don't need your permission to take what's rightfully mine," he said. "And it's not too late for me to eat you for real."

Wilmot did his best to keep his fear in check. "You could have done that already," he said. "But you brought me here instead, which means you must need me for something."

Frogmaggog grunted. "You're a smart one, I'll give you that. This is the Sanctum, at the top of my tower. It's the source of all the city's magic." He looked around the chamber, causing the Hydroboreans to whimper with fear. "Where's the sorcerer?" he demanded. "I need him."

The Hydroboreans all looked to a painfully thin newt woman, who, after a few moments' hesitation, shuffled forward into the light. She held a spiny silver sea urchin in her hands.

"Please, Your Greatness," she said, her voice shaking. "Here he is."

"Give him to the outworlder," said Frogmaggog.

Wilmot, not knowing what else to do, accepted the urchin from the terrified Hydroborean, who immediately retreated. The urchin's spines prickled his palms. "This doesn't look much like a sorcerer," he said.

"Not yet," Frogmaggog replied, and snapped his fingers. The urchin erupted in a flash of light that made Wilmot screw his eyes shut. When he opened them again, he wasn't holding an urchin but a warm, wrinkled human hand, poking out of a dirty white shirtsleeve. The hand, the shirtsleeve, and the arm inside it belonged to a small elderly man with a lined face, an unkempt beard, and a shock of silver hair that stood on end, much like the spines of the urchin had. His eyes were sharp and keen, and they darted around the room before settling on Wilmot.

"Oh no," said the man. "Not you."

Wilmot released his hand and recoiled in shock. He

recognized the man only too well, although he looked far scruffier than the last time they had met, and the beard was a new addition. Someone would have to update the Wanted posters. "Lord Meridi—" he started, before correcting himself. "Aybek! What are you doing here?"

"Wilmot Grunt," Aybek replied. "I could ask you the same question."

Frogmaggog squinted down at them. "You two know each other?"

"Unfortunately," said Aybek, attempting to pat his hair into some sort of order. "Be careful of this one, Your Greatness. He's a troublemaker."

"Me?" said Wilmot indignantly. "You're the most wanted criminal in the Impossible Places."

"Nonsense," said Aybek. "As I explained to His Greatness when I arrived here last week, I am the Chief Librarian of the Ivory Tower and the foremost magical practitioner in the Impossible Places. My reputation is exemplary."

The hollow voice of the book spoke from inside Frogmaggog's fist. "You are Aybek Aranrhod," it said. "Formerly Lord Meridian. Wanted for conspiracy, espionage, high treason, and sundry other offenses. Reward for information leading to capture."

Frogmaggog opened his hand to reveal the book on his palm, and Aybek's mouth dropped open. "But how...?"

"It's alive, it talks, and it absorbs information," Wilmot replied. "Including your Wanted poster."

Frogmaggog laughed at Aybek's look of astonishment. "I always know a liar when I see one," he said. "That's why I've been keeping you as a crustacean when I don't need you."

Aybek looked devastated. He put a hand to a metal collar fixed around his neck and grimaced. "It's an echinoderm, actually," he said. "And what do you need me for now, exactly? More childish enchantments?"

"I want the magic inside this book," said Frogmaggog. "You, this new outworlder, and these other miserable wretches are going to break the spell holding it closed." He picked the book up between thumb and forefinger and thrust it at Aybek.

"But that's mail tampering," said Wilmot, aghast. "No self-respecting Postmaster would ever consider such a thing."

"Then start considering it," said Frogmaggog. "Because your lives depend on it."

Aybek accepted the book with a weary sigh. "There's no use arguing, Master Grunt. I'm afraid he's left us little choice." He raised his eyes to Frogmaggog's. "We'll do as you order, but I can't promise quick results. The binding spell is extremely strong. People in the Impossible Places have been trying to break it for thousands of years without success."

Frogmaggog gestured at the crackling energy bobbing through the air around them. "You're surrounded by pure magic," he said. "If this isn't enough power to reverse the spell then why do you bother to call yourselves sorcerers?"

Wilmot, who thought it safest not to mention the fact that he'd never claimed to be a sorcerer at all, kept his mouth shut. The book, however, was less diplomatic.

"I will not open for anyone but Ina," it said. "Take me to her."

Frogmaggog reddened. "I'm the Master of Magic, not her," he growled. "That means whatever's written on your pages belongs to me and nobody else." He was becoming so angry that fat beads of sweat were breaking out on his skin.

"Dare I ask who Ina is?" Aybek whispered out of the side of his mouth.

"It's a long story," Wilmot replied. Which was true, he supposed, although even if it hadn't been, he wasn't about to trust Aybek with the truth about Ina.

"You don't understand," Frogmaggog shouted at the book. "Without the magic of the founders, we're all doomed. Hydroborea is crumbling and nothing else can stop it!"

Wilmot looked at the titanic figure in bewilderment. His sweat was beginning to give off thick, greenish steam, and the more of it that rose into the air, the smaller Frogmaggog became. He was shrinking before Wilmot's very eyes.

"Oh no!" cried Frogmaggog, looking down at himself in horror. "Not again! It's too soon!" He reached for Aybek, who stepped calmly out of range. "Help me!" Frogmaggog implored. "I need more potion."

"I've warned you," Aybek replied. "The more you use the potion, the quicker it wears off."

Frogmaggog turned his desperate pleas on Wilmot. "You!" he blubbered, a burst of steam escaping from his mouth. "You can make it for me, can't you?"

Wilmot retreated several steps in alarm. "I don't know what you're talking about," he said. "What's happening?" He looked around for support, but neither Aybek nor the Hydroboreans made any move to help.

At last, with a final pathetic gasp of steam, Frogmaggog pitched forward onto the floor, unconscious. He was already half his normal size, and his body continued to shrivel.

Wilmot stood rooted to the spot, wondering what to do. Should he try to help, or to escape? Before he could make up his mind, the wizard clapped his hands for attention.

"Come along, ladies and gentlemen, you all know the drill. The sooner we get this thundering oaf his potion, the sooner he'll be back on his feet and out the door. We all want him gone, don't we?"

The Hydroboreans sprang into action, pulling jars from the shelves, hurrying to workbenches, and emptying ingredients into frying pans and mixing bowls.

With a feeble hiss, Frogmaggog finally stopped shrinking, and the steam dissipated to reveal a figure that was barely larger than Wilmot himself.

"He looks like a normal Hydroborean," said Wilmot.

"Because that's precisely what he is," said Aybek. "You didn't think he could grow to such a gigantic size naturally, did you? He uses the enlarging potion that he forces us to make in this magical sweatshop of his."

"Is that what this place is?" asked Wilmot.

Aybek nodded. "The Sanctum is a prison for anyone in Hydroborea who displays even a hint of magical ability. They're put to work providing His Greatness with whatever spells and enchantments his ego demands, including this nasty little contraption." He indicated the collar around his neck. "Speaking of which, why not make yourself useful and bring me Frogmaggog's signet ring?"

Wilmot shuffled on the spot, instinctively mistrustful. "What do you need it for?"

"To facilitate our escape from this dreadful place, of course," Aybek replied. "The ring gives Frogmaggog a psychic link to the collars. As long as he's wearing it, he can transform his prisoners in almost any way he pleases. He'll be coming to soon, so I suggest you hurry up. And don't let any of the others see you. They can't all be trusted."

Still trying to keep one eye on Aybek, Wilmot stooped down beside Frogmaggog and pretended to examine him. As discreetly as he could, he pulled the ring from the Master of Magic's unresisting finger. It had shrunk along with the rest of him, but it was still heavy and hummed with hidden power. "I don't understand" he said as he slipped the ring behind his back to Aybek. "Why does Frogmaggog need prisoners to do his magic for him? I thought he was already the most powerful sorcerer in the city."

Aybek gave a humorless laugh and slipped the ring into his trouser pocket. "My dear Master Grunt, you probably have more magical ability in your little finger than Frogmaggog has in his whole body."

"Me?" said Wilmot. "But I'm hardly magical at all."

"Precisely. Frogmaggog's a fraud. Even basic spells are beyond him. His only real power is fear, and he's hanging on to that by his fingertips."

Aybek crossed to an empty workbench some distance

from the others and picked a strip of dried seaweed from an open pot, knotting it into a rough circle. Then he drew a stick of coral from a rusty old can full of them, raised it aloft, and caught a passing ball of magic on its tip. With a flick and a whispered incantation, he tapped the coral against the seaweed, which immediately began to reshape itself. Within a few seconds, it had become an exact copy of the signet ring.

"A cheap and nasty illusion," said Aybek as the coral wand crumbled to dust in his hand. "But it should do the trick. Put this back on him, would you please?"

Wilmot took the fake ring and surreptitiously slid it onto Frogmaggog's finger. "Does this mean he can't turn you into a sea urchin anymore?" he asked.

"Thankfully," said Aybek, brushing the coral dust from his hands. "It's a considerable weight off my mind. The rest of the plan, unfortunately, depends on you."

Wilmot started with alarm. "What do you mean?"

"You came to Hydroborea, so I assume you have a means of getting out again," said Aybek. "Is the Express waiting for you somewhere in the city? If so, I expect the crew are attempting some form of ill-conceived rescue attempt as we speak."

"The Express isn't here," said Wilmot curtly. "Suzy and I came in the H.E.C., through the eye of the great void storm."

Aybek cocked an eyebrow. "The great void storm, you say? Why didn't you simply take the direct route?"

"I thought that was the direct route," said Wilmot. "You mean there's another way?"

For the first time, Aybek regarded Wilmot with genuine interest. "How fascinating. You've rediscovered Hydroborea, and yet you don't actually know where it is." A knowing smile spread slowly across his face. "You'll kick yourself when you find out. You needn't have gone to so much trouble."

Wilmot flared his nostrils. "Nothing is too much trouble for a postie," he said. "How did you find your way here?"

"Because I'm the cleverest man alive, of course," said Aybek. "And with the library of the Ivory Tower at my disposal for so many years, I was bound to figure out the city's location eventually. I'd always intended to pay a visit, but my schedule never allowed for it. However, after you and your meddlesome friends relieved me of my duties, I persuaded Tenebrae that he and I should make our way here. We were fast wearing out our welcome in the Union, and besides, I was curious to see if I was right."

"Tenebrae's here, too?" Wilmot looked around the chamber in alarm.

"Don't trouble yourself," said Aybek. "He's probably languishing in a dungeon somewhere, if he hasn't already been eaten." And he dismissed all thought of Tenebrae with a wave of his hand. "Tell me about the H.E.C. Where is it now?"

"It's moored in the abandoned zone down in the Lowertwist district," said Wilmot. "But before you go hatching any schemes, it's inoperable. The engines are burned out."

Aybek's brow furrowed a little. "That makes things trickier," he said. "But is the vessel still watertight? Would it survive a trip to the surface?"

Wilmot's suspicions deepened. "Maybe. But you're not setting foot in it without me, Suzy, and the Chief. And we're not leaving until we've delivered the book to Ina."

"Ever the dutiful Postmaster, I see," said Aybek.

Their conversation was interrupted by the Hydroboreans, who approached carrying a small cauldron of bubbling gray liquid among them.

"It's ready," said the newt woman. "It's as strong as we could make it."

At the same moment, a heavy pounding started on the Sanctum door, making everyone jump.

"Your Greatness!" shouted a Watch Frog voice from outside. "Are you still in there? Is everything all right?"

"Blast," said Aybek as the Hydroboreans scattered for cover. "I got distracted. Quickly, Master Grunt, help me with this."

They picked up the cauldron and lugged it to Frog-maggog's side.

"Open his mouth," Aybek ordered.

Wilmot couldn't think of anything he wanted to do less than touch Frogmaggog's cold and clammy face, but he forced himself to reach down and, very gingerly, part his lips.

Aybek pulled a rusty ladle off a nearby shelf, then thought better of it, tossed it over his shoulder, and tipped the cauldron's contents directly into Frogmag-gog's mouth. The gray liquid disappeared down his throat with a noise like a drain being unblocked, and a bright red glow began radiating from his belly. It spread to his limbs and face, until his whole body was glowing like a light bulb. And as the glow intensified, Frogmag-gog began to grow, quicker and quicker.

Wilmot and Aybek retreated to the workbench as the Master of Magic sat up and opened his eyes. "What happened?" he said, looking at his shining fingers. A few seconds later, the glow faded, and he was his huge, monstrous self again. "Ah," he sighed, stretching his arms until his knuckles grazed the ceiling. "That's more like it."

Aybek looked mildly disgusted. "The effects should last until tomorrow," he said. "But please try not to exert yourself before then. It only hastens your return to your natural size."

Frogmaggog was still getting to his feet when the door burst open and two Watch Frogs leaped into the room, their tridents drawn. They stopped short upon seeing Frogmaggog and bowed.

"Your Greatness!" said one. "Is everything all right? We feared for your safety."

"Everything's fine," rumbled Frogmaggog. "I was just telling these outworlders what I expect of them." He glowered at Wilmot and Aybek. "Open the book and tell me its secrets. Do it quickly, and I'll let you live."

"How generous," said Aybek. His eyes strayed to the two Watch Frogs, who were still standing awkwardly inside the door. "But if I might make a request...?" he said.

"Out with it," said Frogmaggog. "I've got a city to run."

"In the interest of security, perhaps it would be wise to station these two Watch Frogs here in the Sanctum for the rest of the day. After all, are you sure this new outworlder can be trusted?"

Wilmot puffed his chest out indignantly but knew better than to answer back. He maintained a dignified expression as Frogmaggog leaned down and scrutinized him at close range.

"Maybe you're right," said Frogmaggog. "He didn't want to cooperate earlier. You two!" His signaled to the

Watch Frogs. "Stay here and keep a close eye on this outworlder. I don't want him trying to make off with my book."

"Yes, Your Greatness!" The two frogs bowed as Frogmaggog lumbered out, then took up their posts in front of the door, fixing Aybek and Wilmot with some well-practiced scowls.

Wilmot turned his back on them and dragged the empty cauldron to a workbench, where Aybek was already setting out tools and ingredients. "What did you do that for?" Wilmot whispered, pretending to help. "Escaping's going to be a lot harder with those two watching our every move."

"Leave that to me," said Aybek. "In fact, leave everything to me."

"Except this," said Wilmot, picking up the book and holding it tight. "I don't want you tampering with it."

"Oh please," said Aybek. "I spent years trying to open it at the Ivory Tower and got nowhere. I'm hardly going to be any more successful here."

"Only Ina may open me," said the book.

"There, you see?" said Aybek. "Now, please stop complaining. We both have very important work to do."

"What work?" said Wilmot.

Aybek handed him the empty cauldron. "You can wash up."

22

THE HOUSE WITH CHICKEN WINGS

It took a couple of hours for Frederick and the others to find Propellendorf's only pet shop, but once they did it was easy to spot. It was a wooden cottage with a roof of unruly thatch, and it was floating about ten feet off the ground, near the base of the city's southwest roto-spire. Wisps of purple smoke rose from its chimney, and its shutters and doorway were gaily painted with interweaving patterns of wildflowers that had Frederick thinking of the canal boats that plied the waterways of his old home in the Western Fenlands. Unlike the boats, however, the cottage boasted a pair of enormous white feathered wings that sprouted from its sides. They flapped lazily, keeping the house steady in the air, while a noisy chorus of grunts, growls, caws, and squawks came from its open doorway. A painted sign above the door read PALDABRA'S EXOTIC PET EMPORIUM.

"I dunno," said Fletch, looking at the shop sideways. "How is this supposed to help us fix the H.E.C.?"

"I admit it's a long shot," said Frederick. "But if I'm right, they could have exactly what we need." A rope ladder unfurled like a tongue from inside the door as they approached the building, and they scrambled up it.

The shop was full—full of noise, full of the hot, thick stink of living things, and full from floor to ceiling with hutches, crates, tanks, and cages of every shape and size, containing the strangest collection of creatures Frederick had ever seen in one place. There was a cage full of disembodied green hands that scuttled around like spiders on their pointed claws. Another contained a two-tailed cat with fur that seemed to be made of fire. It regarded them indifferently as they passed. Frederick was so distracted by it that he accidentally bumped into a large fish tank, causing a shoal of what looked like miniature mermaids inside it to scatter for cover. It was only when he steadied the tank with his hands and the creatures slowly reemerged from hiding that he realized that, while they did indeed have fish tails, their top halves were hairy and simian-like. A sign fixed to the tank said SEA MONKEYS.

"I'll be right with you!" came a deep female voice from a half-open doorway behind the counter. "Feel free to browse, but watch out for the death worms. Their venom sacs have just grown in, and they like to spit."

Suzy's mom slipped her hand into her husband's. "I'm beginning to think we got off lightly with just the boggart," she said.

The shopkeeper—Paldabra, Frederick assumed— emerged from behind the counter. She *wasn't* an enormous tortoise, but it took him a few moments to realize that, because she certainly looked like one. She was old and hunched, and wore a giant tortoise shell as though it were an armored tank top. The skin of her neck hung in wrinkled curtains, and she blinked at them through a pair of thick spectacles that made her eyes look huge and earnest. Her gray hair was in curlers underneath another, smaller tortoise shell, which she wore like a helmet.

"Sorry to keep you waiting," she said, peeling off a pair of leather gauntlets. "I was in the back room feeding the bunyip pups. They're always a bit feisty." She adjusted her spectacles to get a better look at their group. "Out-of-towners, are you? Looking for a gift? I've got a sale on jackalopes at the moment. Or, if you're after something with a bit more novelty value, I've got a talking mongoose called Geff. I warn you, though, he does like to go on about politics."

293

"We're actually looking for something a bit more specific," said Frederick. "And rare."

Paldabra leaned against the counter, suddenly serious. "Then you're in the right place, young man," she said. "Because rare is my specialty."

"We're looking for a thermo-demon," said Frederick.

Paldabra raised the knobbly lumps where her eyebrows should have been. "That really *is* specific," she said. "And not to be taken lightly. Thermo-demons can be difficult creatures to live with if you don't know what you're doing."

"Oh, we know what we're doing all right," said Frederick airily, only to be interrupted by a tug on his sleeve. He looked round to find Suzy's mom leaning toward him.

"What's a thermo-demon?" she whispered.

"They're a magical and evolutionary fluke," he whispered back. "I remember browsing through a book about them when I was re-cataloging the zoology section last month."

"But do we *want* a demon?" asked Suzy's dad. "Aren't they nasty, fiery, dangerous things?"

"Only a handful of demon varieties are harmful to others," Paldabra said indignantly. "And I don't let any of my creatures leave this shop unless I'm certain they're going to a good home. You've got to give me some assurance you know how to care for it properly."

Frederick raised his hands in a pacifying gesture. "I've done my research," he said.

"How much research?" said Paldabra dubiously.

With a conspiratorial smile at the others, Frederick drew a business card from his pocket and handed it over. "I think this will put your mind at ease."

Paldabra raised her glasses and squinted at the card. "It's blank."

Frederick's smirk vanished. "What?" Paldabra handed the card back and he flipped it over in disbelief. Both sides were completely bare. He rubbed at them with his thumbs, willing the letters to appear, until he realized what was wrong. "Of course," he groaned. "*The Book of Power.*" He tossed the card over his shoulder. "Listen, you can trust me. I'm the Chief Librarian of the Ivory Tower."

"And I'm the Lead Gymnast at the Circus Palooza," said Paldabra. "Now prove you're not a complete nincompoop or get out of my shop."

"How's about this?" Fletch shouldered Frederick aside and slapped his own dog-eared, oil-stained ID card on the counter. "And I can vouch for the boy. He might not look much, but he's got it up 'ere." He tapped the side of his head.

Paldabra picked up the card and pursed her lips. "Impossible Postal Service," she said. "That might be acceptable. But thermo-demons don't come cheap."

"Then it's just as well the company is picking up the tab," said Fletch. "Can you help us or not?"

Paldabra raised the card to one eye, scrutinizing every letter. "You know what?" she said, handing it back with a satisfied smile. "I think I can."

She shuffled out from behind the counter, pausing to retrieve a long wooden pole with a metal hook on one end from against the wall. Then she waved the others aside and moved to the middle of the room, staring up into the rafters as she went. Frederick followed her gaze and saw more cages hanging up there in the shadows.

The shopkeeper turned in a slow circle, tapping one finger against the side of her face and studying the undersides of the cages. "This one," she said, pointing at a large bell-shaped birdcage wrapped in a silk scarf. She reached up with the pole, unhooked the cage, and lowered it gently until it was hanging at eye level. The others gathered round.

"This little fellow's been with me for a while now," said Paldabra, lowering her voice. "I saved him from a sandstorm in the petrified forest of Kulch. He'd got confused and was trying to count every last grain, the poor thing. Another few minutes and he would have been done for. Let me introduce you." She removed the silk cloth.

Frederick stared at the creature in the cage. It was a fat, furry red caterpillar, about six inches long, with a pair of stubby black horns on top of its bulbous head, and a single green eye that blinked at them all with undisguised curiosity.

"*That's* a demon?" said Suzy's dad.

"I call him Maxwell," said the shopkeeper.

"Who are they?" said Maxwell, in a high-pitched buzz of a voice. "Tourists? They look like tourists. All stupid and clueless. I don't like them."

"Charming," said Frederick.

"And this is the stupidest and most clueless one," said Maxwell, pointing at Frederick with his tail. "I bet he gives the others lessons in being stupid and clueless. He's probably got a teaching degree in stupid and clueless, from Stupid and Clueless University. A university they built just for him. Because he's so stupid and clueless."

"Hey!" protested Frederick. "I happen to be a very important librarian." But Maxwell didn't hear him—he was too busy bouncing around inside his cage, making a series of "duuuuh!" noises. "Somebody tell him!" said Frederick.

"I think I'm warming to him already," said Suzy's mom, fighting to keep a straight face. Frederick glowered at her.

"Maxwell?" said the shopkeeper. "These people want to give you a new home. Would you like to go with them?"

Maxwell settled back on his perch and cocked his head

toward her. "Depends," he said. "Will there be work to do? I'm bored here."

"We've got lots for you to do," said Frederick. "Some very important counting and sorting."

"I like counting and sorting," said Maxwell. "I'm best at it."

"So I've read," said Frederick. "So, are you in?"

Maxwell leaned forward on his perch, eyeing each of

them in turn, before settling on Frederick again. "Only if I can call you Professor Stupid."

"No deal," said Frederick.

"Yes deal," said Fletch. "Wilmot and Suzy are running out of time to deliver this book of yours. If you want to get 'em out of the void storm an' save your library, we need to get movin'."

Maxwell stuck his tongue out and blew a loud raspberry at Frederick.

The shopkeeper gave a sigh of contentment. "I never know how to feel when one of my creatures leaves me," she said. "Sad that they're going, or happy to know they've found a proper home at last."

"I'm not sure how happy to feel either," muttered Frederick.

"Let's settle the payment, and I'll let you be on your way," said the shopkeeper. She handed the cage to Frederick and stumped back toward the counter, followed by Fletch.

"Hello, Professor Stupid," said Maxwell, his voice dripping with smug satisfaction. Frederick pressed the cage into Suzy's parents' hands.

"Please stop calling me that," he said.

"Okay, Professor," said Maxwell. "Where are we going?"

"Into the void. Do you think you can handle that?"

Maxwell's eye widened. "You mean the one inside your head? I hear it's infinite!" He laughed so hard he fell off his perch and bounced around the cage like a spring.

Frederick gave him a withering look. "We're on a mission to save our friends, and we need your help. Believe me, if we didn't, I'd leave you here."

"I'm sorry to ask," said Suzy's dad, "but how exactly *can* Maxwell help us?"

"If I'm right," said Frederick, "Maxwell should be able to do the same job as the bifurcator. He'll sort the fuel molecules for the H.E.C.'s engine."

Suzy's mom raised an eyebrow. "*If* you're right?"

Frederick gave a nervous laugh. "I'm pretty sure he can do it," he said. "Can't you, Maxwell?"

"How should I know?" Maxwell replied. Frederick felt his spirits sink.

Fletch returned from the counter, rubbing his hands together. "Some poor soul in the Postal Service accounts department is going to get a shock when they see the bill," he said. "So I hope this idea of yours works, lad."

"So do we," said Suzy's mom darkly.

"You people aren't making any sense at all," said Maxwell. "The Professor's lack of brains must be catching."

"Does he come with a silencing spell or something?" asked Frederick.

"I'll buy you earplugs," said Fletch. He took the cage from Frederick and grinned at the little demon. "Welcome to the crew, Maxwell. It's time to go and rescue our friends."

23
A NIGHT ON THE TILES

Suzy and Ina fled across the uneven landscape of the city's rooftops using every means at their disposal. Ina led the way up old fire escapes, along crumbling balustrades, through derelict attics, and across swaying washing lines high above the streets. It's like some bizarre form of mountaineering, Suzy thought, made even more treacherous by the heavy downpour. Every peak they crested was a triumph, although her body was soon aching with the effort.

The sounds of the Watch Frogs' pursuit had faded, though, and when she paused to look downhill, she saw just how far they had come—Ina's building wasn't even visible anymore.

"You've done this before," Suzy said.

"Every night," Ina confirmed. "It's how I deliver the *Scuttle*. I can't exactly go door to door with it, so I drop it down people's chimneys."

Suzy looked ahead of them, up the city's narrowing curve. "Can we make it all the way to the tower like this?"

"Probably," said Ina. "I just don't know what we'll do when we get there."

Another ominous roll of thunder sounded overhead, making them both flinch.

"The city's never made noises like that before," said Ina. "Whatever it is, it's getting worse. I don't like it."

She wasn't the only one. Doors and windows flew open along the street as scores of Hydroboreans poked their heads outside, searching anxiously for the source of the noise.

As Suzy looked up at the pearlescent roof of the city, she wondered if the cracks seemed to be spreading ... She didn't get much chance to dwell on the question before the rising wail of the Watch Frogs' siren drew her attention to the street below. She joined Ina in the shadow of an ornate chimney and watched a fleet of S-Cargo Units roar past. Each drew a train of detention trailers behind it, loaded with Hydroborean citizens, and there were so many vehicles that it took almost two minutes for the last of them to pass by. Suzy saw Amlod in one of the trailers, trussed up beside the newspaper seller, who was struggling feebly against the kraken's tentacles.

"It looks like they arrested the whole street!" said Ina in disbelief. "Why would they do that?"

"Frogmaggog must have sent them to find *us*," said Suzy. "He wanted to stop me telling you about the book, and stop you trying to reach it."

"But those people don't have anything to do with that," said Ina. "What's he going to do with them all?" A look of horror passed over her face. "You don't think...?"

Suzy nodded somberly.

"*Amlod!*" Ina whispered.

"If we hurry, we might be able to find a way to save him," said Suzy. "How far left to go?"

Ina fought back her distress and looked around. "Too far." She pointed uphill to a large powder-blue building that made Suzy think of a temple or church. Its gilded dome rose a full story above the buildings surrounding it, supported by rows of graceful columns. "That's the Baleen Ballroom. It means we're only halfway there."

"Then let's be quick," said Suzy.

It took Suzy and Ina only a few minutes to reach the building adjacent to the ballroom, and a running jump carried them both across a narrow side street onto a stone balcony that ran around the base of the dome.

"There should be an old fire escape on the other side," said Ina, setting off along the balcony. "We can use it to jump to the next building, but I haven't been much farther than that before. We'll have to make it up as we go along."

Suzy opened her mouth to tell Ina that this was what she had been doing all day anyway, but was drowned out by an almighty clap of thunder that sounded terrifyingly close. She covered her ears with her hands and squinted up into the rain.

"What was that?" said Ina, skidding to a halt.

"I think the city's roof is unstable," Suzy replied.

"Not the noise, I mean that thing, up there." Ina pointed into the gloom overhead. "Something moved, I'm sure it did."

Suzy shielded her eyes with her hands. She could barely see anything through the downpour, but after a few seconds' concentration, she caught a quick, darting movement high above them. It slipped out of sight, only to reappear directly overhead. She got a vague impression of wide-spread wings, and relaxed. "It's just some sort of bird," she said.

She made to move on, but Ina's look of confusion made her stop.

"What's a bird?" asked Ina.

Suzy looked up again, straight into a pair of fiery yellow eyes.

"Look out!" she shouted, screwing her own eyes shut and pushing Ina aside. She threw herself in the opposite direction with barely a second to spare, as Tenebrae arrowed down out of the sky and struck the spot where they had been standing.

"Postie," he snarled, getting heavily to his feet. "At last."

Suzy opened her eyes but kept them on the sharp curve of his talons. "What are you doing here, Tenebrae?"

"Surviving," he said. "Frogmaggog wants you gone and so do I." He advanced on her and she retreated, trying to lead him away from Ina.

"Another outworlder!" Ina exclaimed, too fascinated to be scared. "Wow, you guys are everywhere today."

"Don't look him in the eyes," Suzy warned. "He'll put you in a trance. That's how he attacks his victims."

"Cool!" said Ina.

"I say, that *does* sound interesting," said the Chief, emerging from Suzy's satchel. "Sorry, I'd have popped out to say hello sooner, but I got a bit lost in my own thoughts."

Tenebrae didn't register any surprise at the Chief's sudden appearance, but his pace faltered when the metal collar around his neck gave a crackle of magical energy.

Suzy didn't recognize the collar, but just for an instant, she thought Tenebrae looked scared. She took the opportunity to put a little more distance between them.

"So you work for Frogmaggog now?" she said, still falling back. "He hates people like us. Outworlders."

"And I hate him," said Tenebrae, shaking off his hesitation and stalking after her. "But it's your life or mine."

He lunged at her suddenly, beating his wings for an extra burst of speed. Suzy tried to jump clear, but he was too fast for her and knocked her onto her back.

"Steady on, you ruffian!" said the Chief, raising his fists. Tenebrae simply stepped through him and reached for Suzy's throat. But before he could close his talons around it, Ina cannoned into him from behind.

"Get off my friend!" she shouted. Her blow caught him off guard and he stumbled forward, tripping over Suzy and sprawling on the ground.

Suzy jumped to her feet and joined hands with Ina, and together they fled, hand in hand, around the base of the dome. "Friend of yours?" said Ina.

"I'll explain later," said Suzy. "We're easy targets for him out here. We need to get indoors."

"I know a way," Ina replied, and pointed to a pair of double doors leading into the dome. They swerved toward them and were only a few steps away when Tenebrae landed in front of them.

"That's far enough," he snarled.

He crouched, ready to spring, but before he got the chance, there was a blast of thunder so deafening it drove all three of them to their knees, their hands clamped over their ears. The whole city seemed to shake with it. Cracks ran up the ballroom's golden dome. Windows shattered.

Suzy raised her head as the noise faded to a deep-throated roar that rolled across the rooftops like a break-ing wave, dislodging loose tiles and knocking chimneys askew. "What was that?" she said.

As if in answer, the city's roof split open above them, and a foaming, freezing wall of seawater spewed in. It struck the ballroom's dome and cascaded down its sides, flowing over the balcony like a tidal wave. It swept the three of them off their feet and hurled them into the bal-ustrade. Suzy clung to the wet marble as the torrent tried to pry her off and throw her over the edge into the street.

Then, with a rending crash, the dome surrendered and fell inward. The umbrella of water followed it, and in a moment there was nothing left but a gaping hole in the center of the ballroom, surrounded by the balcony.

Shaken, bruised, and spitting seawater, Suzy and Ina got to their feet. Tenebrae lay beside them, grasping at his head and groaning.

"Are we all still breathing?" said the Chief, poking his head out of Suzy's satchel. "That sounded like a close one."

"Too close," said Suzy. The waterfall was already filling up the ballroom like a leaky bucket. Below the balcony, she heard its many windows and doors bursting outward under the pressure.

"It's a shell breach," said Ina, looking out across the city in dismay. "It's finally happened. Hydroborea's magic has failed us."

Across the Midtwist district, the web of cracks in the city's roof opened wide and the sea rushed in, turning the streets into churning rapids of whitewater. Waves battered the housefronts, smashing open doors and windows, and raising a chorus of panic from every building.

"Get to high ground!" someone shouted.

"Only the Master of Magic can save us!" cried another.

Within moments hundreds of Hydroboreans emerged from their homes into the flood, holding children and possessions aloft as they struggled uphill, one painful step at a time. It was terrible to look upon, but neither Suzy nor Ina could tear their gaze away.

"This is the end," said Ina.

"Not if we can unlock the book," said Suzy. "It's our only hope now."

"But how are we going to get there through all this?"

said Ina as a jagged section of the city's roof fell in and reduced a nearby building to rubble.

"I hate to sound fatalistic, but Ina's got a point," said the Chief.

Suzy shut her eyes against the chaos and tried to think. Between the floodwaters and the crowds, the streets would be impassible, and crossing the rooftops would be slow and dangerous. And she still had no idea how to get into the Gilded Tower when they reached it. Unless...

She crouched down beside Tenebrae, careful to keep out of striking range. "Tell me what you're doing in Hydroborea," she said. "Because I know you didn't come here for me."

Tenebrae sat up. He did his best to look defiant but mostly looked dazed and bedraggled. "It was Aybek's idea," he said, slurring his words slightly. "We were on the run back home in the Union, but Lady Crepuscula was closing in, and we were running out of options." He swiped at her, but it was a clumsy effort, and she easily darted clear. He hissed in annoyance but made no further move to pursue her.

"Aybek said we should come here instead," he continued. "The lost city. It was supposed to be the perfect hiding place, but everything went wrong as soon as we arrived."

Suzy bit her lip. She knew exactly how that felt.

"Now I have to follow Frogmaggog's orders," said

Tenebrae. "Or he'll change me." He tugged at his collar, which gave another snap of magical sparks.

Suzy sat back and thought. She had already formulated an idea—it was clear and urgent, but she didn't like it one bit.

"I think we can help you," she said. "But you have to help us first."

"Suzy, come on!" said Ina. "I thought you said he was dangerous."

"He is," said Suzy. "But he's not stupid. I'm offering to save his life if he spares ours."

Tenebrae snorted. "Why should I trust you?"

"Look around you," said Suzy. "The whole city is dying, and if we keep fighting, we're going to die with it. But if you help us, we might be able to save it."

Tenebrae frowned. "I'm listening."

"Frogmaggog has a book full of ancient magic, more powerful than anything we've ever seen," said Suzy. "If we can reach it, we could use it to stop the flooding, and maybe even repair the city."

"I know the one you mean," said Tenebrae. "I heard your little troll friend's speech just before Frogmaggog ate him." He scoffed at her look of revulsion. "So you want me to get you back into the tower?"

Suzy balled her fists and fought down her anger. "Yes," she said stiffly.

"What's in it for me?" he said.

"You can't be serious," said Ina. "Everyone gets to live. Isn't that enough?" She did a double take and turned to the Chief. "No offense."

"None taken, my dear," the Chief replied.

Tenebrae tapped the point of one talon against his collar. "What about this?" he said. "What's the point in helping you save Hydroborea if I have to live as Frog-maggog's pet canary? I'd rather take him down with me."

"We can use the book's magic to stop Frogmaggog as well," said Suzy. "But we're running out of time, so hurry up and choose. Do we have a deal?"

Tenebrae climbed unsteadily to his feet. "Fine," he said. "Hold still."

He lashed out and caught them both by the wrist. Then he unfurled his wings and leaped into the air, bearing them both aloft.

"Whoa!" shouted Suzy as the balcony dropped away beneath her feet.

"Stop wriggling," he said. "I won't lose any sleep if I drop you."

Suzy clamped her mouth shut and tried not to think of the dizzying fall beneath her. Their lives were suddenly in Tenebrae's talons, and he could cast them aside on a whim. She shut her eyes and hoped that she had made the right choice.

24
NEOMA CALLS

The Express settled back onto the rails with scarcely a bump, and the flock of giant mechanical hummingbirds that had carried it down from Propellendorf disengaged their magnetic clamps.

Frederick stood with Suzy's parents, Fletch, and Stonker on the *Belle*'s gangway, from which they had watched the whole procedure from the start.

"Thank you kindly," said Stonker, doffing his cap at the pilots sitting on the hummingbirds' backs. They waved in return and, with a shimmer of iridescent wings, zoomed off toward the retreating bulk of the city as it drifted away over the dunes.

"I still can't believe it," said Suzy's dad. "We were on a real flying city."

"There are other sky cities out there, you know," said Frederick. "Not to mention walking cities, burrowing cities, and one that only appears by moonlight."

Suzy's dad made a series of appreciative noises as they all made their way back into the cab, where Ursel had already stoked the firebox with bananas. She had also hung Maxwell's cage from one of the hooks in the ceiling, alongside the pots and pans. The little demon sat inside it, counting a pile of lentils into a dish and buzzing happily to himself, although he looked up as the others entered.

"I missed you, Professor," he said. "For a whole five minutes there, I had no one to feel superior to."

Frederick made a point of ignoring him.

"Frrrurnk," said Ursel.

"Yes, let's not waste another moment," said Stonker. "Next stop, the void storm." He released the brake lever, and the Express eased forward, quickly gathering speed. Soon, the dunes of the Tie-Dye Desert were a multicolored blur outside the windows.

Propellendorf was barely a speck above the horizon, when the cab's phone rang.

"Somebody get that, would you?" said Stonker. "I'm busy."

"Grulk," added Ursel, her paws full of bananas.

"Fine, I'll do it," said Frederick. He picked up the receiver from the mantelpiece. "Impossible Postal Express," he said.

"Frederick!" Neoma's voice barked at him down the line, loud enough to make him wince. "I'm calling for an update. I've been following the package using that tracking spell the Postmaster put on it, and it's been sitting in the same spot for ages now. We've only got seventy-five minutes left to save the library, and Wilmot isn't answering his phone. Have you heard from him?"

"Yes," said Frederick. "He and Suzy are stuck on Hydroborea's world, so the crew and I are trying to find a way to get them back."

"What are you talking about?" said Neoma. "They're nowhere near Hydroborea's world."

"Yes, they are." Frederick blinked. "Aren't they?"

"No," said Neoma. "I'm looking at the location of the package right now, and it's on some backwater world in the Mundane Places."

"It's not supposed to be," said Frederick. "Are you sure the tracking spell isn't faulty?"

"Positive," said Neoma. "I've had Mr. Trellis monitoring it ever since the Express left Center Point Station. According to the readout, the book is sitting at the bottom of an ocean on this anonymous no-magic planet. If they've dropped it overboard, so help me, I'll..."

"Stonker, hit the brakes!" cried Frederick.

Stonker jumped in surprise. "What the blazes?"

While he stared in dismay at Frederick, Ursel reached past him and yanked the brake lever. The Express lurched to a halt, throwing them all to the floor. Maxwell's cage swung on its hook, spilling lentils everywhere.

"Nooooooo!" the demon exclaimed. "You made me lose count! That's not fair!"

"Ouch," said Suzy's dad, rubbing his head. "What was that for?"

"I'm sorry," said Frederick. "But Neoma's on the line. She's been tracking Suzy and Wilmot, and the Gold Stamp Special's still giving off a signal even outside the Union. She's got their exact location."

"Great Scott!" said Stonker. "Let's have it, then."

"Thank you for finally asking," said Neoma as Frederick set the phone to speaker mode. "I don't recognize the world they're on, and we haven't got any maps left for me to look it up, but I can send you the coordinates if that phone of yours can receive spells."

"Thrronf grulf rrrrrunk," said Ursel.

"She says it's a top-of-the-range Ether Web connection," said Stonker. "Send it through."

"Roger that," said Neoma.

The line buzzed. It sounded like a large and angry wasp was trying to crawl out of the receiver. Then several

316

wasps. Then a swarm. Frederick held the receiver at arm's length as it started to glow. With a chorus of buzzes, burps, warbles, and pops, the spell emerged into the cab.

It started as a sphere of blue light the size of a Ping-Pong ball that drifted up into the air. Then it began to expand, taking on more detail and color as it grew. Frederick saw landmasses and expanses of ocean emerge on the globe's surface, half-hidden by swirls of white cloud. It was a glowing image of a planet, and it expanded until it almost filled the cab, forcing them all to shuffle back to the edges of the room.

"Hrumph," said Ursel.

"I agree," said Stonker. "What an odd-looking place for Hydroborea to end up."

"This is it," came Neoma's voice from the receiver. "The exact location of the book is marked with a beacon." A winking speck of golden light appeared near the top of the globe, just inside the mass of ice that capped the northern pole.

"That can't be right," said Suzy's dad. "Hydroborea definitely isn't there."

"I triple-checked it," said Neoma. "That's where the book is."

"I'm not talking about the gold dot," said Suzy's dad. "I'm talking about the planet. You've got the wrong one."

"How d'you know?" asked Fletch.

Suzy's parents looked around in consternation. "Don't you recognize it?" said Suzy's mom. "That's *our* planet. That's the earth!"

Stonker regarded the image of the earth floating in the *Belle*'s cab with mild suspicion. "Are you absolutely certain?" he asked.

"We can recognize our own planet when we see it," said Suzy's dad.

"But it's just a big ball," said Stonker. "It didn't feel very round when we were standing on it earlier. Why didn't we all slide off?"

"Because our gravity always works in the right direction," said Suzy's mom. "Unlike *some* worlds I could mention."

"Hey," said Fletch. "Jus' cuz *your* gravity's borin', don't go knockin' ours."

Frederick looked again at the golden beacon. "But if this is your world, how did the H.E.C. get there from the void storm? And why did Suzy go home when she's supposed to be looking for Hydroborea?"

"She'd better not be sitting on her sofa with her feet up," said Neoma, her voice tinny and distant through the telephone. "The Union's had its identity wiped clean and people are going to start rioting once they find out. We need those words back, and quickly."

"We'll head straight to Suzy's house and see what's happening," said Stonker, reaching for the controls.

"Wait a minute," said Suzy's mom. "That dot's nowhere near our house. It's practically at the North Pole."

Stonker paused with his hand on the brake lever. "And you don't live at this North Pole?"

"No one lives there," said Suzy's dad. "It's too cold and empty."

"Then why take the book there?" asked Frederick. "Is there any way to zoom in on the beacon?"

"I think you just prod it," said Neoma.

Ursel, being the tallest in the cab, reached up and jabbed the beacon with a claw. The globe dispersed into a shower of brilliant sparks, which re-formed a moment later into a flat bird's-eye view of crinkly coastlines and a sea full of ice floes, cracked and jagged like broken glass.

"Suzy's under all that?" said her dad, his voice tightening. "But that's even worse than the void storm!"

"Do you think she tried to get home?" said Suzy's mom. "Oh, what if she changed her mind and tried to get back to us, and it all went wrong?"

"Sir, madam, control yourselves," said Stonker. "We don't know what's happened, but if that's where Suzy, the Postmaster, and the Chief are to be found, then that is where we will go. Fletch, can you sort out a tunnel for us?"

Fletch studied the map and smacked his lips. "Should be easy enough now I've got coordinates," he said.

"Leave it to us, Neoma," said Frederick. "We're already on our way."

25

RETURN TO THE TOWER

The avenue leading to the tower was already a sea of refugees, all clamoring and shouting and surging forward together, as if eager to be swallowed by the huge stone frog's head. It was chaotic, and Suzy heard the cries of the crowd as Tenebrae flew her and Ina through the late evening darkness overhead.

"Open the doors! Let us in!"

"Where's Frogmaggog? Why isn't he doing anything?"

"Please! The waters are rising! We need help!"

As they approached the carved stone head of the tower's gateway, she saw a row of Watch Frogs doing their best to keep the crowd at bay, but it was clear at a glance that they were fighting a losing battle. The crush of people was too great, and despite a makeshift barricade of S-Cargo Units, the Watch Frogs were being pressed back against the crimson doors. She spotted Commander Kecker in their midst, but luckily he was too distracted to notice them as Tenebrae swooped overhead and alighted on a window ledge high up in the throne room wall.

"Do you know where Frogmaggog put the book?" Suzy asked.

"No," said Tenebrae. "There's a staircase at the rear of the throne room that leads up through the tower, and I've overheard Frogmaggog and the guards discussing some sort of magical chamber before, but I've never seen it." He pushed the window open and a puff of perfumed steam escaped: orange blossom, Suzy noted.

She put a finger to her lips and leaned in. Through the swirling mists she saw Frogmaggog below them. Her insides churned at the very sight of him. He was wallowing in his bath again and bellowing directions at the teams of Watch Frogs who scurried in and out of the steam. The clouds parted for a moment and she saw Amlod and the other prisoners, corralled within a loose ring of guards.

"Bunch of incompetents!" Frogmaggog roared. "Double the guard at the gates and disperse that rabble. I want them back in their homes."

"But, Your Greatness," said one of the Watch Frogs, pausing in front of the bathtub. "The people are running out of homes to disperse to. Half the Midtwist district is already underwater, and if you don't use your magic soon, the city might—"

He didn't get to finish his sentence before Frogmaggog's tongue lashed out and snapped him up. The prisoners cried out in horror, and Ina turned away in disgust.

"I will use my magic when I see fit," Frogmaggog declared. "Until then, the people need to pull themselves together. How can they call themselves Hydroboreans if they're scared of a little water?"

"He's unhinged!" whispered Ina. "We've got to get Amlod and the others out of there."

"We won't last ten seconds without the book to help us," Suzy replied. "We have to find it and open it. That's the only thing that will solve all this."

Tenebrae clacked his beak impatiently. "Hurry up and find it, then," he said. "And before you do, I need to show Frogmaggog something to make him think you won't be bothering him again."

His words made Suzy's skin crawl, but she unpinned her blank Impossible Postal Service badge and handed it to him. "Use this," she said. "Frogmaggog should recognize it. But how are we going to get down?"

Tenebrae slipped the badge into his pocket. He waited until the clouds of steam obscured Frogmaggog once more, then grabbed Suzy and Ina by the arms. "Don't scream."

"Why would we scr—" Ina began, only for Tenebrae to tip forward through the window and plunge with them both headfirst toward the throne room floor.

Suzy didn't need to worry about screaming—she was too scared to even draw breath. A second before the splattering crunch of impact, Tenebrae spread his wings and glided silently into the shadows beneath the bathtub. No cries of alarm went up. They had made it.

"Hurry," he whispered. Then he was gone again, stealing out from beneath the bath and launching himself toward the rim. Frogmaggog's voice rang out, horrifyingly close, as Suzy and Ina crept away toward the rear of the throne room, hand in hand.

"Ah, my pet has returned. Did you take care of our little problem?"

"Would I have come back empty-handed?" Tenebrae said. "I told you I'd get the job done. Here's your proof."

Suzy risked looking over her shoulder. She saw the back of Frogmaggog's huge head above them as the Master of Magic raised a hand to accept her badge from Tenebrae.

"Excellent," said Frogmaggog. "It's nice to see you outworlders can be properly trained. Now get back into your cage until I need you again."

Tenebrae gave a weary nod and flew up to the cage hanging beneath the chandelier before the steam closed around Suzy and Ina, hiding him from sight. Suzy was glad. She didn't want to feel any sympathy for Tenebrae, but she couldn't help feeling disgusted at his treatment. As ruthless and savage as the owl man was, Frogmaggog was worse in every way.

They stole through the steam, navigating by sound to avoid the hurrying Watch Frogs, until they reached the rear of the throne room, where a sweeping spiral staircase led them up into the main body of the Gilded Tower.

Waves of magical energy pulsed through the gold veins in the marble, racing upward.

"I don't think I've ever seen so much raw magic in one place," said Suzy as they climbed. "It's incredible."

"I told you Frogmaggog was hoarding it all," said Ina. "There's enough for the whole city here."

"Then why doesn't he use it to stop the flooding?" Suzy asked. "It doesn't make sense."

They ducked behind a marble statue of a seahorse as a troop of Watch Frogs thundered downstairs, heading for the throne room. When the coast was clear, they moved on and soon reached a circular landing from which four passageways led.

"Which way now?" said Suzy. "It could be anywhere."

"Wait a second," said Ina. "Let me try something." She pulled her notepad and pen from her pocket and scribbled *HELLO!* in big, untidy letters. Then she held the notepad up and waited.

"What are you doing?" said Suzy, casting an anxious glance back down the stairs.

Then, very slowly, Ina's handwriting peeled off the notepad and dissolved into dark smoke, which spiraled away down one of the passages. "There," said Ina. "Follow that word!"

☙❧

Wilmot carried another stack of filthy bowls to the sink in the corner of the Sanctum, and did his best to look casual as he glanced at the two Watch Frogs standing guard at the door. They glared back at him, and he hurried about his business, carrying a jarful of glowing green eyeballs to Aybek, who was hunched over an earthenware jug at his workbench.

"Here are the kraken eggs you asked for," Wilmot said. He set the jar down and tried not to squirm too much as the eyeballs all swiveled to follow him.

"Thank you." Aybek squeezed a few drops of liquid from a sea sponge into the jug, and its contents started burning with a steady green flame. "I think this is ready now. It just needs to simmer for a bit." He set the jug carefully aside and straightened with a groan.

Wilmot inspected the other contents of the bench. Besides the flaming jug, Aybek had concocted two miniature tornadoes of swirling darkness, which he had trapped in a pair of glass bottles. Even more curious.

"Hey, you. Outworlder," said one of the Watch Frogs. "What's that stuff you're making? It looks dangerous."

Aybek smiled warmly. "I'm simply following Frogmaggog's orders," he said. "These are all necessary unbinding agents for opening *The Book of Power.*"

Wilmot frowned. Whatever these spells were, he knew they had nothing to do with unbinding the book. But as he still had no idea what Aybek's escape plan was, he could only guess what role they might actually end up playing. Aybek certainly wasn't willing to tell him, which only made him more suspicious. He would have to stay alert.

"And what about them?" said the other guard, pointing with his trident to the Hydroborean prisoners, who had retreated back into the shadows.

"They're minding their own business," said Aybek. "But I think you'll find this far more interesting."

He opened the jar of kraken eggs and selected a particularly fat specimen. It jumped in his palm and spun round to stare at him as he produced a gnarled drift-wood wand from a toolbox on the bench. "Observe." He waved the wand over the egg and muttered a brief incantation. The egg quivered like jelly, and then a slender black tentacle wormed its way out of the top. A second followed, quickly followed by a third and fourth. Each tentacle had its own eyeball on the end, and within a few seconds Aybek was holding a fully formed infant kraken. It flailed its limbs and tried to wrap itself around his arm until he carried it to a nearby fishbowl full of water and dropped it in.

"How did you do that?" demanded the first Watch Frog, halfway between wonder and fear.

"With a simple growth-acceleration spell," said Aybek. "Soon there'll be no need to wait for these creatures to mature naturally before you use them in your S-Cargo detention trailers. May I borrow your kraken caller so I can put the beastie through its paces?" He pointed to the silver conch shell on the Watch Frog's belt.

"Civilians aren't supposed to use these," the Watch Frog said.

"I'm not a civilian, I'm an outworlder," said Aybek. "And if you'd like to explain to Frogmaggog why you stopped me doing important work to help maintain law and order, be my guest."

The Watch Frog stepped forward and grudgingly unclipped the conch from his belt. "All right," he said. "But no funny business."

"I wouldn't dream of it," said Aybek.

At that moment a tremor shook the tower, making the jars rattle on the shelves.

"There's another one," said the Watch Frog to his fellow. "What d'you think's going on down there?"

"I don't know," his colleague said. "But I don't like it."

Wilmot remembered Aybek's warnings about the fate of the city and felt his pulse quicken. *I hope you're safe out there, Suzy*, he thought. *I could really use your help right now.*

The thought was still in his head when he turned to replace the jar of kraken eggs and saw the Chief's glowing blue face poking through the door. Wilmot started so suddenly that he almost dropped the jar, but the guards were too preoccupied with Aybek's work to notice.

The Chief grinned, gave him a double thumbs-up, and withdrew.

Wilmot dropped the jar on the nearest shelf and hurried back to the workbench, buzzing with excitement. If the Chief was outside, then so was Suzy.

As casually as he could, he turned to Aybek and said, "I think our delivery has just arrived."

Aybek raised an eyebrow. "I beg your pardon?"

The Watch Frogs straightened. "What delivery?" said one of them. "We weren't told about this."

"I've been looking forward to it," said Wilmot. "It's an *express* delivery." He glanced quickly at Aybek to see if he had understood.

"Ah yes," said Aybek. "*That* one. I was beginning to think it would never get here."

The guards brandished their tridents. "Nothing gets in without us checking it first," the second one said. "What is it?"

"A convenient distraction," said Aybek. "Good-bye." In one quick movement, he picked up the jug with the flaming green substance inside it, and dashed the contents in their faces.

The fire quickly enveloped them in an emerald inferno. Wilmot, appalled, rushed to help them, only to realize that they weren't actually burning. They were shrinking.

"Hey!" one of them shouted, looking down at his diminishing body. "What have you done to us?"

"I've cut you down to size," said Aybek. "Try not to take it personally."

"This is an arrestable offense!" said the second guard in a mouse-like squeak as he and his colleague grew smaller and smaller. At last, when they were barely more than two inches tall, the process stopped.

Wilmot approached the minuscule figures, who

jumped up and down and waved their tridents angrily at him. "I suppose I'd better put you two somewhere safe before you get trodden on," he said.

"Yes, I'd hate to go through the rest of my day with Watch Frog on the bottom of my shoe," said Aybek. "And after that perhaps you'd better let Miss Smith in."

Wilmot scooped up the protesting Watch Frogs in his hands and dropped them as carefully as he could into an empty jar before hurrying to the door. The moment he unlatched it, it was thrown open from outside and he was almost knocked off his feet by Suzy, who rushed in and threw her arms around him. Ina followed close behind her, and the Chief hovered in the air above them.

"Wilmot!" she cried. "I couldn't believe it when the Chief said you were in here. You're alive!"

"Only just," he said. "Frogmaggog spat me out and he's been holding me here ever since. It hasn't been much fun."

"Oh boy," said Ina. "You have no idea how annoying it is not to be able to take notes right now. What a story! SWALLOWED ALIVE: MY TALE OF TERROR BY WILMOT GRUNT. If we live through this, it's going to be my next headline."

"That's rather a big 'if,'" said Aybek.

Wilmot cleared his throat. "Ah, yes," he said. "That's the other thing. Aybek's here."

Suzy folded her arms and gave Aybek her hardest stare.

"We were expecting him," she said. "Tenebrae told us everything."

"That feathered thug's still alive, is he?" said Aybek. "Never mind, I'm sure it won't last." He turned a beatific smile on Ina. "And you must be *The Book of Power*'s new owner. What a pleasure to meet you." He bowed but never quite took his eyes off her.

Suzy took Ina by the hands. "Don't trust anything he says or does," she said. "He's more dangerous than Tenebrae."

"I'm flattered that you think so," said Aybek.

"Don't be," Suzy shot back. "It wasn't a compliment."

Another tremor ran up through the room, making the magic inside its ancient stones flare.

"What's happening down there?" asked Wilmot.

"The city's breaking apart," said Suzy. "The floodwaters are rising, and the citizens are trying to storm the throne room. If we can't save it now, Hydroborea's finished."

"Then we need to hurry," said Wilmot. He dashed over to the workbench and picked up the book. At the same time, Suzy produced the Gold Stamp Special delivery form from her satchel.

"This means we've finally got everything we need in the same place," said Wilmot. "Book, delivery form, and recipient. Do you have a pen, Ina?"

"What sort of journalist would I be if I didn't?" she said, pulling one from her pocket.

"Excellent," he said, exchanging an excited grin with Suzy. "Sign here, please."

Suzy proffered the form to Ina. Wilmot held his breath. At last, after so many dangers and disappointments, they were going to complete the first Gold Stamp Special delivery in living memory. The Express would be free to carry on working as normal, and the book would return every word it had stolen from the Ivory Tower. Everything was going to be all right.

Except, when Ina's pen was hovering just above the form, Aybek picked one of the glass bottles off his workbench and hurled it at the floor.

It shattered, the black whirlwind exploded outward, and the room went dark. Ina yelped, and Wilmot dropped the book in his surprise as Aybek's voice echoed through the blackness.

"I'm sorry to disappoint you, Master Grunt, but the time has come for me to take my leave. And my book."

"Aybek, wait," said Wilmot. He reached blindly in the direction of Aybek's voice, but a hard shove sent him reeling. He regained his footing and stooped to feel for the book, but his hands found only empty floor. "Book?" he called. "Where are you?"

"I am over here," the book replied from somewhere behind him. "I think I am being stolen again."

"You didn't think I would let the greatest magical power in existence fall into anyone's hands but my own, did you?" Aybek's voice seemed to come from several directions at once now, no doubt due to more magic, which only added to Wilmot's confusion.

"The book's useless to you, Aybek," he replied. "Ina's the only one who can open it."

"Which is why I'm taking her, too," said Aybek. The piercing note of the kraken caller rang out. There was breaking of glass and a wet slithering sound, and Ina's scream pierced the darkness.

"Something's got me!" she cried. "Help!"

"Let her go, Aybek," shouted Suzy. "Where are you even going to go? The city's falling apart."

"It deserves to," Aybek snapped back. "Now, if you'll excuse me, the Impossible Places are practically begging for strong leadership, and I'd hate to keep them waiting. Good-bye."

"Stop!"

Wilmot turned, waving his hands in front of him and taking small, cautious steps in what he hoped was the direction of the door. Somewhere nearby he heard a thump, a rattle of pots and pans, and a whispered curse from Suzy.

"Chief," she said, "can you get a glow going?"

"I'm already at full luminescence," came the Chief's voice. "It doesn't seem to be making any difference."

My flashlight! thought Wilmot. He pulled it from his pocket and wound the key, but no light appeared.

"It's no good," he said. "Whatever this spell is, it's designed not to let any light through."

Suzy gave an exasperated groan. "Just when everything was going right for once. But how's he even going to escape the city?"

Wilmot stopped stumbling about long enough to realize he already knew the answer to Suzy's question. "He's heading for the H.E.C.," he said. "He must be planning to seal himself inside and use the conch shell to make the kraken take him back to the surface."

"And once he's there he'll force Ina to open the book, and then he'll be unstoppable," said Suzy. "Which means *we* have to stop him before he leaves."

"That's the stuff," said the Chief. "Now, can anyone find the door?"

They stumbled about, banging into the furniture and each other but getting nowhere. And then came a voice that made Suzy's spirits leap.

"Blimey, who turned out the lights?"

"Fletch?" she said, scarcely daring to believe her ears. "Is that really you?"

"It was the last time I checked," said Fletch. "You got the Postmaster with you?"

"Yes, I'm here!" said Wilmot. "But we can't see a thing. Aybek cast some sort of darkness spell."

They heard Fletch sniff the air. "Smells like a good old-fashioned blackout spell to me. It's thick but it's easy to shift. Just use a fan and blow it away."

"We don't have a fan," said Suzy.

Fletch tutted. "Looks like I'm sortin' out everyone's problems today," he said. "Stonks? Open up the pressure valves and give us a blast of steam, will you?"

There was a great hiss, and a wave of hot, moist, banana-scented air blew across the room. It carried the darkness with it, reducing it to scraps of gray fog and sweeping it out of the open door. Suzy blinked droplets of moisture from her eyelashes and saw Fletch standing outside the door to a storage cupboard, through which she could see the gleaming hulk of the Express. He stepped aside as Ursel and Stonker emerged, followed by Frederick, who was carrying a birdcage containing some sort of furry red worm.

"Hello!" said Frederick. "Are you three all right?"

"Apart from being dead, I've never felt better," said the Chief. "What's that in the cage?"

"Oh, him?" Frederick frowned at the cage. "This is Maxwell. He's here to fix the H.E.C."

"And this is my assistant, Professor Stupid," said Maxwell. "His specialist subject is being absolutely horrible at everything."

Suzy leveled a questioning look at Frederick, who sighed.

"It's a long story," he said.

Before he could start to tell it, Suzy's parents rushed out of the cupboard.

"Is Suzy here? Is she all right?" They skidded to a halt in front of her, and for a moment, she just stared at them. All the words seemed to have evaporated from her head, and she had no idea what to say, let alone what to feel. Relieved, guilty, embarrassed, overjoyed... She was feeling them all at once, and they filled her up so completely she was afraid she might burst into tears in front of them.

"Hello," she said in a small voice. "Sorry."

"Oh, Suzy!" Her parents threw themselves at her and gathered her up in their arms.

"Thank goodness you're safe," said her dad.

"We thought we'd never see you again," said her mom.

"Me too," said Suzy, letting a few of her tears escape. Every one of them felt like a great weight being lifted from her. "I'm so sorry."

"We're here now," said her dad. "That's all that matters."

337

The room trembled, shaking a few jars of ingredients off the shelves.

"Actually, it's not," said Suzy. "The city is imploding. You both need to get out of here while you still can."

"We're not going anywhere without you," said her mother.

"I'll be right behind you," said Suzy. "I promise. But Aybek's here, he's taken the book and a friend of ours, and we've got to get them back. It's the only way to save everyone."

Stonker's mustache bristled. "Aybek, you say? Here?"

Her parents exchanged a quick, wordless look.

"How can we help?" asked her dad.

Suzy blinked. "You want to stay?"

"Suzanne Smith," said her mom. "We've been through an awful lot to get here, and we're not going to just turn around and leave you behind, no matter what's happening. So hurry up and tell us what you need before we change our minds."

Suzy hugged them again, even harder. "We're going to need backup," she said. "Lots of backup."

26

In Pursuit of a Good Book

The throne room was in chaos.

At least it *sounded* as if it was in chaos, but it was too dark to actually see anything. Aybek's blackout magic filled the room, bringing Suzy, Wilmot, Frederick, Stonker, and Ursel to an abrupt halt at the foot of the spiral stairs.

The darkness rang with the sound of Watch Frogs running to and fro in confusion, while the desperate pleas of the crowd trapped on the grand boulevard outside the doors grew ever louder. There was also an erratic clicking noise, like a malfunctioning machine. It took Suzy a few seconds to realize it was the sound of Frogmaggog uselessly snapping his fingers.

"When I find you, old man, I'm going to cut you into pieces so small, the sharks won't even have to chew," Frogmaggog thundered. "Give me back my book!"

"Come and get it yourself," came Aybek's response, once again echoing from all directions at once. "But it sounds as if your people need you. Allow me to show them in."

Suzy heard a squeal of porcelain as Frogmaggog shifted in his bathtub. "Secure the doors. Somebody stop him!"

But it was too late. The doors swung open with a distant creak, admitting a chill breeze that dispelled the blackout fog. The line of Watch Frogs that had been holding back the crowd outside came tumbling in, almost trampled underfoot by the stampede of terrified Hydroboreans who poured in through the mouth of the gateway.

Suzy scanned the chaos and spotted Aybek almost immediately—he was the only figure moving against the flow of people, dragging Ina behind him through the gateway. Her arms were tied by a knot of kraken tentacles.

"There he is!" Suzy said. "After him!"

They started in pursuit, but a full-scale riot was already in progress as the Watch Frogs regrouped and attempted to turn back the incoming tide of refugees. The Hydroboreans defended themselves with whatever they had been able to salvage from their homes—pots and pans, a footstool, pillows. One elderly newt lady was even attacking Commander Kecker with a set of china plates, slinging them at him like Frisbees while he parried with his trident.

Frogmaggog, meanwhile, leaned out of his bath and plucked one unfortunate soul after another off their feet with his long, sticky tongue, reeling them into his waiting mouth.

"Aybek!" yelled Tenebrae, trapped in his cage high above the fighting. "Come back and let me out of here!"

The prisoners from the Midtwist district had broken free of their guards and joined the fray. Suzy's heart leaped when she saw Amlod fighting through the crowd in an attempt to reach Ina, but Aybek had already tossed her into the detention trailer of one of the abandoned S-Cargo Units and climbed into the driver's seat. With a good-bye wave to Tenebrae, he gunned the engine and turned the vehicle away from the tower, scattering Hydroboreans as he went.

"We'll never catch him now," Frederick whined.

"Grrrrawr!" said Ursel.

"She said to climb on," said Stonker. "She'll take care of the rest."

Suzy grinned at Ursel and vaulted up onto her back, settling between her shoulder blades and plunging her hands into her friend's thick fur. "Come on, Wilmot," she called.

"Just a sec." He dashed toward the fighting and retrieved something from the floor—a fallen kraken caller. He returned at a run, holding it aloft in triumph, and scrabbled up Ursel's back behind Suzy. "Ready!"

It was then that Suzy's parents appeared at the bottom of the stairs, sweating and out of breath. Suzy's mom approached Wilmot and held something out for him. His phone.

"You were right," she panted. "We managed to get a phone signal out through the rail tunnel and called for backup."

"We contacted everyone on the list you gave us," said Suzy's dad, resting his hands on his knees. "They're on their way. And can I just say?" He gasped for breath. "Troll phone technology really needs to be more user-friendly."

"But it's really good for your resting heart rate," said Wilmot. "Thank you."

Suzy reached down and took her mom's hand in both of hers. "Thanks, both of you," she said. "I promise we'll be back soon."

Her mom nodded. "Just promise to be careful as well."

"I will," said Suzy. "You and dad should get back on the Express. It's safer there."

"What about the rest of us?" said Stonker.

"Help as many people as you can," said Suzy. "And get ready."

Stonker stood to attention and tipped his hat. "We won't disappoint you."

"Hang on," said Frederick. "Take Maxwell. If anything goes wrong and you can't get back to us, you'll need him." He opened the cage, took gentle hold of the little demon, and offered him to Suzy.

"But what do I do with him?" she said.

"Just point him at the H.E.C.'s engines and he'll figure out the rest."

"Oh yes, let me do all the hard work," said Maxwell. "You can all put your feet up, but not poor Maxwell."

"You don't even have feet," said Frederick.

Maxwell stuck his tongue out and blew a raspberry at him.

"Fine," said Suzy. "He can ride in my pocket." Maxwell performed a graceful swan dive straight into Suzy's coat pocket.

"It smells like old seaweed in here," he said.

"Tough luck." She checked her watch. Only forty minutes remained before the book digested the contents of the Ivory Tower's library. "Let's go."

Ursel raised her head and gave a bellowing roar that cut through the noise of the throne room. The fighting stopped, every face turned to stare at them, and, with a grunt of satisfaction, Ursel plunged forward, fangs bared. Watch Frogs and civilians alike took one look at the enormous yellow beast bearing down on them and fought to get out of her way.

Within a few seconds, Ursel was at full speed and the crowd parted around her like water.

"There's Amlod!" said Wilmot, pointing. Suzy looked and saw him off to one side, defending a group of Hydroborean children from a couple of Watch Frogs.

"Keep fighting, Amlod!" shouted Suzy. "We'll bring Ina back."

He waved at her, then tackled both the Watch Frogs around the waist while they were distracted by the sight of Ursel charging past. The children cheered.

"Stop those outworlders!" roared Frogmaggog. "Don't let them escape!"

A few foolhardy Watch Frogs stepped into Ursel's path, but she put her head down and surged forward. One had the sense to jump clear, but the other two were knocked flying.

"Idiots!" shouted Frogmaggog. "Must I do everything myself?" He heaved himself out of the bath and lumbered after them in pursuit.

"Faster!" Suzy shouted.

They were almost at the huge red entrance doors now. The crowd continued to scatter, giving them a clear run to the exit, but the doorway was narrow with no room to maneuver. Suzy looked over her shoulder and saw Frogmaggog open his mouth wide, his tongue coiling like a spring.

"Look out!" she said.

With a growl of effort, Ursel put on an extra burst of speed. They were suddenly in the gateway. Frogmaggog's tongue shot toward them . . .

. . . and missed, whistling a few inches over Wilmot's head to strike the wall. Frogmaggog gave a yelp of pain and looked down at his foot. Through the crowd, Suzy glimpsed her parents, armed with tridents, jabbing at his ankle.

"Go for it, Mom and Dad!" she shouted. Then Ursel was through the doorway, out of the giant stone frog's head and onto the boulevard, where the endless crowd of displaced Hydroboreans still streamed toward the palace.

"That was close!" said Wilmot.

"That was brilliant!" said Suzy. "Now, keep your eyes open for Aybek. He can't be far ahead of us."

"Rrrrunk!" agreed Ursel.

The crowd parted for them, and Ursel ran on. All Suzy and Wilmot could do now was hang on.

It's a race now, thought Suzy. *Between us and Aybek*. She pressed her face into the deep fur of Ursel's neck and tried not to panic. Because the fate of everything, and everyone, depended on the outcome.

27

THE TRAIN NOW ARRIVING

The battle for the throne room raged on around Suzy's parents, but before they could rejoin it, the shadow of Frogmaggog's huge webbed foot fell over them. "You wretched outworlders are turning into an infestation," he said, glowering down at them. "It's time to put an end to you."

"Don't you dare!" shouted Suzy's mom as she and her husband brandished their tridents.

He brought his foot down, but not before Frederick was able to cannon into both Suzy's parents and knock them clear. The three of them rolled under the bathtub just as Frogmaggog's heel struck the ground.

"I think you made him angry," said Frederick.

Suzy's mom gave a shaky laugh. "Serves him right," she said. "Who does he think he is?"

Frogmaggog gave a dull roar and began stamping his way around the throne room. Hydroboreans leaped clear as his tongue lashed out and struck the crowd again and again, and the tide of people began to turn. Panic spread, and more and more civilians fought their way back toward the tower's entrance, desperate to escape Frogmaggog's appetite.

"Don't just stand there, Kecker!" said Frogmaggog. "Put this rabble in their place. I want my throne room cleared."

Kecker ducked the last of the flying plates that elderly newt was throwing at him. "Yes, Your Greatness!" He raised his trident, and the newt hitched up her skirts and ran. More Watch Frogs fell into line beside him, and together they advanced, driving the crowd before them.

As the crush of people intensified, more Hydroboreans took refuge with Frederick and Suzy's parents under the bath. Amlod, Stonker, and Fletch were among them.

"Things don't seem to be going terribly well, do they?" said Stonker.

"It's Frogmaggog," said Amlod. "He's too big to fight. We need something to even the odds."

"Like what?" said Fletch.

A piercing whistle cut through the noise of the throne room.

"What was that?" asked Suzy's mom.

"It almost sounded like a train," said Stonker. "But it wasn't ours."

The sound came again. A moment later, a tunnel mouth opened in one wall, and a streamlined silver carriage burst out of it, skidding across the polished floor until it came to rest with its nose against the bathtub.

"That's the Silver Zephyr!" said Frederick, jumping up. "The Ivory Tower's private train!"

The Zephyr's doors burst open, and a squad of Lunar Guard piled out, plasma rifles at the ready. Neoma strode out after them, her cape billowing.

"Hello, people of Hydroborea," she said. "We come in peace, unless your name is Frogmaggog, in which case I'm just looking for an excuse to blow you to atoms." She looked up at the gigantic figure standing over her. "I guess that's you," she said.

Frogmaggog's face stretched into an ugly snarl, but before he could take a step toward her, another tunnel mouth opened in the opposite wall. There was no train this time, but a tramp of heavy feet as a team of Lady Crepuscula's statues marched out of the darkness into the throne room. Lady Crepuscula herself followed, carried

348

in the talons of her pet gargoyle. It beat its stone wings until she was level with Frogmaggog's startled face.

"I understand you've been causing trouble," she said, before she was cut off by the sound of a bugle issuing from a third tunnel, which had opened in the rear wall. Instead of a parade of troops, a group of elderly trolls shuffled out into the light. They wore old-fashioned postal uniforms and leaned on a variety of canes, crutches, and walkers. Most of them were chattering animatedly with one another.

"...and so I asked him, 'What are you looking for?' and he said, 'I'm a meteorologist,' and so I went and got him every book we had on meteors, but was he happy? 'Course not."

"Typical academics. They never know what they want."

Gertrude, Dorothy, and Mr. Trellis stood at the head of the group, which fell silent as Gertrude held up a hand.

"Who are you supposed to be?" said Frogmaggog.

"We're the Old Guard," said Gertrude. "Former posties and current librarians. We're here to bring mail thieves and book thieves to justice."

Mr. Trellis shuffled forward, leaning on his cane. "And that means you, sonny."

Frogmaggog clenched his fists. "It's a conspiracy," he said. "Outworlder interference in Hydroborea's affairs."

"You bet it is," said Neoma. "Now stand aside and let us retrieve the book."

"Never!" said Frogmaggog. He leveled a finger at her, quaking with rage. "Watch Frogs, attack!"

As one, the army of Watch Frogs inflated their throats and let out their wailing siren cry. Then they raised their tridents and charged.

28
THE LAST POST

Suzy's hands cramped from clutching Ursel's fur so tightly, but she didn't dare loosen her grip. The great bear jumped and swerved, drifted and jogged her way down through the twisting city, the raging waters surging around her knees. Suzy heard Wilmot cry out behind her as a fragment of the city's roof fell in and flattened a building up ahead. Ursel dodged left into a side street to avoid the shower of masonry, which rattled and cracked against the surrounding houses.

At least no one was in there, Suzy thought. They had passed the tail end of the exodus one level up, and had been racing through empty streets for several minutes now.

"Where are we?" asked Wilmot.

"The upper end of the Midtwist district," said Suzy. "We're almost at the Baleen Ballroom."

"And how much farther from there to the H.E.C.?"

"That depends how high the floodwaters have risen," she replied.

They soon had their answer. As the shattered hulk of the ballroom loomed up on their left, Ursel found herself plunging through water that now reached her shoulders.

"Huuurnk!" she panted.

"Too deep?" said Suzy. Ursel nodded.

"Head for that rooftop," she said, pointing to an angular island of tiles breaking the surface a short distance ahead. Ursel pushed off the bottom and swam for it, fighting to keep her snout above water until she was finally able to claw her way up its slope and collapse, panting for breath. Suzy and Wilmot slid off her back, and Suzy wrapped her arms around the soaking fur of her friend's neck.

"You're brilliant," she whispered. "Stay here and rest. We'll be right back."

"Ronk," Ursel replied with a weary smile.

Maxwell wriggled out of Suzy's pocket, unfurled his wings, and zipped around them at head height. He made a buzzing rasp that sounded a bit like a purr, until Suzy realized he was talking to himself.

"... seveneightnineteneleventwelvethirteenfourteen-fifteensixteen ..."

"What are you doing?" she asked.

"Counting raindrops," he said. "Stop distracting me."

The waters of the flooded lagoon in which the H.E.C. had arrived had risen to swallow half the city. The friends were surrounded by drowned buildings and flotillas of wreckage, and to Suzy's alarm, she could actually *see* the water level rising. It was already creeping up the rooftop on which they stood, and in another few minutes, it would have consumed it entirely. Streetlights still shone here and there beneath the surface, but they flickered out one by one as their bowls cracked and the neon fish scattered into the depths.

"It's risen so far already," said Wilmot, awed.

"And we need to stop it rising any farther," said Suzy. "We just need to find Aybek."

Wilmot scanned the rising flood and pointed. "There's the H.E.C.," he said. Suzy saw the caravan bobbing, half-submerged, some distance in front of them. And there, paddling toward it on a makeshift raft of driftwood, was Aybek, with Ina still in the grip of the infant kraken beside him.

"A little help?" she shouted to them.

Aybek saw them and started paddling faster, scooping water with both hands. Suzy jumped in without hesitating, closely followed by Wilmot. The water was ice-cold, and the shock of it almost squeezed the breath from them both. Suzy forced herself to kick and flail, half dragging the spluttering Wilmot with her. They made a lot of noise and foam, but they also made progress. They were gaining on Aybek.

When he was still a few feet from the H.E.C., Aybek pulled the silver conch he had tricked the Watch Frog guard into giving him from inside his robes, raised it to his lips, and blew. The shell emitted a long and mournful note that made the surface of the water fizz like lemonade.

A kraken tentacle surfaced almost immediately and fixed its large green eye on Suzy and Wilmot. Four more tentacles quickly followed.

Aybek reached the H.E.C., scrambled onto its roof, and turned to them with a look of smug triumph. "Who needs engines when you've got an obedient sea monster?" he said. He blew on the shell again, and one of the tentacles scooped Ina up and dropped her onto the roof beside him.

"Let me go," Ina protested, trying in vain to wriggle free of the infant kraken's hold.

Suzy tried to call out but swallowed a mouthful of seawater by mistake. "We're not going to make it," she choked.

"Wait a sec," said Wilmot, clinging to her in an effort to stay afloat. He held up the kraken caller he had found in the throne room and blew hard on it. The note he made in the few seconds before he sank beneath the surface was high-pitched and wavering, and when Suzy reached down and fished him back up again, he spat an arc of seawater.

"Did it work?" he said eagerly.

Suzy shook her head. The kraken still reared over them. It didn't even seem to have heard the conch.

"I congratulate your effort, Master Grunt," said Aybek. "But it seems my beast isn't impressed by your musical abilities."

Wilmot blinked water from his eyes. "I wasn't calling to your beast," he said, and pointed to Ina.

Aybek turned in time to see the infant kraken release its hold on her. Suddenly free, Ina jumped to her feet and kicked the shell from Aybek's hands. It sailed out over the water and disappeared with a splash.

"No!" he cried. "What have you done?"

"You stole my book," Ina said, grappling with him. The H.E.C. pitched and rolled beneath them as they struggled.

"Well done, Wilmot" said Suzy, towing him toward the caravan. He grinned, accidentally swallowed more water, and spat it back out again.

"Mom made me take trombonamaphone lessons when I turned seventy," he said. "It looks like they finally came in handy." He threw his own kraken caller as far into the waters as he could. "Now Maxwell is the only one who can take the H.E.C. anywhere," he said.

"Hopefully he won't need to," Suzy replied. "Let's just get the book, the form, and Ina, and then head back to the tower before things get any worse."

At that moment, there was a bellow of thunder from overhead, and a jagged section of the city roof, five hundred feet across, fell in. It plunged into the water nearby, throwing up a wave that almost swamped the H.E.C. and broke over Suzy's and Wilmot's heads. Without Aybek's conch to command it, the kraken retreated into the depths as an avalanche of water crashed in through the wound in the city's shell.

Suzy and Wilmot resurfaced, coughing and spluttering. "Quick," said Suzy. "We need to get on board."

The two friends scrambled up the H.E.C.'s side and onto the roof, where Ina and Aybek were hanging on grimly. It was like riding a bucking mule, as the waters churned around them.

This wasn't just a flood anymore; it was a tsunami, rushing up through the city like a gigantic bulldozer, smashing buildings and peeling off roofs. Suzy looked for Ursel, but the roof on which she had been standing was already gone.

"Ursel!" she shouted. "Maxwell! Where are you?"

A furry red bullet whistled past her ear and began circling her head.

"... onebillionsevenhundredandninetysixonebillion-sevenhundredandninetysevenonebillionsevenhundred-and ... oh, you made me lose count!" snapped Maxwell. "Now I'll have to start again. Onetwothreefourfivesix—"

"Get inside," Suzy said. "And where's Ursel?"

"Do you mean the big, loud, yellow one?" said Maxwell. "She's behind you."

Suzy turned and, to her immense relief, saw Ursel clinging to the roof with her claws.

"Frunf," Ursel said, spitting water. She pulled herself up and swept Suzy, Wilmot, Ina, and even Aybek in through the sunroof, before squeezing in after them. It looked like an uncomfortable procedure, and when she landed inside, she left almost no room.

"I don't believe it," said Aybek, who was wedged up against the front window. "Moments away from achieving my life's ambition, and now I'm going to die in a caravan, asphyxiated by a bear."

Suzy clambered over Ursel's back and pulled the sunroof shut. "Maxwell," she said. "We need the engines working. Can you do it?"

"Show me," he replied.

Wilmot ducked under one of Ursel's forelegs and

opened the cupboard beneath the sink, revealing something that looked like a big hourglass lying on its side. Instead of sand, the glass bulbs were full of purple steam that sparkled and fizzed. A small metal plate divided one bulb from the other, and set over it was a charred stump of ruined machinery. "Here," said Wilmot. "You can see where the bifurcator's burned out."

Maxwell leaned forward on his perch and eyeballed the bulbs of steam. "What a mess!" he said. "There's no order to these molecules at all."

"But can you fix it?" said Suzy. "Because we're going to get smashed to pieces if you can't."

Maxwell settled on the burned-out bifurcator, took a moment to make himself comfortable, then looked down at the glass bulbs and tutted. A crackle of electricity snapped from one of his horns to the other. As it did so, the metal gate dividing the two glass bulbs of the machine flickered. It seemed to disappear for a split second, and then it was back. "That's a bit better," he said. "But still so much to do."

"What just happened?" asked Wilmot.

"I'm sorting," said Maxwell, without taking his eye off the glass bulbs. His horns crackled with electricity again, and the gate flickered and reappeared. "Tidying up the fuel molecules. Now, shush! This is tricky."

He stared intently at the bulbs, and his horns snapped

and crackled with energy every few seconds. The gate became a constant flicker that Suzy found impossible to focus on. Slowly but surely, the fuel in one of the bulbs was turning red, and the fuel in the other blue.

Suzy snapped her fingers. "It's thermodynamics!" she said. "The different types of molecules have different amounts of energy, so by separating them out..."

"He ends up with one bulb of high-energy molecules and one of low energy," Aybek finished for her. "This is all very basic."

The fuel in the bulbs suddenly ignited with cherry-red and ice-blue glows, respectively. There was a hum of power, and the lights on the console flickered on.

"He's done it!" said Wilmot. "He's got the power back. Maxwell *is* the new bifurcator!"

Maxwell was ignoring them entirely now. He leaned forward in his seat, his eye wide and unblinking, darting back and forth between the two bulbs. His horns crackled ceaselessly now, and the metal gate was flickering so quickly it was virtually invisible.

"Get us out of here, Wilmot," said Suzy. "This flood's about to hit the throne room and we've got to get there first."

Wilmot shuffled out from underneath Ursel and jumped at the controls. "Hold on," he said. "This might be rough."

He pressed the launch button and the H.E.C. leaped upward, blasting clear of the flood waters in a pall of flame. Wilmot gripped the console and steered their course up through the city, weaving between buildings and punching headlong through sheets of falling water as the tsunami crashed at their heels.

"Ten minutes left," said Suzy, checking her watch. "Have we got enough power to reach the palace?"

"More than enough," said Wilmot. "I'm just not sure we've got good enough brakes to stop when we get there."

The tide of battle in the throne room was shifting. The Lunar Guard and Crepuscula's statues charged at the Watch Frogs together, breaking their ranks and keeping them away from the civilians, while Frederick helped Suzy's parents, the Old Guard, Fletch, and Stonker shepherd as many new civilians as possible in through the entrance to the tower.

At the same time, Neoma and Crepuscula were doing their best to distract Frogmaggog, alternating between blasts of plasma-rifle fire and icy magic. A stray shot had broken Tenebrae's cage open, and he joined the attack, swooping at Frogmaggog from above and striking with his talons.

"I'm going to eat the lot of you," Frogmaggog said,

trying to stamp on Neoma. "I don't care how much indigestion it gives me."

He came within a few inches of swatting Crepuscula's gargoyle from the air, when the shockwave from the collapse of the Midtwist district hit the throne room, throwing him off balance. The blast was followed by a rush of cold air and the steady roar of the approaching tsunami.

"That doesn't sound good," said Suzy's dad, helping a procession of elderly frogs across the threshold. "Is there any sign of the others?"

Frederick fought to see out over the heads of the crowd. Apart from the last few stragglers outside, the grand boulevard was deserted. "Not yet," he said.

The ground shook, the wind blew stronger, and a wall of dirty seawater thundered into view around the curve of the boulevard. Frederick felt his heart drop into his stomach—the wave stretched from the road to the city roof, tearing open buildings as if they were made of paper.

"Close the doors!" shouted Stonker.

"But what about Suzy and the others?" said Suzy's mom, carrying a young newt girl to safety. "They're still out there."

Frederick pulled the last refugee—a frog in a pinstriped suit—inside as the throne room doors started to swing shut, but it was a painfully slow process and the

water was already halfway along the boulevard. Then he spotted a bright flash amid the carnage. There, riding a trail of fire in front of the wave, was the H.E.C.

"It's them!" cried Frederick. "They're coming!" And then, in a sudden panic, "Hold the doors!"

The gates paused, three quarters closed, and Frederick had to will himself not to look away as the H.E.C. hurtled toward them. The gap was barely large enough.

"Got you!" In all the confusion, Neoma had taken her eyes off Frogmaggog for a second, and he stooped down and picked her up. She struggled against his tightening grip.

"I'm going to squeeze you until you pop," the Master of Magic declared.

The H.E.C. shot in through the gates with barely a foot to spare on either side. Frogmaggog just had time to look up before it struck him full speed in the chest and knocked him off his feet. He dropped Neoma, performed a neat backward somersault, and came crashing down in the bathtub while the H.E.C., its forward momentum suddenly arrested, dropped sputtering to the floor.

"Now for goodness' sake, get those doors shut!" yelled Stonker. "Quickly!"

The enormous doors swung closed a split second before the water struck them with a noise like a train crash. They groaned, the throne room trembled one last time, and then an eerie quiet descended. The fighting stopped.

Suzy's parents were already running to the dented wreck of the H.E.C.

"Are they all right?" said Suzy's mom, trying to see in through the windows. "Is anyone hurt?"

The sunroof popped open and Ursel squeezed out, staggering drunkenly before plopping down on her haunches.

"Frowlf," she said.

"Travel sick?" said Stonker, reaching her side. "I'm not surprised after that."

Suzy, Wilmot, and Ina all came tumbling out, shaken and dizzy.

"That was quite an entrance," said Suzy's dad, helping her to her feet.

"I told you I'd be back," she said, and accepted the ferocious hug that he and her mom pulled her into.

Gertrude and Dorothy ran to embrace Wilmot, and a battered but jubilant Amlod shoved his way out of the crowd and threw his arms around Ina.

"You made it!" he said.

"Of course," she said. "As if you ever doubted me."

Maxwell emerged from the wreckage, buzzing contentedly. He performed a lazy loop-de-loop and landed on Frederick's shoulder wearing a big, dopey grin. "Hey,

Professor," he said, nuzzling Frederick's ear. "That was good fun."

"You did a brilliant job, Maxwell," said Frederick, rubbing the demon between his horns. "You saved them."

Maxwell gave a sleepy giggle. "Yeah, but you're my favorite," he said, and promptly dropped off Frederick's shoulder into his breast pocket, where he began snoring.

Suzy looked around at the hundreds of people, trolls, and statues filling the throne room. "It worked," she said. "Everyone came. But where's Frogmaggog?"

All eyes turned to the bathtub. The steam rising from it was now a dark and bilious green.

"This is an outrage!" came a tiny voice from inside it. "Surrender immediately, or I'll have you all executed."

A small figure appeared on the rim. It was Frogmaggog—bruised, winded, and shrunken to his natural size. Scandalized whispers ran through the crowd of onlookers. Frogmaggog shook his fist at them.

"Why have you stopped fighting, you disgusting cowards?" he shouted at the Watch Frogs. "Bring me Commander Kecker. I'll have his head for this."

A few Watch Frogs looked around nervously, but none of them moved.

Amlod cupped his hands around his mouth and booed. With a huge grin, Ina joined in. Then Suzy and Wilmot.

Then some of the civilians. Then a few Watch Frogs. One by one, the chorus of disapproval spread until almost everyone in the throne room was booing at Frogmaggog, who ranted and stamped his feet in vain.

"Stop it! How dare you? I'm the Master of Magic!"

Lady Crepuscula sidled up to Suzy and the others with a conspiratorial smile. "Do you know what I've always wanted on my mantelpiece?" she asked.

They looked at her blankly until Frederick said, "A frog in a snow globe?"

"Precisely," she said, and raised her cane. A bolt of magic leaped from its tip and struck Frogmaggog, enveloping him in a large glass bubble. He beat his fists against the inside but only succeeded in rolling himself off the lip of the bath. Everyone in the throne room let out a collective gasp as he plunged toward the ground. But the bubble was already shrinking, and when Lady Crepuscula caught it neatly in one hand it was no bigger than a tennis ball. Frogmaggog, still trapped inside it, was barely two inches tall. Suzy and the others clustered around to look.

"Please!" said Frogmaggog in a high-pitched squeak. "Let me out. I'll do anything!"

Lady Crepuscula held the ball up for everyone to see. "I think a little while at this size will do you good," she said. "You need to learn to look up to others. Then I'll hand you over to your own people and they can decide what to do with you."

Frogmaggog went white. "No! You can't! You don't know what they'll do to me. Please!" His protestations ended abruptly as Lady Crepuscula's shadow peeled itself off the floor, reached up, and seized him in both hands. The sphere fell away into the shadow, as if into a deep pit, and was gone.

"That takes care of one problem," said Lady Crepuscula. "Now, where's my good-for-nothing brother?"

There was a groan from the H.E.C., and Aybek crawled out of the sunroof.

"I was hoping you'd forgotten about me," he said. "And before you say another word, yes, I surrender." He got to his feet and raised his hands.

Tenebrae landed in front of him with a soft thud but was immediately surrounded by a squad of Lunar Guard. "It's not her you should be worried about, old man," he snarled. "You left me for Frogmaggog."

"Oh dear, Aybek," said Lady Crepuscula, clearly enjoying the spectacle. "You have been making yourself popular, haven't you?"

"Never mind that right now," said Suzy. "Where's the book?"

"I am here," said the book from somewhere inside

Aybek's robes. "You have one minute remaining." Aybek withdrew it and handed it to Suzy.

"I suppose you want this as well," he said, offering the crumpled delivery form to Wilmot, who snatched it from him, smoothed it out a little, and passed it to Ina.

"Could you sign it here, please?" he said, his hands shaking a little with excitement as he pointed at the bottom of the sheet.

"And as quickly as you can!" added Frederick.

Ina pulled out her pen. "Are you sure about this?" she said. "I still don't think I'm qualified.

"Your handwriting is quite messy," said the book. "But you alone sought the truth when others accepted lies. You asked questions when others were offered easy answers. You understood the limits of your knowledge and sought to overcome them. For these reasons, I have chosen you."

"Wow," said Amlod. "And all this time I thought she was just nosy."

"She is," said the book. "And that is a very good thing."

Aybek tutted and turned away.

Ina laid the form and the book beside one another on the floor. Suzy and Wilmot clasped hands as she pressed the nib to the paper. Then, with a quick scratch and a flick, she signed her name.

"Done," she said.

Wilmot took the form as though it were made of glass and held it up to the light. A curl of black ink emerged from between the book's pages and drifted to the form, blotting its surface. The blots became letters and lines, and within a few seconds the form was complete again. Ina's signature glowed briefly, and the stamp attached to the book evaporated in a little puff of gold smoke.

"It's over," said Wilmot, a huge smile slowly spreading across his face. "We did it."

"Oh, jolly well done, you two!" said Stonker.

"Three cheers for the Postmaster and his deputy!" said Mr. Trellis. The Old Guard whooped and applauded and flung their hats in the air.

Suzy threw her arms around Wilmot. "Congratulations," she said. "Whatever else happens now, you'll always be a Gold Stamp Postmaster."

"And you'll always be a Gold Stamp postie!" he replied, hugging her back.

"The postal spell is broken," said the book. "Command me, and I will open."

"Yes, please," said Ina.

The book almost purred with satisfaction. "You might want to stand back." It sprang open, its pages turning as if riffled by unseen hands. Suzy caught flashes of dense text, colorful illustrations, and richly illuminated letters. They blurred together, the pages turning faster and

faster. And not just turning but unfolding, opening out of the book like origami blossoms.

Then it launched into the air in a whirl of fluttering pages. It continued to unfold as it wheeled through the heights of the throne room, until it wasn't a book anymore but a flock of pages, thousands upon thousands of them, all interconnected and moving as one. Their passage through the air was like the sound of a thousand wings, and Suzy saw a shape forming from their chaos.

Some of the Hydroboreans screamed as the form emerged. It was an enormous feathered serpent, with scales of overlapping parchment and eyes as black as ink in its arrow-shaped head. A long black tongue flickered out of its mouth, tasting the air. Then it lowered its head toward Ina in a reverent bow.

"I am the Book Wyrm," it said. "The living embodiment of Hydroborea's knowledge and culture. All its stories, all its histories and learning, are in me. And they are yours to do with as you wish."

Ina approached the Book Wyrm slowly. She raised a hand and it rubbed its papery snout against her palm. "Are you a . . . a library?" she asked.

"I am," it replied.

"Wow!" Frederick bounded to Ina's side. "This is incredible. I just got a serious case of library envy."

He was still admiring the Book Wyrm in wide-eyed wonder when Neoma limped up, supported by a couple of Lunar Guards. "Neat trick," she said. "But can you help us do anything about *that*?"

Suzy followed Neoma's pointing finger and saw, to her horror, that the entrance doors were bowing inward. Tiny spurts of water forced their way in around the frame, and a web of hairline cracks was working its way out across the walls. The crowd panicked and there was a small stampede toward the rear of the throne room, only to find that water was already trickling down the spiral staircase.

"We have to get everyone into the tunnels," said Frederick.

"There are too many of us," said Neoma. "We'd never get everyone out in time."

Suzy turned to Ina. "You're our only hope now," she said urgently. "We need the power of the founders."

Ina's eyes were wide with fear, but she turned them on the Book Wyrm. "Can you help us?"

The Book Wyrm cocked its head to one side. "Yes, I think I have what you need. Try this." Its scales rustled, and some of them fell away from its body like autumn leaves. But instead of scattering, they fell together into a single blank volume. The Wyrm lowered its head and touched the pages with its tongue, staining them black. The stain began to change, forming rows of words.

Finally, a leather cover grew across the pages, and in a few seconds, a finished book lay on the floor at Ina's feet.

"*Hydroborea: An Operation Manual for Beginners* by Hill and Walker," Suzy read over Ina's shoulder.

"Why does a city need an operation manual?" said Wilmot.

"Because Hydroborea is not just a city," said the Book Wyrm. "It is a machine for gathering and sharing magic. And it has not been used properly for a long time."

"Machine, eh?" said Fletch, ambling over. "Give us a look." He leafed quickly through the pages. "Cor," he said. "If I'm readin' this right, we're standin' in a giant transmitter. The city sucks magic up through the spiral and beams it out from the top of the tower."

"So that's why the Sanctum is so full of magical energy," said Wilmot.

"The tower is no longer broadcasting, so the magic has nowhere to go," said the Book Wyrm. "But it can be reactivated."

"How?" said Ina.

The throne room doors groaned, and water began to fountain up through new cracks in the floor. They had only seconds left.

"Quickly!" said Suzy.

"Try page thirty-seven," said the Book Wyrm.

Fletch flipped to the appropriate page, read the entry, frowned, and read it again. "Is that it?" he said. "Looks a bit simple."

"Whatever it is, just do it!" said Frederick, jumping to one side as a trickle of water made its way through the roof and down the back of his neck.

"All right, keep your hair on." Fletch pulled the stubby metal rod of his troll wand from his tool belt and raised it in the air. "Hydroborea, I command you," he said. "Up!"

Nothing happened.

"That can't be right," said Neoma. "You can't move a city with a single word."

"I'm only doin' what it says in the instructions," said Fletch.

The palace trembled underfoot, and Suzy ran to her parents. They hugged each other tightly as the shaking grew worse.

But the tower wasn't disintegrating, she realized. It was rising.

"I think it's working!" said Ina.

Suzy felt the same pressure in the pit of her stomach that she sometimes got when riding in an elevator. Faster and faster, Hydroborea rose from the icy depths. The doors stopped bowing, and the spurts of water forcing their way in through the cracks in the walls lessened to dribbles, then stopped altogether. With a sigh and a rumble, the city came to a halt.

"Are we here?" asked Wilmot. "Did we make it?"

"There's only one way to find out," said Suzy. "Open the doors."

The day was as bright and sharp as a knife edge. Hydroborea stood like a mountain on the ocean's surface, the sun gleaming off its pitted gold shell for the first time in countless generations. The retreating flood waters poured out of its broken sides and the waves created by its surfacing rolled away toward the horizon. High above it all, the summit of the tower flared like a torch, releasing a corona of magical energy into the atmosphere.

Slowly, tentatively, Suzy and the crew led the shell-shocked Hydroboreans out of the throne room into the remnants of the boulevard. Not a single building remained, but through the huge rents in the city's shell, they could see the world outside. The dark swell of the ocean's surface was studded with diamond-white ice floes, while the vibrant blue sky seemed to stretch forever. The air was bitterly cold and tasted fresh and sweet in Suzy's mouth.

Some of the Hydroboreans appeared captivated by these new sensations, while others turned away and wept. Most of them just stood there looking dazed, as if it was all too much to take in.

"There's so *much* of it," said Amlod. Ina slipped her hand into his, speechless.

Suzy spotted the newspaper seller and gave him her best attempt at an encouraging smile. He did not smile back.

"What do we do now?" he said disconsolately. "We've lost everything. Even Frogmaggog failed us." He nudged a fallen brick around with his foot. "What are we supposed to do?"

With a painful start, Suzy realized she didn't have any answers for him.

The awkward silence was broken by a long foghorn blast from outside the city. Suzy looked down and was puzzled to see a large cruise ship floating a short distance from the base of the city. She could just make out the name PRIDE OF OSLO on the prow, and its decks were crowded with elderly tourists, all of whom were pointing and taking pictures.

"Oh, yes," said Suzy's dad. "In all the excitement we forgot to tell you: We're on Earth."

Suzy turned to him in astonishment. "We're *what*?"

"Somewhere northeast of Iceland, I think."

She studied his face to see if this was some sort of joke,

but her mom nodded in confirmation. "I don't believe it," said Suzy.

Her mind was filling with so many new ideas that she couldn't keep them in order, and she turned excitedly to her parents. "Don't you see what this means?" she said. "Earth isn't ordinary, it's magical! Or a little bit magical, anyway. But that still counts!"

"This world was steeped in magic once," said the Book Wyrm, sticking its long nose outside the shell to taste the air. "Hydroborea drained it all to maintain itself during its exile. Now the last vestiges are being returned."

Suzy looked back through the gateway and saw the ribbons of energy zipping through the throne room's walls. *Earth magic*, she told herself.

"If we're making Earth magical again, what does this mean for us?" said Suzy's mom. "What happens to normal life?"

"It'll probably be a bit less normal from now on," said Frederick.

Suzy's mom pursed her lips and mulled this over for a moment. "I can live with that," she said, and put her arm around Suzy.

A man's voice, amplified through a PA system, reached them from the cruise ship.

"Attention, Unidentified Floating Object," it said in a

377

Scandinavian accent. "We come in peace. Do you require assistance? And, um...is that a *dragon* you have with you?"

A lot of confused chatter broke out among the crowd.

"Well?" said Lady Crepuscula. "Would anyone care to make a decision?"

"I would," said Suzy. She turned to the newspaper seller. "You asked me what you should do now," she said. "How about a cruise?"

29

ONE LAST SCHEME

Several hours later, the last of the Hydroborean civilians had been ferried to the fleet of rescue ships that now surrounded the city. Three more cruise liners, a scientific research vessel, and several dozen fishing boats had arrived, and after some rather complicated explanations, the baffled captains had agreed to take the city's inhabitants to the nearest port.

Only Ina and Amlod remained behind. They stood with Suzy, her parents, the Chief, and the crew, watching Crepuscula's statues pick up the Zephyr and set it back on the train tracks inside the tunnel mouth. Aybek, Tenebrae, Kecker, and the other Watch Frogs sat in a miserable-looking huddle at the foot of the giant bathtub, watched over by the Lunar Guard. Lady Crepuscula had removed Tenebrae's collar but had bound his wings with a length of magical thread to stop any escape attempts.

"I still can't believe it's happening," said Ina, caught between trepidation and excitement. "We're leaving Hydroborea."

"The one thing no Hydroborean was ever supposed to do," said Amlod.

"It's certainly going to be strange for you," said Wilmot. "And sometimes it will be difficult. But we trolls have learned a lot about being homeless recently, and if you or any Hydroborean ever need help, just come to Trollville. You'll always find a welcome."

"And just think," added Suzy, "your people are going to need a good reporter now more than ever. Someone has to tell their story to the world, and to help them understand others in return. They don't have Frogmaggog feeding them fake news anymore."

Ina smiled. "Good point," she said. "But I think Amlod and I will spend a bit of time at the Ivory Tower first. The Book Wyrm has to return all the words it took, and I've got quite a lot to learn about managing a library."

"Frederick's the best in the business," said Suzy. "You'll be fine."

"And I'm very low-maintenance," added the Book Wyrm, coiling in the air above them.

Ina laughed. "Don't think you and Wilmot are getting away without a full interview for the *Daily Scuttle*, by the way. You'll be seeing me again soon, I promise."

"I look forward to it," said Wilmot.

Frederick approached them from the direction of the Zephyr, with Maxwell circling his head. "We're ready," he said. "Neoma says we need to get a move on before the tower transmits the last of its magic."

"Why, what happens then?" asked the Chief.

"Hydroborea sinks again," said the Book Wyrm. "Forever."

The friends exchanged rapid hugs while Maxwell zipped in and out between them.

"I'm going to live in your H.E.C. now," he said. "So many molecules to sort! And Professor Stupid says I can visit him and catalog library books on my days off!"

They made for the Silver Zephyr while Crepuscula's statues crossed the floor to relieve the Lunar Guard of their duties. It was as the prisoners were being handed over that Aybek made his move.

"Catch!" he cried, pulling a squirming mass of tentacles from inside his shirt. It was the infant kraken that he had used to trap Ina, and he hurled it at the nearest Lunar Guard, who staggered back and threw up her hands to defend herself. Aybek was past her in a flash, stooping to grab a discarded trident.

"Stop right there," he ordered Ina, leveling the prongs at her. "If I can't control the book, I'll make you do it for me. And don't think I won't poke her full of holes, Selena." This last warning was directed at Lady Crepuscula, whose shadow was creeping across the floor toward him. "I'm sorry to have to refuse your hospitality once again, dear sister, but I have no intention of going back into my cell."

"Aybek," said Lady Crepuscula sternly. "You're being uncharacteristically stupid. Let the girl go while you still can."

"Why should I?" said Aybek.

A shadow fell over him, but it was not Lady Crepuscula's. The Book Wyrm had reared up, and its enormous head was poised over him. Aybek greeted it with a wild grin.

"Listen to your mistress's instructions, Book Wyrm," said Aybek. He grabbed Ina's wrist and hissed into her ear. "Tell it to grant me anything I ask. The secrets of the city's founders. Unrivaled magic!"

Ina took a deep breath. "Never," she said. "I've just escaped from one tyrant, and I don't want to live under another."

"Ina?" said the Book Wyrm. "Duck."

Ina stamped hard on Aybek's foot and he released her with a cry. She dived to one side, and in a single movement, the Book Wyrm struck. Aybek just had time to cry out before it swallowed him.

Silence descended on the throne room for a second. Then the Book Wyrm's scales rustled once more, and a new book formed. It was thicker than the previous one, and its cover, when it grew into place, was pristine and shining silver. Ina seemed reluctant to pick it up, so Suzy stepped forward and did it for her. The book's title was picked out in crisp black letters. *Aybek Aranrhod: A Life.*

"I don't understand," said Suzy. "Is this . . . him?"

"Everything that he was," said the Book Wyrm. "We are all just stories in the end."

Lady Crepuscula approached, leaning heavily on her cane. "Oh, Aybek, you fool," she said, although her voice carried none of its usual bite. "Always trying to have the last word." She reached down and traced the embossed title with her fingers. "I think I'd better look after this, if you don't mind, Ina," she said. "If it's a complete account of Aybek's memories then it contains a lot of very dangerous secrets. Including the haircut I gave myself when I was thirteen." She smiled, but Suzy saw the sadness in it.

"Of course," said Ina. "If that's what you want."

Lady Crepuscula snapped her fingers, and one of her statues took the book from Suzy. As it did so, the ribbons of magic in the throne room walls flickered and the city trembled slightly underfoot.

"Time is so rarely in our favor," sighed Lady Crepuscula. "I would advise you all to stay out of trouble, but experience has taught me not to waste my breath, so instead I will simply say good luck." Her eyes met Suzy's for the briefest of moments. "The door of the Obsidian Tower is always open to you." Her gargoyle launched itself from its perch on the rim of the bath, picked her up in its claws, and swooped into the waiting tunnel, followed by the statues and their prisoners. Their footsteps faded away and the tunnel mouth winked shut.

Frederick turned from Suzy to Wilmot with a look of astonishment. "Was she just *nice* to us?" he said.

"I think so," said Wilmot. "I think I quite liked it."

The Silver Zephyr's whistle blew and Neoma leaned out of the driver's cab. "Last call for the Ivory Tower," she shouted. "Hurry up unless you want to swim home."

The Lunar Guard trooped onboard, a few of them still struggling to pry the baby kraken off their friend.

"How are you going to fit?" Ina asked the Book Wyrm. "You're bigger than the train."

The Book Wyrm purred. Then, in a matter of seconds, it folded itself back up into a book and dropped into her hands. "I am portable," it said.

"Wow," said Frederick. "*So* much library envy."

Suzy hugged him. "Thanks for coming after us," she said. "And good luck with everything at the tower."

"I still owe you the tour, remember?" he said. "Will you be visiting anytime soon?"

"I don't know."

They both turned to Suzy's parents.

"Don't look at us like that," said Suzy's mom. "Your father and I only decided to stop you visiting the Impossible Places because you promised us you were safe, and we didn't believe you."

"And since then you've run away from us, been sucked into a void storm, got trapped at the bottom of the ocean, almost been eaten by a giant frog, almost drowned, and, to top it all off, your new friend has a pet dragon-thingy that turns people into books," said her father.

Suzy's face fell.

"But if you can come out of all that with a spring in your step, I suppose it's pointless trying to stop you," said her mom. "So yes, your father and I are going to age prematurely from all the worry, but as long as you promise to be careful and at least a *little* bit sensible, please, then I don't see why you shouldn't carry on. Especially now that Earth is a little more impossible, too."

Suzy felt so full of joy she thought she might burst. "Thank you!" she said, and threw herself at them, catching them both in a hug.

"As long as it doesn't interfere with your schoolwork," her father added.

"Wilmot, did you hear that?" Suzy said with tears in her eyes. "You're stuck with me."

"I wouldn't have it any other way," he said.

They waved good-bye to Frederick, Ina, and Amlod as the Zephyr pulled away, then climbed the spiral staircase back to the Sanctum, where the Express waited. The chamber was gloomier now, and the pulse of magic within the walls had faded almost completely. The city groaned again, and Suzy felt it drop slightly beneath their feet.

"So that was Hydroborea," said the Chief as they climbed the steps to the *Belle de Loin*'s gangway. "As lost cities go, it had some highlights. I'd probably put it somewhere in my top five. What do you think?"

"I think I want to go home," said Suzy.

"Then let's do that," said Stonker.

They followed him into the cab, and a minute later the Express pulled away into the tunnel mouth. At the same moment, the final spark of magic left the tower and soared high into the atmosphere. With no power left to maintain it, Hydroborea sank, unseen, beneath the waves and was gone.

30

THERE'S NO PLACE LIKE HOME

The Express pulled to a stop, not in the fridge, but in the cupboard under the stairs, which was now the size of a school gymnasium. Suzy and her parents stepped out into the hall. After the chaos and terror of the previous few hours, the quiet stillness of the house felt very strange to Suzy.

"Everything *looks* normal," said Suzy's mom, with obvious suspicion.

"'Course it does," said Fletch, following them out. "What did you expect?"

"Honestly? A soaking-wet ruin," she said. She led the way into the kitchen. It was spotless, although four troll teenagers lounged around the table watching the television on the worktop, supervised by a portly older troll in a gray uniform.

"Finally," said the troll as the others walked in. "I was beginning to think you were never coming back."

"Sorry about that, Marv," said Fletch. "The job turned out to be bigger than I thought."

"Same here," said Marv. "That boggart of yours is a cantankerous little devil. We finally got it cornered, though. In there." He pointed at the microwave. "Stick it on a low defrost setting every hour or so. That seems to keep the little fella happy. And Lara here figured out what was making it so upset. What did you say it was again, Lara?"

"Lactose intolerance," muttered one of the youths, without turning from the television. It was showing a live news broadcast, with helicopter footage of some of the rescue ships heading for shore and blurry, long-lens shots of the Hydroboreans on deck. The headline at the top of the screen read *Magical Asylum Seekers Emerge from Ocean Depths*. A scrolling ticker tape of news beneath the footage said *Loch Ness Monster Sighting Confirmed* and *Ghost of Elvis Announces Comeback Tour*.

Suzy's mom picked up the remote and switched the set off. "Let's worry about all that tomorrow," she said. "I'll put the kettle on."

"You're a treasure, Marv," said Fletch, clapping his

388

friend on the shoulder. "You lot put the place back together perfectly."

"How much of it did you take apart to begin with?" asked Suzy's dad. He moved around the kitchen, opening and closing cupboards, searching for anything out of place.

"Our pleasure," said Marv. "Mind giving us a lift back to Trollville?"

"It's a long walk otherwise," said Fletch. He and Marv cackled together and headed back to the hall. The youths slouched after them.

Stonker tapped the little window on the front of the microwave. Something inside tapped back. "I suppose we'd better find the little chap a new home," he said. "I wonder if that place in Propellendorf will take it."

Suzy pulled on her mom's sleeve. "Let's keep it," she said. "Please?"

Her mom rolled her eyes, but she was smiling. "Did you hear that, Calum? We make one concession and she thinks we're pushovers." She laughed. "If the world's going to be full of fairies and who knows what else from now on, I don't suppose having a boggart around the place will hurt. But you'll be responsible for it."

Suzy chewed her lip. "Does the convenience store sell almond milk?"

"And soy," said her dad.

"Then you've got a deal," she replied. "See? Our house was magical *before* it was cool."

"Splendid," said Stonker. "Well, if you're all settled here, we'd best be off." He shook Suzy's parents by the hand. "It's been a pleasure having you aboard," he said. "I hope we haven't seen the last of you."

"Hrrrolf frrrunk grorwl," said Ursel, pulling them both into an unexpected hug. To Suzy's surprise, her parents hugged her back.

"You'll have to come for dinner again," said Suzy's dad.

"And I'd better get back to the lads on LA ROUQUINE and tell them all about our discoveries," said the Chief. "They must be itching to get out there and tour the Union again. Think of all the things we could see."

"Grrrolf," said Ursel.

"Yes, very true," said Stonker. "Map reading isn't my strongest suit, so I could always use some help in the *Belle*'s navigation room. A team of resident experts would be just the thing."

"That's a great idea," said Suzy. "And it has panoramic windows, so you'll always be able to see where you're going."

"Huzzah!" said the Chief. "I feel like I've got a new lease on death."

"We'll make the Topaz Narrows our next stop, then,"

said Stonker, taking the Chief's skull from Suzy. "Are you coming, Postmaster?"

"I'll be right with you," said Wilmot. He waited until the others had left, then gave Suzy a bashful smile. "It looks like the Express is going to be quite busy from now on."

"You certainly won't be lonely," she said. "And I'll be back next weekend to help out."

"I'm already looking forward to it," said Wilmot. "We're scheduled for a run out to Nethertown. I'll remember to pack some anti-vampire spray for you. And then there's the medal ceremony, of course, for the Gold Stamp Special. And our names on the post office wall of fame." He was becoming increasingly animated. "And the official re-dedication of Trollville's coming up in a few months and that's going to be *huge*! The king's promised a week-long party, and after that I thought maybe you'd like to put in for the Postal Proficiency Exams so you can become a full postal operative and not just a deputy, because that's the first step to becoming a Postmaster, which I think you'd be *brilliant* at, and…" He finally ran out of breath. "And I just wanted to say how happy I am that we don't have to say good-bye."

Suzy blinked away a tear. "Me too," she said. "Well done, Postmaster."

Wilmot drew himself up and straightened his cap.

"Congratulations, Deputy Postal Operative," he said. "See you next weekend."

Suzy and her parents followed him to the cupboard under the stairs, and waved as the Express slid back into the darkness of the tunnel. When the steam cleared, the cupboard was back to normal—just a vacuum cleaner and some mud-encrusted Wellies.

"I don't know about anyone else, but I could use a cup of tea," her dad said.

Suzy drifted after her parents, back into the kitchen. She was already looking forward to everything that lay ahead. There were worlds out there she hadn't even begun to imagine yet, and she would see them all one day.

For now, though, the kettle was boiling, the boggart was purring in the microwave, and her parents were laughing and chattering together. She was home again. And she was happy enough with that.

ACKNOWLEDGMENTS

The more time I spend writing books, the more convinced I become that they should end with a roll of closing credits, just like a movie. Because books, like movies, are the result of lots of hard work by all sorts of talented people. So here's a list of just some of those without whom *Delivery to the Lost City*—and indeed Suzy's previous adventures—would never have made it into your hands:

My wife, Anna, who's remarkably patient with me at the best of times but went to tremendous lengths during the COVID-19 lockdown to make sure I had the space and time to finish the final drafts. Thank you for always being there.

Our boys, Aurelien and Théo, both of whom are now legitimately better at Mario Kart than I am. (I promise I'm only slightly bitter.) Please, never stop asking for bedtime stories—it's my favourite part of the day.

My editors, Anna Poon and Liz Szabla at Feiwel & Friends, and Becky Walker and Rebecca Hill at Usborne.

They're the ones who've spared you from my fudged plot points, meandering characterization, and bizarre leaps in storytelling logic. It's been a tremendous privilege working with you all for the past three years, and I couldn't have asked for better support and guidance along the way. Suzy's success is yours as much as mine.

My powerhouse of an agent, Gemma Cooper, who continues to steer me safely through the strange world of the publishing industry. Thank you for doing so much to champion me and my books, and here's looking forward to new stories in the future!

Whichever side of the Atlantic you live on, Suzy's adventures look absolutely amazing thanks to the talents of two brilliant illustrators: Matt Sharack, for the US editions, and Flavia Sorrentino, for the UK. The pictures in my head when I write pale in comparison to their work. Thank you, both of you, for realizing the worlds of the Impossible Places so brilliantly.

Before the lockdown took hold, I made a habit of doing some of my writing at the Coffi House, Cardiff. I'd like to thank the staff there for always making me feel welcome, and for serving the best coffee and cake in the neighborhood. I can't prove it scientifically, but I'm sure they made the words flow more freely.

Claire Fayers will have to back me up on that, as we've

been meeting at the Coffi House to work on our respective books for a few years now. Claire's the one who, upon reading my first draft of *The Train to Impossible Places*, told me I had something worth publishing, and has been a tremendous source of advice and reassurance ever since. Thank you for being such a good friend in what would otherwise be a too-solitary profession.

Mum and Dad; my brother Chris; Heather and Serge; Jayson, Tascha, Luc, and Alyssa: the best family that anyone could ask for in any circumstances. Thanks, all of you, for your love, support, and encouragement. I hope by the time you read this we'll be able to approach within two meters of one another.

There are many more people I could and should mention, but I want to finish by thanking my readers. A story is no good unless you've got someone to share it with, and I'm deeply touched by how many of you have enjoyed Suzy's adventures and taken them to heart. Over the past three years, I've had the privilege of speaking with thousands of you all around the world, and I hope to meet even more of you in future. Always remember that, if you're ever feeling bored, or lost, or lonely, the Impossible Places are waiting to welcome you. Pay them a visit, and you'll see that our own world is more magical than it first appears.

Thank you for reading this Feiwel and Friends book.
The friends who made **DELIVERY TO THE LOST CITY** possible are:

JEAN FEIWEL, PUBLISHER

LIZ SZABLA, ASSOCIATE PUBLISHER

RICH DEAS, SENIOR CREATIVE DIRECTOR

HOLLY WEST, SENIOR EDITOR

ANNA ROBERTO, SENIOR EDITOR

KAT BRZOZOWSKI, SENIOR EDITOR

DAWN RYAN, SENIOR MANAGING EDITOR

KIM WAYMER, SENIOR PRODUCTION MANAGER

ERIN SIU, ASSOCIATE EDITOR

EMILY SETTLE, ASSOCIATE EDITOR

FOYINSI ADEGBONMIRE, EDITORIAL ASSISTANT

TRISHA PREVITE, ASSOCIATE DESIGNER

ILANA WORRELL, SENIOR PRODUCTION EDITOR